Frankie

Book 1: Paradise

ROBERT CARTER

dlw
publishing

www.frankiefoxybabe.com

Published by DesignWave Pty Ltd

www.designwave.com.au/publishing

ISBN: 978-0-9925711-1-5

ROBERT CARTER

A full-time writer and film director, Robert has won international awards for his work and received outstanding reviews from around the world. As writer, his first novel won the A&R Fellowship and was shortlisted for the Miles Franklin and 3 Premier's Awards. As director, Robert won Best Feature Film at the Hollywood Film Festival in 1998. He has been awarded Residencies and Fellowships to Paris, New York and Los Angeles. Robert's latest film, *THIRST*, awarded 4 stars, had packed screenings in 2012/13. *FRANKIE: Book 1: Paradise* is the first of a new thriller series.

Other Publications

The Sugar Factory: *HarperCollins* Australia 1986, 1987, 1991. *Atheneum/MacMillan* USA 1987. *Gallimard* France 1989, 2006. U.K, Denmark, New Zealand, Brazil, Germany.

The Pleasure Within: *HarperCollins* Australia 1987. *Atheneum/MacMillan* USA 1988, *HarperCollins* UK.

Prints in the Valley: *Heinemann* Australia 1989. *Pan Picador* Australia 1990. *Secker & Warburg* UK 1989.

The Collectors: *HarperCollins* Australia 1993. *Morrow* USA 1994. *HarperCollins* UK 1994.

Online:

Email: hello@frankiefoxybabe.com
Twitter: @robbycart
       @frankiefoxybabe
Facebook.com/frankiefoxybabe
www.frankiefoxybabe.com
www.thirstthefilm.com

There is no confusing the touch of a knife blade pressing against the sensitive part of the throat. You know it is a knife. You know nothing will save you if the person holding it decides to slide it like a lover's lips across your flesh. The room is pitch black. His knee scrunches the pillow beside your face. You pretend to be still asleep. You are afraid to open your eyes or move. You know this is not a dream – a nightmare. You are naked – you are always naked in your bed. You don't care if he wants to rape you. You don't care if he wants to cut you or do degrading things to your body. You just don't want to die. You haven't lived yet. Not enough. You haven't loved deeply enough. You haven't lifted your wings. You haven't proved yourself to be something – anything – something outstanding: someone who deserves to live.

1

It was way too cold for me to be wearing so little but I didn't care. On my last day as Frankie Bennetti I was at least going to look the part. Silly high heels pok pokked along the concrete. Basically, I'm a boots and skirts and jeans girl – but this was my last day. My last day! Painful as it was, I couldn't help the smile as I thought of my door painted in gold letters with a black shadow:

Frankie Bennetti
Debt Collection
Missing Persons
Investigations

All I ever wanted was painted on that door. To be honest, the Frankie Bennetti part wasn't really mine, it was already on the door from the previous tenant – a shonky accountant. I figured he wouldn't mind seeing as how he tried bungee jumping off his desk wearing an electric extension cord as a necktie. If you think about it – an extension cord is not the best choice if you are intending to hang yourself rather than go for decapitation. Who knows what pushed old Frankie over the edge – whatever it was, he cured it.

I didn't ask too many questions about Frankie but I did promise to burn a candle for him for getting the rent into my price range and for getting me nice new carpet. I could have kept my own name: Diane Boyle but hey, who you gonna hire to collect your debts Diane Boyle or Frankie Bennetti. Diane Boyle is going to say please, she might even hurt your feelings. Frankie Bennetti is not gonna say a thing but she might hurt a lot more than your feelings.

Truth is I do have a violent streak. Principal at my old high school said just before he suggested I leave rather than be expelled: "Boyle, you have this nasty, twisted, violent... (He was struggling for the word here)... *thug* inside you."

I was an angry little hornet at the time and thug sounded about right. Anyway that was a long time ago. I always knew I'd be good at investigating and collecting. Along with my inner thug, I have this inbuilt, unstoppable drive to do the impossible: get people to be responsible for the bad things they do. And let me tell you people do bad things, very bad things.

#

It had taken me a long time to get here, half a lifetime if you count that it started twenty years ago when I was sixteen and my brother disappeared. Okay, he didn't really disappear, he left a note. It took me eighteen months to track him down. Besides being labelled a thug I have been called, stubborn, persistent and dogged. Anyway, when I located my brother, I caught a train from Central Station, a bus and a taxi and surprised him. He was two years older than me and I just wanted to know why he did it, why he hadn't considered telling me face-to-face, and how he could have left me alone with the clinically insane – our mother. His answer hit me like a slammed door: 'I tried to kill her,' he said.

"What?"

"I tried to drive over her in the car."

Well, we cried a lot then. I wasn't sure whether I was sorry he tried to run over our mother or that he had missed her. Okay, that sounds a little harsh – but hey, you don't know the woman. When I was five she told my brother and me she wished she never had children and that we were the reason our father left. It gets worse. She said to me one tear-soaked night that she would prefer, rather than him leave her, that I contracted a terminal illness. I did wonder at the time why *I* had to have the terminal illness.

Anyway, I've forgiven her as much as I can, maybe she couldn't help it. Montaigne said we are all foolish and don't know why, and there is nothing we can be sure of and not much we can do about it. Okay, now I sound like a philosopher, but my ex-boyfriend made me read a truckload of it – said it made him horny to talk philosophy while we made love. Unfortunately towards the end of the relationship I found the philosophy way more exciting. Once, he placed down in front of me a glass with some water in it, and asked: 'okay, so this is our relationship, is this glass half full or half empty?' I was tired – he had a smug look – I picked up the glass, drank the water, slammed it down and said, 'empty.'

#

Standing outside the street entrance I couldn't believe my heart was hurting like something squeezing it. The steel door was always open in the day and it lead to a staircase and landing with two other offices. And there was mine. How could some gold letters on a door bring such joy? But they did. And now it was all over. Lease up a month ago, in debt to my armpits. Six months with five clients who never came back after the first meeting. If I wasn't a confident person I could begin to think there was something wrong with me. Montaigne would have said:

'there is something wrong with all of us, honey so don't worry'– but I only read a condensed version.

And then there were two shocks for me. One, the door wasn't locked and two, as I opened it, a woman was sitting on my rented sky-blue divan staring directly at me.

"The gentleman let me in," she said in private boarding school English.

I knew the gentleman was my landlord who was no gentleman and no doubt had come to collect rent. I recovered quickly and smiled as I crossed the room holding out my hand, trying to keep my enthusiasm under control.

"I'm Frankie... I'm not a guy..."

"I'm surprised anyone has ever made that mistake."

"Ha ha ha," I said, suckie as hell. "Some people assume... you know..."

"I would like to employ you..."

"Hire," I corrected her.

"Pardon?"

"You want to hire me."

She stared at me now like she hadn't really noticed me before. I made a mental note not to correct people, it's annoying.

"Quite right," she said.

She was slim, angular, confident with Ferragamo shoes that would have paid my back rent and given me a week in Bali. Ordinarily she and I would unfriend faster than her immaculate eyebrows could rise, but now I was ready to be a surrogate birth mother for her, my new best friend, my first client who looked like she could actually pay me something.

"Okay." I took out a heavy red journal from the desk drawer.

"How quaint, I haven't seen anyone use a pen in years."

We made eye contact and I wondered whether she was doing payback for the employee/hire thing, although I couldn't see any malice.

"I enter the details in my laptop later," I said as evenly as I could.

"My name is Patricia Wheeler." She passed me a card with her phone number as I scribbled in my quaint journal, hoping she couldn't see my shitty handwriting.

"I'd like you to collect something for me."

"Uh-huh."

"From a soldier... He's being discharged, his name is Travis Pike."

"Pike? His name is Pike and he's a soldier?" I grinned, but Patricia stared back at me blankly and I tilted my face and my quaint sense of humour back to my quaint journal. But I knew I had to ask the hard question. "So what is the something you want me to collect?"

"There is no reason you have to know that... it's personal."

"Ah well... see Patricia... a debt collector is kinda like a priest, or in my case like a nun." I glanced upwards here in case lightning was coming for me. "You've got to tell us everything so we can intervene on your behalf." I have to say old Patricia never batted a golden eyelash, she reached into her Prada handbag and placed on the desk a neatly folded bundle of $50 notes held together with a bank slip. I'm crap at math except with my favourite designer's work. Without touching it I knew there was at least twenty-five beautifully designed works of art on my desk. "I haven't mentioned my fee," I said without taking my eyes off the bundle.

"Take what you need."

"To be honest, Patricia that wouldn't leave you with a lot of change." She took back the money and I tried to hide my disappointment. I decided to elevate my tone towards posh. "What I need to know is exactly what might be involved here so I can confidently serve your needs."

"Letters."

"Letters? Your letters?"

"Yes."

"To Mr Pike?"

"Captain Pike, his ship is docking at Circular Quay terminal tomorrow afternoon at five thirty."

"How come you didn't use emails or phone him?"

"He was in what the military called a black area.. with restricted contact.. letters they could check."

"Why don't you just go collect them yourself?"

"Because I don't want to see him again."

"Okay."

"Before he went overseas we thought we were in love..."

"And he still thinks so?"

"Something like that. I'm also a coward."

"Anyone calls themselves a coward, Patricia is never going to be a coward. "A flash of affection crossed her face as I continued. "What do you want me to do with the letters?"

"I shall pick them up from you in a week or so. "She dropped a snapshot of a good looking man on my desk. "This is the only photo I have, it was taken before he left for duty overseas." She looked uncomfortable and avoided looking at the photo, as she made movements to go.

"Excuse me asking this Patricia, but is the captain likely to take this hard?" For the first time Patricia hesitated, slightly off-balance, as if we had just come off her script. I pushed on. "I guess I'm asking whether he might be... aah... disagreeable, like violent or suicidal?"

"Oh no, not Travis..."

"So... no risk for me or for him?"

Now, she seemed downright flustered. She stood up, obviously eager to leave. "No, no of course not," she said, as she shook my hand once, twice – forced a smile, wheeled like a catwalk model, and was out the door before I could explore the niggling feeling that something here wasn't quite right.

#

Sydney Harbour on a spring afternoon was so beautiful you should have to pay to look at it. Passenger ferries ploughed white furrows, racing yachts danced like moths, the green of the botanical gardens framed the water's edge – life outdoing art.

At Circular Quay, the warship had been discharging soldiers for an hour and the flow was slowing to a trickle. Handmade welcome banners flapped in the breeze, mothers cried, embarrassed children kissed strange fathers. Soldiers were excited and awkward as a bad brass band played something that was supposed to sound triumphant. Despite myself I was moved. Not because they were soldiers – I personally feel you have to score high on the psychopath scale to sign up to kill people – but because of the emotion. Okay put your finger down your throat if you have to but I am moved by the innocent, unguarded display of genuine human love.

I had a photo of the captain and I kept glancing from it to the faces flowing off the ship. I was beginning to think he may not have been on board or was not getting off. Eventually no one came at all and a metal gate was swung into place across the gangplank. In my head I saw the $50 notes on my desk go marching in little military lines into the distance. Maybe Patricia got the date or the ship wrong. Maybe I failed to recognize him. Nearby, a soldier in a wheelchair rolled around as if looking for someone, and as he turned I caught a glimpse of his face.

"Shit!" I said too loudly. I looked around to see if anyone heard. I'm okay appearing crude but not insensitive. I made a beeline for the captain who was wheeling away at some pace. I caught up and touched his shoulder, wondering whether this was some kind of no-no behaviour for the disabled.

"Captain Pike?" I asked. He spun the wheelchair around to face me. It was him all right – only Brad Pitt could play him in the movie.

"That's right," he said, with a killer smile. "Did Patricia

send you?"

I tried not to stare at the chair or where his legs were covered by a grey blanket. "She didn't tell me you were... injured..."

"I don't think it has fully registered with her yet."

"Really?" I said, thinking Patricia didn't look simple minded.

He stared at me as if figuring how stupid I might be. "You know, like painful stuff you shove back into your unconscious."

"Yeah," I said. "I've got a few ex-boyfriends there." He laughed. I like anyone who laughs at my jokes. "Wanna get a drink?" I asked.

"You got a thing for crippled guys?"

"Not yet." I smiled, knowing he was aware of his good looks.

#

The bar was post-modern glass, granite and steel with halogen lights and stools designed by people who hated people with arses. I was perched so far above Travis we almost needed to text each other – but I did notice he had an unusually comprehensive view of my legs, both of which I am disgustingly proud. The bartender waved Travis's money away with a little salute and I watched him drink. He was a quick drinker, vodka and bitter lemon and he was surprised when I ordered a Coke. I used to drink a lot but discovered I was an idiot after four glasses, and the day after a big night I was as sharp as a brick.

Travis looked up at me with a twinkly grin. "So you're some kind of private eye?"

"Yeah, the good kind."

"And she wants her letters back?"

"Seems to be the case."

He looked away. "Did she pay you enough to console me?"

"Console you?"

"Sleep with me."

"Come on Travis not even Patricia has that kind of money." He laughed genuinely and I liked him a little more.

"Want to take me home?" He asked.

"No."

"No?" He paused and cocked his attractive head to one side. "Do you want the letters?"

#

Travis's apartment was thankfully on the ground floor. The block was an old cream brick, tiny-windowed money-maker from the middle of the last century which probably looked shabby eleven minutes after it was built. I pushed old Travis through the doorway.

"I can manage," he said.

"I need the exercise."

"You look in good shape to me."

"It's a facade, Travis underneath I'm a crumbling wreck."

"Yeah, I could tell that from your legs." I couldn't help feeling pleased as old Travis wheeled away down the corridor. "Have a seat," he said. "I'll be back."

I looked around the room, it was seriously devoid of personality. No books, or personal stuff anywhere just K-mart prints on the wall and vinyl chairs and synthetic carpet – unlived and unloved. I started to feel sorry for old Travis and tried not to wonder whether Patricia had dumped him before or after the legs went.

"What's your name?" Travis called from further inside the apartment.

"Frankie... Frankie Bennetti," I shouted.

"Cool," he called out, sounding impressed. And then I heard the rubber wheels squelching down the corridor and he was looking straight at me, a taped up brown envelope

9

in his lap. "I used to wonder... before I got these," he slapped his legs with distaste. "What it would be like doing it with a cripple." Okay, I was beginning to feel uncomfortable now. "There was a girl in high school had a car accident... I used to wonder..."

"Well frankly Travis, I have never wondered that." Travis looked at me as if he didn't believe me. He sighed and tossed the envelope to me. I could feel the pull of sympathy sex – not something that has worked out well for me in the past. "So... You'll be okay now huh? Not gonna have a close shave with a sharp object..." Oddly, his expression changed... softened, as if he was about to change his mind or confess something. I decided not to go there and headed for the door. "Look after yourself," I said lamely.

"Listen, Frankie..." He started to say and then stopped himself. "You be careful... Okay?"

I opened the door and paused. "'Cause I certainly can't be good." A quick wink and I was gone.

#

A tide of red taillights rippled down the highway as I followed mindlessly in my old Ford Falcon, the hole in the muffler making me sound like a fat biker on a Harley. I lied to old Travis, I did wonder what it would be like doing it with a cripple. I mean would he get the mechanical part to work... If he couldn't feel anything, would he just stare blankly while you had your way with him? Maybe it would last longer than usual? Ya gotta admit it's an interesting area of exploration which I did as the traffic washed on and the radio hummed too low to understand.

My apartment block was only slightly more interesting than Travis'. Down the hallway to my door on the second floor a smartly dressed man appeared from the opposite stairwell. He was young and very well built and if I hadn't been tired I would have flirted with him. He had a confident smile as I passed and I caught a whiff of a classy cologne. With my handbag strap between my teeth, I unlocked the door and pushed it open. The first surprise was the hair at the back of my head. It hurt. And then between my shoulder blades a distinct hand pushing hard, and I flew into my apartment, leaving the floor. I saw the package sail across the room as I sprawled face first on to my very ugly carpet. Fortunately the handbag strap was still clenched between my teeth and buffered my face hitting the floor. I heard the door slam behind me and I looked to where the guy's legs might be: it was Mr Well-built from the hallway. I calculated my chances of overpowering him with a shin scraping kick – as I have trained to do, but was lifted to my feet and immediately recognized superior strength. A gun was carefully rested against my mouth and a large hand patted over my waist and chest. I watched the hand searching for a weapon. Professional, I thought. The gun was pressing my bottom lip against my teeth and it hurt.

"Your gun?" He whispered into my ear. I took my baby Glock from a cloth holster I had specially made to strap to my inside leg above my left knee. I could get it out in three hundredths of a second, I've timed it. Instead of handing it to him, I turned around and pointed it at his powder blue right eye.

"Do you know that a dying person's fingers automatically spasm?" I said in my calmest news reader voice. Well-built had not thought of this before. He stared back at me blankly, long enough for my confidence to grow. "Let's both of us take the guns away at the same time... shall we?" I said reasonably. He was not convinced. "We can talk," I suggested. "Okay, I'll count to three and we'll both drop them on the floor, okay? One... two... three..." Neither of us was that stupid. "Okay, let's just relax..." I said.

In one movement he knocked the gun from my hand, slammed the butt of his pistol into the side of my head and down I went, the room spinning like a fun park rotor. I saw him kick my gun away and watched it skitter across the carpet spinning madly. I tried for humour as I struggled to rise to my hands and knees. "Do you realize how many people are injured by careless gun handling?"

"Whatever he gave you, give it to me," he said evenly.

"Who?" This must have sounded like an invitation to stand on my fingers with his size fifteen Brogues. "Owww... Jesus!"

"Where?"

"In the bag.. oww..oww.." He looked at my bag near the doorway which should have had my face imprint on it, lifted his foot from my fingers and placed the gun in my ear.

"Bring it here."

I could feel a trickle of blood down the side of my face. I was scared. And angry. I deliberately acted a little woozy, trying to give myself time to think. "My head hurts."

"Bring it over here... and by the way I will blow away the top of your head before you can even think of doing something stupid."

"Okay, that should fix the headache..." I said, hoping what I read was actually true about humour being the fastest way to bond with a stranger. I took my time picking up the bag and deliberately swayed a little as I stood up.

"Bring it to me," he said. I knew in that moment, from his eyes, that he had no intention of leaving the room with me still breathing. I unzipped the bag as if looking for something and upended it, spilling a normally embarrassing amount of personal crap across the floor. His face darkened as he strode quickly towards me, arm outstretched, gun pointing at my forehead. I bent down and picked up my little leather diary with all my cringe-worthy secret thoughts and offered it to him. He snatched it without taking his eyes from me, but he couldn't resist, he flipped open the diary. I waited, rubbing my head as if I was too dizzy to do anything dangerous. I waited, coiling my body till he used his gun hand to flip over the first page. With open palms, and all my body weight, I leapt against his gun arm, crushing it into his chest and knocking him backwards. As he fell, I charged madly for the open bathroom, kicking the envelope through with me, slamming the door shut and locking the old iron lock. Two quick shots splintered the door as I rolled to the side. And then silence. Several seconds ticked by. Nothing. I hated the silence.

And then, wham the door rattled and vibrated from what must have been his size fifteens. I looked around the bathroom for something that might help as the door wouldn't survive many more hits. The window high on the wall looked as if it had been sealed shut during the Second World War with steel security bars.

"If you push what I want under the door, I give you my word I will leave," he called through the door with surprising calm.

"Someone will have heard the shots," I said lamely.

"Undoubtedly, but by the time the nearest police car arrives you will be dead and I will be gone."

My heart was trying to climb out of my throat. Above the window there were mouldy old curtains on a rod with white plastic spearheads on each end. I climbed onto the edge of the bath and unhooked them from their rusted brackets. I slid the curtains off one end of the rod and replaced the plastic spearhead.

His voice cut through the door. "I'll count to five and then I'll come in and shoot you in the head... okay?"

"That sounds fair," I said.

"One... two..." I looked at the makeshift spear in my hands and shook my head. I'd never be able to use it. "Three...four..." I dropped the curtain rod. "Five..."

Wham! The door near the lock partly shattered from a massive kick. I grabbed the envelope and shoved it under the door, my stomach joining several other organs wanting out through my mouth. Silence. I figured he was reading. I put my ear up against the door. Nothing.

"Did you get it?" I asked politely. Nothing. I counted to twenty-five. "Are you still there?" I switched off the light and looked through the keyhole. I couldn't see him anywhere. This felt good. My breathing began to steady. I had no intention of unlocking the door for at least two hours. For the first time I thought about what the hell could be so important in the envelope and how come Patricia or Travis didn't warn me. Then I remembered Travis's odd, 'be careful'.

Crunch! The door almost shattered, splinters of wood flew into the bathroom. I screamed before I could stop myself. One more kick and it would be gone. I braced myself in the dark against the bath, clutched the curtain rod and stopped breathing. The next kick did it, the lock broke and the door flew open. I heard the gun firing and saw his shape come at me in the dark. I was screaming. The gun kept firing and I felt pain. I wondered where I'd been shot. There was blood, lots of it. I was bleeding down the side of my face, but not as much as Mr Well-built who was impaled through the throat by the plastic curtain rod.

2

Karl Muntz stared at me with exaggerated anger but underneath I could see he was genuinely concerned. A young cop with an old-time heart who partnered with my father up until the night he was gunned down. Muntz still blamed himself for not being there, even though my father was off duty and eating in the swankiest restaurant in town with the woman he left my mother for.

"I'm gonna charge you... you know why? Look at me..." He said, taking my chin firmly but gently. I felt the lump on the side of my head and picked at the dried blood down my face. "Don't do that... and don't do that sympathy crap on me... he didn't hurt you... your head's thicker than your old man's..."

I realized I hadn't been shot in the head, it was blood from when he whacked me with his gun. A rush of pleasure at not being dead or dying, surged through me.

"Have you got a cigarette?" I asked.

"No, and I wouldn't give it to you if I had." He looked around at the photographer taking a snap of Mr Well-built. I couldn't help looking again at the plastic spearhead sticking through his neck and the buckets of blood. When he charged through the door my eyes were shut and the rod was braced against the bath, his body weight would have done all the impaling work.

"Do you know what your old man would do now, huh? He'd smack that lump on your head and say, hey! is there anyone home?"

Karl got drunk once and let spill that my father asked him to keep an eye out for me as a personal favour. As Karl wouldn't hesitate to take a bullet for my father, it made me love my father a little bit, at least for a while.

"What was I supposed to do, Karl? He was about to shoot me..."

"You're not supposed to do this stuff at all... is your gun licensed?"

"Oh shit..." I looked around for my baby Glock.

"It's all right, I know the patrol cop, he didn't see any gun. Not that this girly little thing could actually hurt anyone." He passed the gun to me distastefully as if some girly hormones might rub off.

"I have the ammunition specially made, Karl – they'd stop the Hulk on an angry day – and yes it is licensed."

Karl lit a cigarette and I noticed his hands were shaking almost as much as mine. I took his hand and he tried to be a tough guy and pull away but I clung on. I was always a problem for Karl. With my father gone, Karl felt looking after me was a lifetime command, that he had to be kind of parental, only trouble was, a part of him wanted to get naked with me whenever he got within ten feet of me. I was never going to tell him that I had thought about it, kinda like a fantasy... and it wasn't half bad. A young detective noticed our handholding and grinned. Karl dropped my hand and glared at him and the grin froze in place.

"This is what the guy was after," I said.

I handed the envelope to Karl who turned it over and pulled off the sealing tape. He slid out several pages of paper, turned them over and flipped through them. Blank. He looked at me suspiciously.

"What kind of bullshit is this?"

I grabbed the papers and fanned through them with my thumb. I turned them over and held them up to the light. Zero. Nothing. I was shocked and shaken and annoyed – for this – blank paper, I was almost murdered? "I'm not holding back on you... I don't get it either," I said.

As the paramedics arrived, Karl looked at me with sympathy. "Here, take my keys, you can't stay here," he said to me, warning the other detective away with a threatening glance.

I raised my eyebrows at him suggestively, half in tease, half in a flush of affection.

"Oh, Karl this is so sudden..."

"Shut up you idiot, it's a crime scene for Christ's sake," he said as gruffly as he could. As I took the keys, I winked at him and he blushed.

Fortunately the paramedics intervened and rescued him as much as me. I protested that I didn't need to go to hospital, but I was grateful when they carried me out on a stretcher. I felt like shit. I didn't tell Karl about Patricia or Travis. I told him I found the envelope under my door. I don't think he believed me but he knows me well enough to know that if I don't want to tell him something, it would take more torture than he was willing to apply to get me to open my mouth.

#

Late that night I tried to sleep in Karl's hard-as-a-rock bed. I hadn't heard him come in and I wondered whether he was deliberately staying out late and whether he would slip into bed beside me without waking me. Even with my sore head and Mr Well built's blood sloshing around in my brain, I found the thought very exciting. Karl had lived alone the last five years since divorcing his attractive, celebrity chef wife for putting herself on the dessert menu of a coal mining magnate. He had steadfastly refused to accuse, condemn, or even talk about her since.

Earlier in the day, against the advice of the crusty old IC unit doctor, I checked myself out of the hospital and took a cab to Captain Travis Pike's apartment. As I expected, it was empty. The next-door neighbour told me it was a rent-by-the-day for the local girly bars which I would have realized if I hadn't been so distracted by Patricia's wads of cash and Travis's good looks. I called the military who refused to tell me anything and politely suggested I make a formal complaint when I told them that I paid their salaries and that technically they worked for me.

I'd been set up in some way. But why? Why me? Was Patricia part of the deal? I called the number she gave me and got a telco recording that no such number existed. Great. Well done, Frankie Bennetti, idiot debt collector. I searched 'Patricia Wheeler' on my cell phone. Nothing.

In my mind, I debated telling Karl the whole story – Karl lost. I knew he would never let me get involved or even tell me if he managed to track down either of them.

At the tip of my awareness, something was trying to emerge. That was how my mind worked. If I was trying to remember something, I could sort of feel it floating from my unconscious to the surface like a bubble from the ocean floor. Something about Patricia, something to do with her handbag. No. With the wad of money. What was it? It was near the surface – I could feel it. The money? If my head didn't hurt... the money was new...it had a bank slip holding it together. Something printed on the slip. What was it? 'Honest?' No. Something starting with a P. Promise? Yes. Promised...something. Promised Land! That was it – Promised Land Bank!

I leapt out of bed, pulled on one of Karl's white T-shirts which covered the important bits and went searching for a map or road directory in Karl's meagre little shelf of books. Bingo, an old road atlas with its cover missing. And there it was, the Promised Land, smack on the edge of the desert – about 12 hours' drive west. Population 4,000 –

formerly an opal mining and cattle grazing area, site of a low security female prison and a closed abattoir. No airport nearby. A key rattled in the door making more noise than an apprentice in a metal shop. Then repeated knocking and slowly the door eased open. Karl stood in the doorway staring.

"Are you okay?" He asked, genuinely concerned. I put the book back and pulled down on the T-shirt. He tried not to stare at my legs. "I didn't want to spook you... especially seeing you have a gun."

"Yeah, I'm fine," I said.

"What were you looking at?"

"Nothing. I couldn't sleep."

He stepped into the room and headed to the kitchen. "You want a drink?" He asked with his back to me, and his voice full of tension.

"A hot chocolate would be nice." He spun around to see if I was serious.

"Chocolate?"

"Some warm milk would be fine."

"I don't do a lot of shopping..."

"Water is good."

He nodded and filled a glass. "Guy you speared... doesn't have a record from his prints. Doesn't have a name or address either... not one piece of info on him."

"Really? What does that mean?"

"It means he is either very professional or a head case."

"Great. Professional killer or psychopath – I feel much better."

"You would if you told me everything."

"Karl, if I told you everything I'd have to kill you."

"Yeah? Well seeing Mister curtain rod I reckon you could carry that out."

I tried not to laugh, but hey, life is short. I don't feel you have to respect the dead if they were trying to kill you.

I insisted Karl sleep in the bed alongside me rather than on his grubby little couch which he once told me was rejected by the pickup truck of the Salvation Army. It was weird. For both of us. There was no avoiding the sexual tension in the air – it could have been cut with an eighteen inch chain saw. I fell in and out of sleep for an hour or so edging my leg towards him and pulling it back. He kept his back towards me and never moved. Eventually I fell exhausted into a deep unconsciousness. And dreams of trying to catch a bus running and running in high heels, expensive shoes covered in blood – trying to wipe them clean with $50 notes – and someone feeling my chest – a well-built someone searching my body with strong hurtful hands and I am reading a letter to him and there is nothing on the paper. And it is Karl's arm around me and I move closer to him and he kisses me, slowly, gently with soft lips, his fingertips thick and rough, barely touching between my legs and I close them tightly around his hand and force his finger inside me. I want to come and Karl is too gentle, too kind. I want to be fucked angry, I want to fight, I want to hurt and be hurt. I want to scream out anger and pain and craziness… to keep me sane.. to keep me alive… and there is yellow light and heat and I don't want to wake up, as sun floods the room and Karl is not in the bed nor in the apartment. I am fully awake and I shut my eyes and try to go back to the dream. Stuff reality. And I use my own fingers – even though the dream is gone.

#

"Cubby, I need to borrow your Audi," I asked my brother.

"You only call me that when you want something," he said evenly. It was true, my brother knew me well. I couldn't remember when Kevin became Cubby but I always thought it suited him better.

"Kevin, I need it for a few days – you can have my Ford Falcon."

"Let me think, my top-of-the-line four-wheel-drive Audi for your T model? Aah so tempting."

"I need a reliable car."

"What for?"

"A long drive... its work."

"Where to?"

"Out west."

"How far out west?"

"The Simpson Desert."

"Are you nuts!"

"The Audi's designed for the outback."

"That's outback of outback! And you're not having it. What the hell are you doing out there?"

"Its work... Just five or six days..."

"You're not wrecking my car..."

"You want me to go out there in my Falcon...?"

"No, I don't want you to go out there in my Audi."

"Okay, I'll rent it."

"Excellent... Hertz has some great offers."

"From you... you know I can't afford Hertz."

"I'm sorry I have to go."

"Keep watching the news for a body found slumped in a Ford Falcon in the desert..."

Bastard. I didn't blame him – I borrowed his pushbike at eleven and sold it to Rennie Vincent for a kitten that didn't even belong to Rennie Vincent. I'm not the most reliable borrower nor the hottest trader. Dearest mummy took care of the kitten, she took the train for an hour and left it in the wash basin of the ladies room on the station platform. I know this because she sat me down and carefully told me every detail.

I threw underwear, clothes, toiletries and two boxes of hollow nosed bullets into a backpack, kissed the dashboard of my main man Mr Ford Falcon, told him I loved all his cylinders and drove off for the Promised Land.

3

There is just so much music and talkback radio your brain can take on a long drive. I can take six to seven hours then I want to pour coffee into the speakers or hurt someone. I worry about my mother's crazy genes floating around in my head. I swear once on a long drive I headed back towards a radio station with the express intention of shooting the shock jock talkback idiot who was bullying a caller. I'd been driving for eight hours and he'd been rabbiting on about justice and crap about women who choose to marry violent men deserving everything they get. The caller was actually sobbing on the phone as she tried to explain how her husband wasn't violent in the first years. But the jock was performing for his redneck listeners. I stopped at a payphone and called and told the show's producers I wanted to tell the jock something personal and shocking on air. They put me through in two minutes, sensing a ratings coup and I told him I was impressed with his take on justice – so much so that I was going to achieve some justice for his listeners – I was coming in to the station to put several bullets into his tiny brain. I don't think it went to air – they have a delay button which I am sure they pushed. But hey, I loved the idea of the prick looking over his shoulder or maybe losing some sleep.

I realized then that long drives can render me a little unstable. With that in mind, I overnighted at a Roadies Motel after nine hours of driving – five of them dead straight roads through dust-dry countryside with the most exciting thing being where I will pee next.

Two hours into the next day's drive, after turning on to a gravel road pointing to the Promised Land, in the middle of the red, flat, sandy desert – old faithful died. Black smoke wheezed from under the hood and I cursed my brother and his Audi. I peered at the engine in total ignorance. It was ticking with a radiating heat and smelling of burnt oil and rubber. I had an extra drum of fuel on the back seat advised by the last service station but that wasn't the problem. No cars had passed in the last hour since I'd been on the gravel road. I had plenty of water, also advised at the service station, and half a dozen chocolate bars and a banana. Things could be worse. My phone worked surprisingly well and allowed me to Google road assistance and then died just as they picked up.

The thing that surprised me when I gave up trying to start the car was how quiet it was. Stunningly, beautifully, still and silent. I could hear myself chewing and breathing as I sat in the shade of the car. It was eerie but nice. A mob of skinny, grey kangaroos loped by as the temperature began to drop slowly. I thought of what I was doing. What was I doing? Karl told me not to leave town, not to carry my gun, not to hold back any information. At least I was consistent – I disobeyed everything. It wasn't the money, much as I needed it – it was being used that got to me. Patricia or Travis or both had used me and I felt foolish, not to mention the fact that I was almost murdered and forced to skewer someone.

A warm breeze brought the smell of sand and eucalyptus and the sound of regular soft thudding. A gentle tapping as if it was on my forehead. The smell wafted into animal sweat and the tapping was on my forehead. My eyes sprang open, I must have dozed off. There was a huge dark hand tapping my forehead and behind him three gigantic camels grinding their teeth and looking bored. I leapt to my feet on autopilot, grabbing the thick fingers and bending them back with all my weight.

"Hey... hey..!" The guy yelled and slapped the side of my jaw hard enough for me to let go. He was huge – legs like tree trunks and a body the size of a mountain gorilla. "I thought you needed help," he said, massaging his fingers.

"Sorry... I was asleep..."

"For a little girl you got a big grip."

"How far are we from the Promised Land?"

"Aarr... We're all closer than we think to the promised land..."

"Okay, if I laugh at your joke will you tell me?"

"Sorry, the tourists usually like that kind of shit. It's about four hours walk, about two by camel.. and by the look of it, a lifetime by your car."

"Are you going to the town now?"

"Yep."

"Could you tell a mechanic or someone to come look at my car or pick me up?"

"I could..."

"But?"

"But, Rodney, he's the garage guy, doesn't make calls. Fact is, no one's ever seen him leave the garage – has his groceries delivered... his skin is really white..."

"Well how do I get some help?"

He held his hand out. "My name's Edgar... you like camels?"

#

I hate camels. I threw up chocolate bars and banana all the way to the Promised Land. Camels were worse than boats and I got queasy looking at a picture of a wave.

As we swayed down the main street, I wondered what confused soul could have called this place the Promised Land. Perhaps he had a sense of humour. Believe me, the only promise about the place was that you vowed to leave it as soon as possible. A one-pump Shell gas station, a cafe with three plastic chairs and a torn umbrella out front, a corner hotel, a sandstone bank building, a grocer, hairdresser, newsagent, a scattering of other sad buildings and a massive town hall built in 1896 before the opals ran out. This was the Promised Land? I waved to two old men and a young woman all wearing moleskin jeans and wide brimmed hats, chatting in front of the bank. They stopped talking and stared at me – no wave back. Okay, bad-mannered or unfriendly – I had a lot to look forward to here.

Edgar found me a room above the Railway Hotel (no, there was no railway line, go figure). He offered to get my car towed into town and to talk to Rodney the agoraphobic garage guy who never spoke to strangers. He insisted on buying me dinner in the Paradise Cafe and as I sat opposite him I began to feel that Patricia was unlikely to live in a place like this no matter what was promised, that perhaps she just used the bank here to make it more difficult to be traced. Each time I tried to order from the menu, Edgar grimaced and shook his head until finally I said I'll have what he's having. When the waitress left, he leaned forward and said. "If you don't want to go to the other promised land, you've gotta order beefsteak rare as hell – that way it will still be overcooked but won't be black and crispy."

"Listen, Edgar... this is important to me... I'm trying to find a friend... her name could be Patricia but she might have changed it and I think she could live around here somewhere." Edgar was delighted.

"I know everyone for two hundred miles around here. What's the girl look like?"

"Woman, she's a woman, Edgar - girls are under

sixteen."

"Right, gotcha ..what's the chick look like?"

I knew he was teasing me so I ignored it. I described Patricia from her hair to her expensive high heels. Edgar grinned. "I know someone like that – name's not Patricia."

"Really?"

"Phillipa Ericsson.. lives on a huge old grazing property called Billabong, about an hour out of town – husband's some big shot in the city – hardly ever see him. I can take you out there."

"I am never, ever, under any circumstances ever riding a camel again."

"I have a Land Rover."

"Thank you Edgar, I appreciate that but I'd just as soon go by myself."

"You'll never find it girl – there are dozens of tracks out there.. change all the time.. wind blows sand off 'em and on 'em all the time."

"Edgar, you're wasting your time – I'm in a relationship," I lied.

"That's nice... I'm kind of in one too..." He seemed genuinely pleased for me.

"Oh, good," I said, also genuinely pleased.

"Well, I will be... you know... In a relationship soon... I have a plan."

"Okay... planned relationship that sounds good. Listen, I'm sorry I've been a bit prickly, you've been very kind and generous... so thank you."

"Ahh.. Prickly... So that's what you've been. I just thought you were being a prick."

For two seconds I was taken aback and then we both burst out laughing. It felt good. I realized I hadn't laughed from my gut for a long time. I held out my hand in peace.

"I'm Frankie, Frankie Bennetti." He shook my hand and grinned.

"Frankie?... suits you." We chuckled again. "As far as being prickly, Frankie – Only things I know need to be prickly, got a reason to be.. gotta protect a too soft centre."

I already liked Edgar but now he was special – a fellow life philosopher. I smiled warmly at him as the meals arrived. Edgar's steak was three times the size of mine. He winked at me. "Should have told them you were called Frankie, you might have got the boy size.."

I laughed. Edgar was way more fun than most of the dates I'd been on.

#

Billabong was tucked away behind a man-made oasis: eucalypts, palms, hedges, tree ferns and jacarandas. A dozen motorized sprinklers slowly rolled away across five acres of lawn. "Bore water," Edgar said. "They must have drilled to the centre of the earth".

"It's stunning," I said, seriously impressed.

Edgar parked the car at the gate and turned to me. "I'm gonna wait here."

"Really?"

"Yeah... well I'm not sure they would be pleased to see me."

"Because?"

He sucked in air between his teeth. "Kind of a long story..."

"I've got time."

"Couple of my camels got lose and ate a few of his vegetables."

"Is that all?"

"Well kind of.. twenty-three camels and five acres of cabbages."

"Okay. Right. You stay here."

As I dodged sprinklers and headed up the driveway I thought I could hear dogs barking. Thankfully it was only the throb of the pumps. I pushed through the greenery and the house suddenly appeared – impressive, expensive, post-modern concrete, glass and steel. A BMW four-wheel-drive was parked in the circular driveway in front of the house, two of its doors wide open. There were voices floating out. A man's voice, sharp and angry. I felt the baby Glock against my thigh for a confidence boost and moved forwards. At the door, I paused – the opportunity to hear the owners unguarded was too good to resist. I pressed my ear up against the door and hoped no one was about to open it any time soon. Inside the house I could hear footsteps echoing on a timber floor. They were coming towards me. I had just enough time to spring back and knock.

The door flew open and a tall, olive skinned man, in a white linen shirt and tailored slacks carrying two suitcases stared at me, genuinely surprised.

"Oh hi... I'd just started to knock," I said cheerfully, going for ditzy tourist. "I hope I'm not bothering you but I need to use a bathroom... I took a tour with this man, Edgar something or other and I think he's just been driving me around and around..."

"Edgar Wilson," the man interrupted without expression. "The village idiot... You're not taking one of his camel tours are you?"

"Oh goodness no."

The man turned his head back into the house. "Phillipa," he shouted.

I saw her at the precise instant she recognized me and I enjoyed her moment of horror. Impressively, she quickly erased the shock from her face. As the man faced me again, I pulled off a dopey grin.

"Hi," I said. He took a good look. I could almost hear him thinking 'halfwit'.

"This unfortunate woman has been tortured by Edgar Wilson and needs to use the bathroom... well, *your* bathroom now," the man said with venom, as he pushed past me towards the BMW.

"Oh, please come in," Phillipa said, her eyes begging me not to spill the beans in front of mister angry.

The bathroom was the size of my apartment with a glass skylight and more maidenhair fern than a plant nursery. When I came out, she was talking through the driver's window of the BMW, her face anxious and worried. Mister angry looked at her with a blend of hatred and serve-you-rightness. He closed the window in the middle of her sentence and drove away while she was still leaning on the car causing her to almost fall. I could see why she might prefer sexy Captain Travis to this shithead.

Inside the house, she offered me a drink which I refused even though I was thirsty. I had my pride. And I had my anger.

"Thank you for not... you know... in front of my husband..."

"Don't thank me..."

"How did you find me?"

"It's what I do. I'm a professional finder... and you're a professional liar."

"I'm sorry..."

"For what?"

"Deceiving you."

"What was that about Patricia... Phillipa?"

"It's... It doesn't matter now... I can pay you. How much do I owe you?"

I took a step forward and slapped her hard on the side of the head with my open hand, knocking her off her feet. She remained sitting on the floor, struggling not to cry.

"I deserved that," she said.

I reached into my jeans and pulled out my baby Glock. "No, you deserve this," I said as I pointed the gun at her. Finally the tears came.

"We needed to find out whether my husband knew about Travis and me..."

"What?"

"Travis thought Heyden, my husband, may have been watching us... and if he had been he would have intervened... and then at least we would have known.."

"Intervened?"

"My husband is... is.. he can be very vindictive. So when Travis told me no one bothered the two of you I was so relieved.. I can't tell you. I have already sent your fee to you in the mail."

"So you used me like some kind of ..bait."

"I'm sorry."

"You could have warned me."

"He has my daughter..." Now the tears came in a flood. As always, faced with someone crying, whether I caused it or not, I felt like a miserable bully. I helped her up off the floor and onto a massive white lounge.

"What do you mean he has your daughter?"

"I asked him to move out before... before Travis and me..." More tears. "We had no relationship, my husband and I, he was always working at his office in Sydney, in a plane or overseas on some project or other. He was very angry with me..." She broke down and spoke between sobs. "Carol... our daughter.. She's just a twelve-year-old and she'd do anything to get his attention. He said if he found I'd been sleeping with someone else then I'd never see her again..." The tears seemed genuine and at least half my anger was gone.

"Do you realize that you almost got me killed?" I said, feeling around for the rest of my fury.

She stopped crying and looked at me with a mix of fear and horror. "What?"

"Someone did intervene, he shot holes in my bathroom door, smacked me on the side of the head a lot harder than I hit you, and guess what?... He's dead... With a curtain rod sticking out of his neck.. And I have the police crawling up my Levi's looking to lock me up."

"Oh God... Oh God... I'm sorry." Then she panicked. "He knows then... he must know…"

"Maybe, maybe not. If he sent the guy to get the letters,

it means he wasn't sure and he never got any letters, so he might still only have his suspicions."

#

We sat talking for so long that Edgar came looking for me. He stayed quietly in a corner while Phillipa poured out her heart about how miserable her life had been before Travis and how Carol made the whole marriage bearable and that in the beginning her husband had been really really nice. In the middle of her apologizing again for what happened to me, she suddenly got up, disappeared into a back room and came out with a stack of photographs of her daughter and a stupendously attractive bundle of $50 notes even larger than the chunk she dropped on my desk. Edgar sweated so rapidly at the sight of the money he had to ask for a glass of water.

"That's a lot of money, Patricia..."

"Phillipa."

I stared at her, needing to give myself time to think. "Okay, Phillipa... that's too much money."

"Please, I want you to have it... it's the least I can do." She took hold of my arm and looked directly into my eyes. "I want to hire you – genuinely this time."

"What's that saying – once bitten...?"

"I want you to find out where my daughter is... and if at all possible for you to bring her back to me."

"Why don't you call the police? That's what they're for."

"No! If Heyden thought I'd called the police..."

"The police would protect you from him."

"You don't understand my husband... he's made a lot of money... and a lot of important friends. He gives donations... large donations all the time... he has favours owing everywhere..."

"Okay, so why would you think I'd be able to cope with all that?"

She stared blankly at me for several seconds, then more tears. "I don't know... I shouldn't have asked... I'm sorry.. I just thought you being... being..."

"A woman?"

"I'm sorry, Heyden can be... better around an attractive woman."

"Great, Phillipa."

The tears stopped suddenly. "Put yourself in my position – your twelve-year-old daughter has been taken..."

"Okay. Fair enough," I said. I thought to myself, it wouldn't be the first time I'd used what she was suggesting I use to influence a guy. With mixed results.

Across the room, Edgar signalled he wanted to go. I got up, told Phillipa I'd think about her offer, and having no intention of making the same mistake twice, scooped up the bundle of notes and left. As I walked back to the car, I broke up the notes and stuffed a chunk of them into four different pockets of my jeans. They felt as warm and erotic as any hand that had ever been there.

#

On the drive back, I let myself feel the excitement of having a real case... a serious case   finding a mother's daughter and bringing her back home. I wondered whether Phillipa was lying to me again. Edgar asked me what I was going to do, whether I would be staying in town or heading back to the city. I knew I would take the case from the moment Phillipa offered it. Edgar told me my car needed more replacement parts than his grandfather – the one who'd been dead for ten years.

"Rodney said parts for your car only existed in wreckers yards, city dumps, and your imagination. But don't worry I'm gonna lend you my car..."

"Really?" I said with suspicion.

"For nothing."

"I'll rent it from you."

"I'd be insulted."

"Okay," I said. "I'll give you a tiny amount and you can be slightly insulted." That made us both laugh.

"All right, there is something..."

"I knew it."

"I just need... some advice... some business advice."

"Business advice? Why would I have any business advice to give, Edgar – my own business is hanging by a thread."

"I just saw you get paid. Anyone earns that much has gotta be a business genius."

I shook my head at Edgar and felt the wads of notes in my pockets and a warm flush of business genius coursed through my body.

"Hey Edgar, in your humble opinion, do you think Phillipa is telling the truth?"

"Well girl, my opinion's never been called humble, but the tears looked honest and the money looked real."

I got Edgar's point and began to feel comfortable driving along with him.

"Would you say I'm a bit paranoid?" He asked.

"What?"

"Paranoid... you know.. illogically suspicious."

"Don't know you well enough. Are you?"

"Never thought I was..."

"You're making me uncomfortable here Edgar."

"I think there's been a car following us since we left the homestead." I turned around but there was nothing to see but our dust well into the distance.

"How do you know?"

"Sun reflected off their windscreen... and when I slowed down they never caught up."

#

Back at my hotel I got a call from Karl. I debated whether I should answer or not for a few seconds and then surrendered.

"Hi Karl."

"You idiot... You're about to be held in contempt of court."

"Oh shit!"

"I told the coroner a relation of yours suddenly got ill."

"Can you stall them a few more days..."

"No. You're doing something connected to that guy you killed aren't you?"

"Can you not say.. 'guy you killed?'"

"Okay, that guy you speared through the carotid artery with a curtain rod."

"Karl, two days... that's all I need." He went silent for a few moments.

"We traced the guy."

"Really? Who is he?"

"Come back and I'll tell you."

"Karl, I promise I'll be back in three days – four tops. It really means a lot to me... like I'm having nightmares I killed some guy with five kids... so tell me who is he?"

Silence for several seconds.

"Ex-army... Some kind of field trainer. You do not tell anyone you know this."

"Don't insult me."

"Okay, the guy did have a son."

"Shit, I knew it..."

"That he hadn't seen for seven years. Probably because he killed the boy's mother."

"He killed the boy's mother? You're just saying that to make me feel better."

"Make *you* feel better? Sometimes you can be a little self-absorbed."

"You know what I mean."

"They couldn't prove he did it, in fact they suspected him in two other killings."

"He's a professional?"

"We think so."

35

"Shit!"

"You got lucky, Frankie I'm serious you need to come clean about everything you know."

"Karl, I will, I promise as soon as I'm back I'll tell you everything I know."

"No, tell me now."

"Two days, Karl... stall them please."

"Where are you?"

"I can't tell you."

"I know where you are."

"What?"

"I put a satellite tracker on your car."

"You bastard."

"What are you doing in a place called the Promised Land? And don't give me any bullshit."

"I've got to go, Karl... there's someone here... wants some business advice."

"Hey! Don't you hang up on me!"

"Love and kisses Karl."

I hated hanging up on Karl but I didn't want him rushing up here like I'm a naughty adolescent. I knew he would cover for me with the coroner's court. His loyalty and protection was dear to my heart.

#

Edgar ushered me through the door of a rambling old building on the edge of town that a hundred years ago was a Hall of Arts. I was truly surprised as I stepped inside. Like stepping back in time, it resembled a dozen drawing rooms of about the 1970s. Old padded lounges and recliners, cedar tables and chairs, collections of alarm clocks and old cameras and iron pots, a pinball machine and pool table, a monster coffee machine – the whole thing brought to life by the orange glow of a dozen tasselled floor lamps. I turned to Edgar.

"I love it!" I said, meaning it.

"It's lovely isn't it, my wife started it twenty-five years ago. She loved the place a lot... here every day and most nights. She called it an Introduction Agency in those days."

"A dating agency?"

"Uh huh... before the internet. People used to love coming here... stay all day... lotta lonely farm and mining boys out here."

"Okay," I said as I walked through the place, noticing myself smiling. "What you need is a website, Edgar."

"That's what Roxy said, but you know that wouldn't bring people in here would it? They just e-mail in pictures of themselves taken twenty years ago.. and stay in their bedrooms..."

"Who's Roxy?"

"She's tucked away down the back here." Edgar got a dopey grin on his face as he pulled aside a curtain strung along the back wall to reveal a tiny, dark haired woman sitting at a computer. "This here's Roxanne Tilbury," he said with a soft tone and love-struck eyes. "Roxy, I'd like you to meet Miss Frankie... ahh..."

"Bennetti," I helped him out.

"You from the council?" Roxy asked.

"Ah no," I said politely.

Roxy glanced at Edgar. "Ain't no way she's a client."

Edgar laughed. "No, no she's giving me some business advice."

"Business advice?... She giving you...business advice?..." Roxy looked at me suspiciously, her eyebrows raised. "Best advice I can see is change the introduction agency to an escort agency..." Edgar ignored the suggestion and turned to me.

"Roxy was a godsend..."

"Work release send, actually," Roxy said.

"Pardon?" I said.

Edgar cut in. "From the correctional institution just out of town... They like to place the girls in work situations prior to their release."

"Excellent," I said, thinking OMG rather than excellent. At this point I noticed a lanky farm boy standing alongside me holding his wide brimmed hat over his crotch and staring at me.

"Is she available?" He said to Edgar.

"What?" Edgar said. "No, you idiot she's my business adviser."

"Oh," he said, disappointed.

Edgar grabbed the boys arm. "Come with me." He turned to Roxy and me as he dragged the boy away. "You two have a business discussion."

Roxy watched them disappear down the room through the furniture and turned to me. "Listen Bennetti..."

"Frankie," I said.

"Whatever. If you're here to rip this guy off," she said intently. "You better think twice –'cause he's a dickhead for sure but a goodhearted one who's seriously helped me out."

"Hey, he's all yours... I'm just returning a favour..."

"Okay – favour away, what's your business advice?"

"I don't have any."

"Well I do." She stared at me in silence.

"You want to share the advice? I asked, beginning to get annoyed.

"And let you take all the credit?"

Now I was pissed off. "Listen, Roxy Whatever... I don't want your credit, or Edgar... nor do I care for your opinion but I will get politeness from you."

"Or what, little city girl?"

I could feel the angry little hornet inside me starting to buzz. I lent on the back of her chair, my face up close to hers. "Or this." I pushed hard on the chair back and watched Roxy flip backwards and land on the floor with the chair on top of her.

She leapt to her feet immediately, scrabbling at the desk for a weapon and finding a stapler. I whipped out my baby Glock and held it at her head between her eyes. From another room, Edgar's voice sounded concerned.

"Are you girls all right out there?" Silence. Roxy and I glared at each other.

"Yeah, we're like besties..." I called out to Edgar.

He called happily back. "I knew it – I knew the two of you would get along.."

Suddenly it was very funny. I started to grin and Roxy couldn't help herself, she dropped the stapler, straightened the chair, and slumped into it giggling.

"Sheez girl," I said to her. "You may be the first person I've found angrier than me."

"Sorry," she said, sticking out her hand. "I get social worker types who want to fix me and save me from myself... and nervous ninnies that think prison is catching... by the way that is a cool little gun."

"Yeah, it's my real bestie."

"Can I have a look?"

"Sure..." I started to pass it to her and she slapped my hand away.

"Fuckwit... Don't ever give a stranger your gun!"

There was a stunned silence and then we both fell about laughing.

#

Later when Edgar walked back to my hotel with me, he told me Roxy was in detention for a confrontation with her sister's violent boyfriend who regularly used her sister as a punching bag.

"How come she got time for that?" I asked.

"Well, she confronted him with a ten inch kitchen knife in quite a few places."

"Okay. Still sounds like a civic duty to me."

Edgar laughed. "So, Frankie girl... can you do me a favour?"

"Probably not."

"Seriously, the correctional institution's social worker

actually won't renew Roxy's work-release authority with me. She doesn't believe there's any work."

"Is there any work?"

"Not really. Frankie girl this is serious... Do you have a business registration?"

Now I was beginning to get edgy. "Maybe..."

"Do you or don't you?"

"Yes, I do... but..."

"You can hire Roxy yourself.. To work for you. The social worker will love the fact you're a woman... I think she has special feelings for women..."

"Jesus, Edgar does Roxy know how you feel about her?"

"Oh no... well... maybe... probably... But look at us, could you find a worse fit... she barely comes up to my belt buckle and her waist is about the size of my wrist."

"Yeah, those are serious wrists, Edgar, you could lose a few buckets of lard."

"I know... I know, that's part of my plan! See the camels don't put on weight do they? No matter how much I feed them... "

"True, I haven't seen a lot of fat camels."

"So when I take a tour group, I'm gonna walk and carry the same load as them."

"The tourists?"

"No, the camels."

I looked closely at Edgar to see if he really had been out in the desert without a hat too often, but no, he looked serious. "Good plan," I said.

After farewelling Edgar, I decided to go find out about my car before going to the hotel room. The garage was locked up but there were lights on inside. I looked through a dust caked window for the agoraphobic Rodney. I saw my car at the far end of the workshop, it was in pieces spread out over the concrete floor. I was shocked and ready to shoot Rodney if I could find him. The window was gummed shut with age and grease. I looked around for something to lever it open with. And then I got the disturbing sense that I was being watched. Perhaps I was imagining it, encouraged by Edgar telling me a car was following us when we left Phillipa's place. I looked around in the fading light. No one. I'd thought about smashing the glass out of the window but who knows how Rodney might react to a break and enter – *eccentric*, I believe, is just the hillbilly cousin to insane.

"Rodney!" I shouted.

From behind me, the shock of a deep voice spun me around.

"He'll never answer you." Wheeling towards me, a big grin on his face, was Captain Travis Pike. "I've never actually seen him, and he's fixed my van twice."

"Have you been following me?"

"Phillipa told me you paid her a visit. Are you going to slap me around too?"

"I would," I said, "only I never hit the weaker sex."

Travis laughed with his handsome head thrown back, and my anger with him scooted off like a bunny rabbit in the desert.

"Frankie, I'm sorry for what you went through... we had no idea it would get violent."

"Well now you know."

"Phillipa is afraid he'll take Carol away from her."

"There are courts to stop that."

"Not so simple, Frankie. Carol is twelve, she thinks her mother unfairly threw her father out – if she found out about me..."

I remembered myself at twelve: I knew everything... and hated everyone. "Okay, so what about hubby? Is he capable of hiring a murderous armed professional just to get some love letters?"

"I don't know. I've known him for a few years, his company does the financial stuff for the army bases overseas. I was assigned as liaison to escort him to meetings in Kabul and later in Paris for meetings with the

UN. That's also where I met Phillipa. A large part of my time was spent showing Paris to Phillipa at Heyden's request. He used to do four or five meetings a day."

"Workaholic?"

"Probably."

"So where do you think Carol is now?"

"Could be at his city apartment – he's used professional child-minders before, or his sisters place."

"Phillipa wants me to bring her back."

"I know. Carol is a good kid really."

"What do you mean – really?"

"She's twelve, she's angry, desperate for her father's attention, and ready to go to war with her mother."

"So am I supposed to kidnap her against her will and take her from her father – a guy who probably hired a professional killer..."

"This is why I wanted to talk to you – if you find Carol, you could call me and I can talk to her. She likes me – probably because of this..." He hit the rubber tires of the wheelchair.

To myself, I think the film star good looks wouldn't hurt either.

#

After Travis left I sat in the bar of the hotel sipping a glass of Coke and ice the size of a fish tank. A part of me thought I should tell Karl and let the cops figure it out. Another part of me, perhaps the most interesting part sensed there was more to Travis and Phillipa's story. Something didn't feel right. Like someone hiring the services of a professional just to get some letters – serious overkill – as well as the amount of money Phillipa was thrusting at me. I wanted to find out more.

"G'day girl," Edgar's voice made me jump. Alongside him, Roxy stood awkwardly, holding a bunch of droopy desert flowers. They both seemed relieved and pleased to see me.

"Want a drink?" I asked.

"Can't drink alcohol on work release," Roxy said.

I held up my Jacuzzi of Coke. "It's all soft..."

"Soft it is," Roxy said.

"I'll have a... a... Coke too," Edgar said.

"You can drink whatever you like," Roxy said to him.

"I like Coke," Edgar said.

"Really?" Roxy said, squinting at him.

Edgar was so dopey-eyed with love, there was no way he could look at her directly and lie. "I hate it," he said.

Roxy raised her eyebrows at me in a 'how-do-men-even-get-dressed-by-themselves' look.

"Edgar wants me to employ you," I told her.

"Really? Oh shit, really?"

"Only need to sign an employer's form, that's all," Edgar said.

"Would you do that?" Roxy asked with genuine surprise.

"I have to go back to the city," I said.

"She could work where she is at the agency – she's not allowed to leave the Promised Land. You realize you'd be saving her from having to go back to prison," Edgar said.

I tried to avoid his lovesick eyes but hey, I've always been a sucker for love.

#

As I headed back to the city in Edgar's borrowed Land Rover, I realized how ridiculous life was – a few days ago I was going out of business, fighting failure, depression, boredom, with mounting debts. Now I was in the desert, my pockets stuffed with fifty dollar notes – I was the business advisor of an outback dating agency, I had a new employee, and a new case: a missing girl case. How good was that. I was on a roll, what could possibly go wrong.

After three hours of interviews and form filling at the correctional institution outside town, I was cured of wanting a life of crime. And this was a minimum security prison – clean as a hospital, all stainless steel and comfortable furniture. The women I passed looked bored and subdued. The social worker didn't believe I was a real employer for a minute but there was nothing she could do. I had the business registration and signed every document she could come up with to release the prison from any responsibility.

The road out of town was straight and flat as far as I could see which was a seriously long way. I had come to like the desert and even made peace with the heat, the flies and the grit that blew into your eyes and stuck in your throat. Behind me a vehicle had been gaining on me for a few minutes which was impressive because I was travelling well over the limit. It never occurred to me that it was a police car until the lights started flashing. The road at that point had been built up over a 'once in twenty years' floodplain and was narrow. Pulling over meant parking on the edge of a considerable drop. It wouldn't be my first speeding fine, and as I saw in the rear vision mirror the middle-aged cop getting out of his car, I wished I'd worn something more girly. I got out of the car and he waved at me.

"Too hot... stay in the car," he called out. I was happy to get back into the car. I rolled down the window and beamed most of my teeth at him. He came up slowly, took off his hat and smiled back. This was good. He was sweating as he leaned into the car.

"Hi, officer," I said breezily.

"Do you mind?" He said, as he opened the rear door and climbed in behind me. This was not good. He had a bulb of a stomach and burnt, blotchy skin. I could smell cheap aftershave and garlic as he pulled the door shut.

"I'm Frankie," I said, twisting around and passing my license to him.

"Hi Frankie. I'm Hugo... Hugo Ravic." His hand reached over my shoulder and I shook it.

"I think I may have been travelling a little over the

limit," I said, as sweetly as I could – which may not have been sweet at all – I have got sweet wrong in the past.

"I saw you in town," he said, looking at the photo on my license.

"Really," I said. Dim-witted response but it was getting hotter in the car with the engine and air con off.

"You here for something in particular?"

"Aahh... yeah."

"Mind telling me what?"

"Aahh... Officer Hugo... have you stopped me for speeding?"

"I wouldn't get too friendly with the camel guy."

"Edgar?"

"Uh huh... ran his wife's introduction agency into the ground."

"Well... the internet..."

"Do you know the Ericsson's?"

"Aah well... Patricia... I mean Phillipa..."

"The husband, Heyden virtually gave the town its swimming pool."

"*That* is really nice."

"Now that sounded like city sarcasm."

"Really? I think sometimes I come across like that officer... I don't mean to but some of my friends have pointed it out to me..."

"Here's the thing, Frankie we're very protective of each other out here – got to be – not a lot of interest from outside. So I make it my business to know what's happening and what might happen because I don't like surprises."

The angry little hornet was beginning to buzz. "Okay, Hugo what's going to work for me is that you give me a ticket and a little lecture on the dangers of speeding, if that's your thing, and I'll drive off, and you can go have a nice cool swim in the town pool – how does that sound? Because unless someone dug Stalin up, this is still a democracy."

I twisted around and saw his expression had changed. I could almost hear his thoughts calculating – his pension entitlements versus smacking me around. He got out of the car and stood alongside the driver's window, turning my license over and over between his fingers. He looked at it and read my name.

"Okay, Miss Frankie Bennetti, I believe you are some kind of debt collector or investigator."

"And how would you know that?"

"I know everything that happens in my jurisdiction."

"Look, give me a ticket or I'm going to go."

"Do you carry a firearm?"

"Yes, I do."

"Is it licensed?"

"Yes it is – and I'm surprised you didn't know that."

"May I see it please?"

A spasm of fear joined my anger. I stared back at him. "Why would you need to see it?"

"I'm sure you are aware we are authorized to inspect firearms."

I reached into my jeans and pulled out the Glock. When I turned towards him holding it out butt first, I saw that he had drawn his .38mm and was pointing it at my forehead.

"Now before you could get that safety off, I could have two neat holes in your head. Does that sound reasonable to you, Miss Bennetti?"

"Very reasonable."

"And I would say that when I pulled you over for speeding, you drew your gun and I had no option... You following me?"

"Every word."

"Now, a couple of things for you to consider – one, I don't want you to come back here and two, I don't want you to have any contact, connection or dealings with the Ericssons."

"Mrs Ericsson has hired me!"

"I don't care."

"If you like the Ericssons, why wouldn't you care – she wants my services."

"People don't always know what's best for them, Frankie."

With his gun at my head, I thought what's best for me is to shut up. But I wasn't known for doing what was best for me. "This is her husband.. isn't it?" I asked. "Getting you to do this?"

"Now you're going to do as I ask and stay away aren't you Frankie?"

"Cross my heart and hope not to die..."

"See that kind of smart-mouth city shit talk is... it.. drives me crazy..."

"Sorry... I won't come back."

"Give me your gun."

"No."

This truly surprised him but I remembered Roxy's advice – not to be a fuckwit and give up your gun. He was unsure what to do. The sound of a car approaching made him glance down the road and back at me. I could see how quickly his confidence faded – he was never going to shoot me – he was just pissed that a girl, a city girl, would not get all teary and frightened. He looked at me with some kind of hatred that I knew had less to do with me than some other female from his past. He was looking for a way out with dignity and I tried to give it to him.

"Look, I'm sorry, I was smart mouthed... I'm just trying to do my job."

The car was getting closer – he looked at it and back at me and then in a quick movement, threw my license as far as possible into the desert. It lifted and fluttered on the breeze as I kept watching so I would be able to find it. Without waiting for any smart mouthed putdowns, he wheeled away back to his car and took off with a squeal of tires, throwing gravel and dust up into the air.

I waited till the approaching car passed, waving at a

white-haired old man bent over the steering wheel before I climbed down the steep embankment. And then I realized I was shaking and exhausted, and I threw up into the dry desert sand.

And I cried because no one was there. I cried about the man I killed even though he might have deserved it – and I cried about being frightened by the bully cop and about being lonely and about life itself.

And then the phone rang and it was Roxy.

"I just wanna say thanks.. for signing the work release forms."

"Aah, Roxy... I needed that."

"What?"

"Oh nothing... Just feeling a bit sorry for myself."

"Are you crying?"

"No."

"Something's up, I have radar for shit like that."

I sighed and realized I had a deep tiredness. "Roxy, do you find life... like disappointing sometimes?"

"No. I find life disappointing all the time."

This struck me as particularly funny and I started laughing and couldn't stop.

"Whoa girl... I'm not that funny," Roxy said.

I took a deep long breath and let it go. And deficient as they were, my brain and heart were back. "Okay... listen Roxy, what do you know about the town cop?"

"Ravic?"

"Yeah."

"The guy looks like he swallowed a weather balloon? I've heard some of the worst bad boys he picks up in his police van seem to end up in bandages."

"If he threatened you, would he be serious – like should you be worried?"

"Did that prick threaten you?"

"Maybe."

"I know people Frankie... I can have his legs bend in the wrong direction."

"Aah thanks, Roxy that's okay. What about the Ericssons – Phillipa and Heyden Ericsson?"

"Not much. He's a hero around town because he's got a shitload of money and a few drachmas get dropped in town from time to time."

"What about a soldier – a Captain Travis Pike?"

"Pike? Ya gotta be kidding?"

"No. He's wounded – probably in Afghanistan and he's in a wheelchair."

"Never heard of him."

"Seeing as you are now an employee of Frankie Bennetti Investigations, could you find out what you can about all of them?"

"Woo hoo... I'm a private eye!"

"No, you are not... Roxy you are...a...a... an assistant."

"Assistant? That sounds boring. Can I be a.. investigator?"

"No."

"Okay, how about... researcher?"

"Okay, you can be a researcher."

"Can I be chief researcher?"

"Goodbye, Roxy."

"Wait, wait... I wanna ask you something."

"I'm driving so make it quick."

"I had this terrific idea to get the introduction agency firing for Edgar... you know there are a gazillion farmers, miners and other guys on the books and we never have any women to match them with – well we do now, da daa – the prison! There are a hundred and fifteen lonely women locked up and primed to go..."

"Are you nuts?"

"Listen to me...more than half of the prisoners are allowed out on supervised visits to town..."

"You are nuts."

"And we could hold a dance...in town...invite all the..."

"I'm hanging up Roxy..."

"No, seriously it's a great idea..."

"Take your medication and go do some.. investigative research."

"Hey that's it... I'm an investigative researcher."

4

On the steps of the coroners court, Karl was waiting for me with his angry, protective face. I was so relieved at the finding of 'death by self-inflicted injury during an assault', that I flung my arms around him. To his credit, he didn't pull away even though I knew it would not look good for an investigating officer to be so obviously close to an investigatee.

"There's a cafe under the bookshop a five-minute walk that way," he said. "Meet me there in ten minutes. Now let me go, thank me, and walk away."

I let go of him and thanked him very loudly, shaking his hand vigorously. "How's this... only strangers shake hands," I said with a big smile.

I walked away without looking back – also something you do only with strangers.

The bookshop cafe was snug and smelt of coffee and what I imagined was something like printer's ink. As I slid into a booth with a sugar loaded, long black, I wondered whether this was a place Karl might come to on a regular basis. I realized I knew very little about his personal life. I also realized how pleased I was to see him as I watched him enter the cafe and head for my cubicle. As he sat opposite me, I was about to apologize for running off to the desert when he held up a hand.

"Shut up. I don't want to hear how sorry you are..."

"Okay... but I'm really..."

"I mean it, shut up!" He stared at me for several seconds.

"So are we going to sit here in silence?"

"No. I'm going to decide whether I take your license away."

"Really?" I said. He was angry but I could see in his eyes he would never hurt me. "I was on a case, Karl."

He grabbed my wrist. "The cop from the Promised Land did a departmental search on you."

"Ravic?"

"Christ, you even know his name." He let go my wrist and shook his head.

"He's a pig...he threw my license..."

"I don't care what he did – you probably deserved it."

"That's not..."

"Shut up. Lucky for you they put him through to me..."

"Okay...thank you."

"This stops now, Frankie – you tell me everything you know – otherwise I swear I'll pull your license."

My mind raced trying to figure how much I should tell him. If he knew about Phillipa and Travis, he'd talk to them immediately and they'd know it was me and never trust me – and more importantly never hire me. And I was really liking the way the fifties filled out my jeans.

"The second I know anything worth telling you, I promise I will."

"Not good enough."

"You have to trust me."

"Why?"

"Because that's what a good relationship needs."

"Relationship?"

"You know what I mean." This seemed to have thrown him a little.

"That guy you killed – he's out of your league, Frankie...you got lucky."

"I know that."

"Okay, good."

The relationship thing had completely disarmed him. I could feel the little risk taker inside me start to open its mouth. "Listen, Karl... I was thinking...would you... you know... sometime like to... you know aah.. Go out to dinner...you know like real people...?"

My phone chirped that I had a text from Roxy.

"A date?" Karl was shocked. Now he was definitely turning pinkish.

"Uh-huh," I said, as casually as I could, focusing on the text. Roxy had listed Heyden Ericsson's home and office address.

"Ah, I'm actually seeing someone at the moment," Karl mumbled. This slapped my face hard. I kept staring at Roxy's text to hide my horror.

"Oh really... oh good... I just thought... listen I've got to go." I held out my phone as proof of my need to go. I got up, careful not to knock over his coffee. I'd watched this scene in the movies a dozen times – if I'd been wearing a dress it would be ripped off, snagged on the table, I would trip and sprawl across the floor and my handbag would burst open and twenty-seven tampons would roll across the cafe and into the kitchen.

"Frankie!" He called after me. I turned at the entrance to the cafe and tried to salvage some pride by smiling and waving – I had bypassed embarrassment and gone straight to humiliation. Then I got the hell out. The level of my suffering told me I must have been fooling myself about Karl being hot for me and that it was obviously the other way around.

5

I loved the 21st century. I could sit in a car painted with camels outside a city office tower in a no parking zone, using a counterfeit emergency services sticker downloaded from the Internet, ordering car-delivered coffee by iPhone. And if I wanted I could play scrabble with someone in Kazakhstan, while I listened to a podcast on 'how best to use your time'.

I knew Heyden Ericsson was there in his thirty fourth floor office because I phoned the front desk and pretended I had an appointment. I also knew this guy possibly hired some kind of professional to track me and possibly kill me. I checked his city apartment address that Roxy found for me and he hadn't been there for weeks. I needed to know where he was staying now – presuming his daughter, Carol was there with him.

My first stakeout and I was beginning to hope he hurried up and came out because I was going to need to pee. I hadn't needed three soy lattes but I kind of got a kick out of the cafe guy knocking on the window with my delivery.

I tried not to think of the humiliation with Karl. But on the positive side it did tell me clearly that maybe I felt something for him that I was unaware of. Unaware was a good word for me regarding relationships. With various guys I have dated, I have been unaware of being ignored, betrayed, and lied to. I was also, on occasion, unaware some of them saw me as a needy, angry, demanding and criticizing bitch. Okay, I was aware of the angry bit. A therapist I used to see, said that with an abandoning father and sociopathic mother, it was a wonder I hadn't shot up a school or beheaded cats.

Two skater boys were practicing jumps up and down the gutter by swinging off parking meters. They weren't wearing protective gear and I loved to watch their careless energy. I wondered whether it was too late for me to learn skateboarding at the precise moment the younger boy snagged his wheels and spilled forward onto the concrete. I phoned the cafe to deliver two sweet, milky coffees to them and watched their astonished faces as the cafe guy pointed me out. They rolled up to my window, unsure what to say.

"You guys have been entertaining me," I said. "The coffee is appreciation."

They looked at each other and back to me and hopefully saw that I didn't have any sinister motives. They smiled warmly at me.

"Thanks," the older boy said, slightly embarrassed and excited. "Are you like.. a camel herder or something?" He said, indicating Edgar's camels on the side of the Land Rover.

"Ahh, no – it's a friend's car."

They rolled away and up the pavement still holding the paper cups and continued gutter jumping with obvious awareness now of being watched. I wondered whether this could be their first ever coffee and that maybe I should have ordered hot chocolate. I wondered about having children, my own children, and decided to shut that alarm off before it frightened the horses and got me pregnant.

With about fifteen minutes left in my bladder, Heyden Ericsson appeared through the doorway of Ericsson

Financial Services. I was expecting his BMW to come out of the underground car park and it took me unawares. I got out quickly and locked the Land Rover as he walked quickly away from the CBD, and without waiting for the traffic lights, crossed a side street.

I was excited with my first real tailing. I had practiced on unknown strangers and believed I was pretty good. I was tempted to text Roxy so I could enjoy it more but Heyden Ericsson was moving too quickly. I dodged cars across the side street as they honked angrily at me but I kept him in sight, just. I praised God that I was wearing runners and not my sexy ankle snappers. At the next intersection he crossed into a busy park where office workers sat in groups finishing lunch, joggers trotted by, and kids yelled at each other as they wrestled on the grass or tossed balls. With dopey luck I was still carrying my foam coffee cup which helped me to appear like a lunchtime worker.

Ericsson headed for a shrubby corner of the park and momentarily I lost sight of him. I cut through a dog obedience group and two teenagers twisting together on the grass and there was my man seated on a bench alongside a guy – maybe mid-forties, in an expensive cashmere suit. The guy was eating something from a brown paper bag – he didn't look like someone who ate out of a paper bag.

I sat on the grass to the side of their eye line and sipped my cold coffee. I was out of earshot but they appeared to exchange a few pleasantries and nod and smile like strangers. Ericsson lit up a cigarette and I realized he had just ducked out for a naughty private cigarette. I was disappointed. I could see the park toilets a stone's throw away and it sent a signal to my brain that my bladder must be obeyed – like immediately. I was sure Heyden Ericsson was going to puff away for at least another few minutes, and even if he left he would be going back to his office.

In the toilets, which were disgusting, I tried to hold my

breath as long as possible. The relief though, was worth the toxic aroma. I emerged a new woman – two percent lighter and Heyden Ericsson was nowhere in sight. I calculated a quicker way back to his building and took off, dodging pedestrians and cranky car drivers.

I cursed giving into my bladder and mumbled apologies as I pushed past slow-moving groups. I reached my car out of breath and promised myself to get back to the gym tomorrow or maybe this week or soon anyway. The older skateboarder was still jumping gutters and waved to me. I was relieved the coffee hadn't revved him up to try skateboarding on top of the cars. At the far corner on the opposite side of the street, Heyden Ericsson came into sight and I was delighted my first tailing wasn't a complete disaster. Then I noticed he was carrying something. It looked very much like the lunch bag of mister cashmere suit from the park. I was truly puzzled – he'd had no time to buy lunch – it had to be the same bag. Why would he have taken the guy's bag? I made a snap decision – not always my best ones. I signalled the skater boy, who immediately rolled up, and in a show-offy way flip-caught his board and smiled at me.

"Can you do me a big favour?" I asked.

He frowned – maybe the old lady really was some kind of pervert.

"Like what?"

"See that guy opposite...the one with the lunch bag – do you think you could rock by him and snatch up the paper bag? It's kinda like a prank – he's like... my boss."

The kid looked at me with his brain going a million miles an hour.

"Here's fifty dollars now and another fifty when you go around the block, wait ten minutes and bring the paper bag back to me here. You'll have to decide quickly – he's headed for that building."

The kid was uncertain, he looked from the building to Ericsson and back to me.

"I'll buy you another coffee..." I said, with a wink.

He found this funny, grinned back at me, and took off across the road, weaving between the moving cars like a slalom skier. I wondered whether I had lost my mind. Karl's disapproving face appeared in my brain.

I got into my car and watched in the rear vision mirror Heyden Ericsson heading towards his building and skater boy heading towards him at warp speed. The closer the two got, the more regretful I became. I was reckless just like my old principal said – I didn't think things through.

As if in slow motion, skater boy snatched the bag from a truly shocked Heyden Ericsson who spun around and watched helplessly as the boy disappeared down the edge of the road against the run of traffic which swerved and honked and shouted at him. Ericsson took off after him but it was obviously futile. The boy rounded the corner on the road travelling faster than the traffic. At the corner, Ericsson stopped chasing and dialled on his phone.

My heart was pounding – I had broken the law or worse – incited a minor to break the law. Maybe I was not really cut out for investigating work. But at the back of my mind I knew that the way Ericsson reacted there was something more than a sandwich in that lunch bag.

#

Five minutes ticked by slowly and I began to calm down. Ericsson quickly tracked back to his office, phone to his ear all the way. I called Roxy to keep my mind off what I had just done.

"Roxy?"

"Yeah."

"I might be joining you in prison."

"Frankie this isn't a prison, it's a Low Security Correctional Facility...big difference... think country club.

"I paid a minor to break the law..."

"A miner? Are we talking gold or coal?"

"Minor!... a fourteen-year-old kid I've never seen before... I paid him to steal something."

"I like you more all the time."

"Seriously Roxy..."

"What did he steal?"

"I don't know."

"Okay... that makes sense, pay someone you don't know to steal something you don't know."

"A brown paper bag..."

"With what in it, for God's sake?"

"I don't know...a sandwich maybe?"

"Wow, you must be seriously hungry."

"It's not a joke...the guy I asked you about, Heyden Ericsson, he went to the park and... ahh... look...it doesn't matter..."

"I've been investigating... errr.. researching the Ericssons."

"And?"

"Not a lot...father spends most of his time in the city – he's head of some big financial company. The mother keeps to herself in her big homestead and is considered pretty much a snob by the townspeople. They have a daughter, Carol who's twelve and a handful. Apparently she has too much money – buys too expensive presents for the other kids, especially since she doesn't need to – apparently she's got the drop dead blonde model look."

"That's it?"

"Hey, there's not a lot of people here will talk to me."

"Sorry, I know... I'm just a bit tense."

"Okay. By the way, Edgar and I may have a surprise for you..."

To my horror I saw a parking officer coming towards me. "Gotta go!" I said to Roxy and hung up.

The parking officer looked at my emergency sticker and punched the keyboard of his hand-held, Nazi computer. He indicated to me to roll down my side window.

"How much are they charging for those now?"

"Pardon?" I said, knowing exactly what he was talking about.

"The fake sticker."

"What do you mean fake?" I tried for as much indignation as I could. He shook his head.

"You need to move now, or I will message the police. You will receive a ticket in the mail in the next seven days."

"Look officer, I just need to be here another five minutes."

"I'm sorry..." He looked at his computer and read the screen. "Edgar Wilson. Are you Mrs Edgar Wilson?"

"Aahh... That's right," I said.

"Do you want the police to move you? You are not only breaking the law with the false sticker, but you are actually parked in a *no stopping* zone."

"Okay," I said, starting the car engine.

He moved back and watched as I made the world's worst back and forth attempts to leave a car park. I continued to look for the skateboard boy but he was nowhere in sight.

The parking officer called out to me. "I can send a message about your resistance to obey a legal direction..."

"I'm trying... you prick!" I said to myself, to calm my inner hornet, forgetting the window was still down.

"What did you say?"

"I said I'm trying to be quick..."

With the car free, I decided to stall it by discreetly yanking the park brake on.

"Okay, that's it..." he said.

"I'm going! I'm going!"

I restarted the car and pulled out very slowly. Coming towards me, around the corner, I saw my skater boy. I stopped and rolled the window down. Cars behind me went nuts with their horns and shouted abusive things about my IQ. The kid rolled up alongside and tossed the bag through to me. I held out the fifty and he winked and

61

smiled but didn't take it. He indicated the parking officer.

"I saw him hassling you. He's a dickhead... moves us on all the time. Watch this..."

He jumped the gutter, rolled towards the parking officer and picked up speed. As he passed, he snatched the Nazi computer from the hands of the officer to his horror and mine.

I did not wait to see what happened. I took off with a squeal of tires and hurtled off into the traffic. In the rear vision mirror I caught the reflection of my own eyes. "That went well," I said to myself.

6

It was dark as Heyden Ericsson stopped his BMW outside a large, beautifully restored Victorian terrace in Glebe. I followed half a dozen cars back and was surprised that we were only five minutes' drive from the city centre in a student dominated precinct surrounding the University.

I waited until he went inside and parked a little way past and opposite his house. After the dickhead parking officer had moved on back in the city, I returned to my original stakeout opposite Ericsson's building and waited until he emerged from his car park. The lunch bag contained only a thumb sized USB drive, still in its new plastic wrap. He must have bought it on his way back after having his cigarette in the park. It was disappointing – and a relief at the same time. He was unlikely to pursue the theft of a ten dollar computer drive. In the terrace house there were lights on and I strained to see any sign of Phillipa's daughter.

Sitting and waiting is not one of my strengths, and having sat today longer than a breeding turkey, I slipped out of the car for a closer look through one of the church like Victorian windows which all had steel security bars. I edged cautiously along the side of the house. Inside, I could see a tastefully furnished sitting room and beyond that a small dining room. No people anywhere. I moved further along to another window which had white lace curtains and was lit by a soft stream of light from a hallway. It appeared to be a bedroom. I suddenly remembered my phone and scrambled to turn it off before someone called and made it squawk.

I cupped my hands against the window in order to see better. And then received a nasty shock – a face was staring back at me. The window popped open and a young girl pointed a kitchen fork at my face.

"You're from my mother, aren't you?" She said confidently.

"Whaa... I'm..."

"I saw you pull up in the camel guy's car."

"Right," I said, my mind racing to find something intelligent to say as I cursed Edgar's camel safari signs all over his Land Rover.

"She sent you, didn't she?"

"Aahh...well...now..."

"I'm not going home...back... I'm staying with my dad. You can tell her... it's her fault."

I saw the fork was not really a weapon, she was eating some kind of spaghetti dish that looked like it came out of a can.

"Carol?" I asked.

"She didn't tell me.. or even talk to me before she told dad to leave – so I don't have to talk to her."

"Sounds fair."

This stopped her. She looked at me and finally saw *my* face rather than a substitute for her mother's. "So what are you doing sneaking around looking in our windows?"

"Actually... I'm a pervert."

This got a tiny smile of respect. "I'm not going back," she said and her teenage fear and doubt wafted over me, taking me back for a few seconds to those horrible, wonderful years.

"Would you phone her?" I said gently. "So she can

know you're okay."

"No. She doesn't deserve it."

I took out my phone. "What if I called her and you just said a few words."

"No. If you call her, I'll call the police and report you as a pervert prowler."

"Okay." I hesitated. "But can you report me as an attractive and polite pervert prowler?"

This got a reluctant smile. "Look..." she started to say, then a man's voice from within the house called out.

"Carol? Are you talking to yourself in there?"

Her face changed to concern, she turned away and called out into the house. "I'm practicing a speech I have to give at school, dad." She turned to me and whispered as she closed the window. "Go...now."

I handed her a card. "My number – call me after you've thought about it or if you want someone to talk to, okay?"

As I headed back to the car, I realized she could have given me away, but she didn't. That was kind or generous or protective of her father. Perhaps she was glad that her mother cared enough about her to send someone after her – she was angry but amongst the anger was hurt. As I got into the car I made a mental note for the 'Handbook for Investigators' I intended to write in my old age: *the best vehicle for undercover work is not a Land Rover painted with a string of camels.*

Before I could pull away from the curb, the passenger door opened and Heyden Ericsson climbed in.

"So, are you looking to use my bathroom again or start camel tours across the city?"

I recovered quickly. "I just wanted to speak to Carol..."

"Phillipa sent you?"

"Hired."

"She hired you?"

"Yes."

"You're some kind of investigator?"

"The good kind."

"Hired you to do what?"

"To talk to her daughter and get her daughter to talk to her."

"And how did that go?"

"She's angry with her mother and won't talk to her."

"Surprise, surprise."

"Her mother's worried that's all."

"Carol just needs a little time."

"Yeah, I know."

"Meanwhile, you have something of mine."

"Pardon?"

"A brown paper bag snatched by your skateboarding friend on the street outside my building to day."

"I don't know what you're talking about."

"One of my staff was laughing about the camel car parked opposite our building in a no parking zone."

"Really?"

"Look, Ms..."

"Bennetti.. Frankie Bennetti"

"Bennetti... You seem like a nice enough person..."

"Not everyone would agree with you but thanks."

"You're a bad liar. If you give it back to me, it's all forgotten."

"Can't give you what I don't have..."

"Look, you could get hurt here, seriously hurt..."

I wanted to tell him that the last person he sent after me didn't get what he wanted and did get seriously hurt – but I thought better of it. Maybe he didn't know it was me that did the serious hurting. He looked around the car, presumably for his package but I had stashed it under the driver's seat – a little habit I picked up after having stuff stolen from my car.

"You want to search...?" I offered.

He stared at me for an uncomfortably long time and then opened the car door and got out still holding the door open.

"You know where I am," he said. "Please, for your sake

and mine, give it back to me."

"I'm here for Carol – to get her to go back to her mother. You know that's the right thing...please tell her."

Ericsson shook his head and took a deep breath. "You probably only have a few hours..." he said. He stood there hopefully for a few more seconds before slamming the door and walking away.

#

I was grateful Karl was out as I let myself in to his apartment. My laptop and a few other things I'd left behind at my apartment were neatly stacked on a coffee table. I wondered whether Karl's girlfriend had folded my clothes and the thought brought back the humiliation from the bookshop cafe. I needed to look closer at Heyden Ericsson's paper bag. If he was so keen to get it back, it had to be more than a ten dollar USB drive.

As the laptop booted up, I looked around for any tell-tale signs of what kind of woman Karl was seeing. Nothing. No feminine touches anywhere. I was annoyingly pleased. I was also annoyingly exhausted, I hadn't slept for way too long.

The USB drive asked whether I wanted to open files which was odd as it shouldn't have had any files on it, being brand-new. I clicked on it and a spread sheet opened with three columns without headings. The first two columns consisted of five digit numbers, the third column looked like dollars and cents – amounts which varied from hundreds to thousands. The list went on for pages and pages. I scrolled through the whole document – same thing – pages of numbers without headings or descriptions. Meaningless to me. I closed the file, pulled out the drive and dropped it in my bag. I decided to return it to Heyden Ericsson, I had no wish to have another gun carrying, door kicking visitor. Whatever it was – industrial secrets or whatever had nothing to do with me or what I was hired for. I was way too tired.

I called Heyden Ericsson's number and got his voicemail. I decided against leaving a message and literally crumpled onto Karl's bed, falling asleep before the bed stopped rocking.

#

I woke to the smell of coffee and the realization I wasn't on top of the bed clothes but under them. In my underwear. Karl was standing in the doorway sipping coffee.

"You've been asleep quite a while," he said, staring at me like a worried parent.

"Can I have some?" I asked him.

"Uh huh."

"Thanks...for putting me to bed." I smiled at him and he turned and headed to the kitchen.

"Your clothes are on the chair," he called out.

"I like your bed better than mine," I called back, then immediately felt like an idiot for what it could sound like. I leapt up and dressed, determine to get out quickly and head for my own place regardless of the blood and memories.

At the kitchen bench, Karl sat opposite me, he'd made toast and sliced up an avocado and some cheese. I was touched that he'd obviously made an effort.

"You're welcome here whenever you want," he said, without looking at me.

"Thanks Karl, but I need to get over... you know... with my apartment."

"Our cleaners are very good."

"I'm sure."

"We've also got good counsellors."

"Yeah I know. Did my dad ever go to counsellors?"

"You mean like after a bad job?"

"Uh-huh."

"Yeah... yeah... I think he did."

"He didn't, did he, Karl?"

"No."

"What was he like to work with?"

Karl looked away and pretended to do something in the kitchen, taking his time to answer. "Hard."

"In what way?"

"Demanded...a lot… and gave a lot."

"Was that good?"

"Best partner I've ever had." He looked at me squarely.

"Good." I smiled and refused to get emotional. Maybe I did need to talk to a counsellor.

Karl stopped fiddling in the kitchen and turned to face me. "You know our conversation in the cafe?" He asked quietly.

"Let's not go there," I said.

"I'm not seeing anyone."

"But you said..."

"I know – I just made it up."

"Why?"

"I don't know... something scary about it... and I'm ten years older."

"You could have just said thanks, but no thanks."

"But I *would* like to... go on a date..."

"Uh-huh," I said. My face was composed but my heart was like a five-year-old with a can of Red Bull.

"How about tonight?"

"I don't know, Karl... I've just started seeing someone..."

"Oh really?"

"No, I'm kidding. Tonight would be great."

7

My apartment reeked of solvents and bleach which somehow seemed reassuring. In the bathroom I kept having flashbacks of the shower scene from Psycho but I was determined not to be intimidated out of my own place. And it was my place – not my *home*. My home was an ideal – a fantasy I kept tucked away in some corner of my mind. I wasn't sure I'd even recognize a real *home* home.

After a shower, I felt better and sat on my tiny little balcony, eating an out-of-date vanilla yoghurt. I phoned Heyden Ericsson again to tell him I would be returning his USB drive. Voice mail again so I hung up. I tried not to think about dating Karl – yeah, right. Would it be a mistake? He was nearly ten years older but hey, he was in great shape. Would we sleep together? Before I could dissolve into that little fantasy, a sharp knocking on the front door shocked my yoghurt over the balcony. Fortunately no one was underneath.

Through the peephole, I could see nothing but black – someone's hand was over it. I got my Glock from the bedside table and listened up close to the door.

"Hey Frankie!" It was a woman's voice. I was flooded with relief and swung the door open.

"Roxy, what the hell... and Edgar!"

I was surprised how pleased I was to see them. Together, they looked as if they had stepped out of a sideshow of the bizarre: a child prostitute and a bear dressed in clothes that wafted 'essence de camel'. Roxy made for the bathroom and I turned to Edgar. "I thought she wasn't allowed to leave the Promised Land?"

"That's okay. I forged your signature as her employer that you gotta have her for three days in the city and you'd be responsible for her."

"Jesus, Edgar!"

"It's my plan. You know... my relationship plan. We have to spend some time together so she'll get to know me."

Roxy emerged from the bathroom and grinned at me. "We brought your car back," she said.

Edgar cut in. "Rodney adapted a few parts, it's kinda like new."

"Really? That's fantastic," I said, cheering up.

"Yeah, he put an old tractor engine in it – so it makes a bit of noise."

"What?"

Edgar shook his head. "Geez, Frankie, you city people are so gullible."

I laughed. I was feeling better by the minute. "So where are you staying?" I asked.

"Boss, we wouldn't think of leaving you by yourself," Roxy said.

"There's only one bed..." I protested.

"We have Edgar's Safari swags – better than a bed."

"Okay," I said, wondering if it was okay. Normally I would shoot anyone who even suggested staying over as I'm a very private person but somehow I liked the idea of these two moving in for a few days.

"So, boss... can we go shopping?" Roxy asked. "I have a credit card."

"Really, whose?"

Roxy blinked for a moment and then realized I was joking, she laughed and slapped my back. "You are so my best friend."

#

Roxy wanted to buy clothes and refused Edgar permission to come. She wanted the Julia Roberts, Pretty Woman makeover: slut to fox. I told her she'd nailed the first part beautifully which cracked her up.

Getting to fox took several hours and included a hairdresser, Italian shoe store, and lingerie specialist. Roxy had several credit cards. I didn't ask.

The transformation was astounding. She didn't quite make Julia Roberts but she made hot little fox. As we drove back to the apartment in my beloved old Falcon which was performing like new, thanks to Rodney the agoraphobic mechanic, I saw how excited and pleased she was.

"Do you think people can change, Frankie?" She asked.

"Big question," I said. "With a lot of answers."

"But what do you think?"

"Maybe, maybe not. Hard to tell whether someone changes or whether they were like that all along."

"I guess."

"Some people look like they've changed but maybe all along...like underneath, they were always someone else."

"Do you think I can change?"

"To what?"

"Shit, Frankie I'm a con! It's all upward from here."

I looked at Roxy. "No."

"No?"

"Because you don't need to – you're cool the way you are. And I don't think you're a con."

Roxy beamed love at me. "Two cool, foxy chicks – that's us."

"Foxy chick? – that's a chicken with fur or a fox with

73

feathers?"

Roxy slapped me as she giggled like a little girl. "You're absolutely the funniest boss I ever had."

"And you are definitely the funniest employee I've ever had."

"Hey Frankie, I have a little problem."

"Okay?"

"I need some money – like an advance."

"Okay."

"What do you mean, okay."

"Okay you can have an advance."

"You can't just give money away like that!"

"I trust you, and I like you."

"Now I don't want it."

"Okay."

"Stop saying that – I have to have a tattoo removed."

"Uh huh."

"It's on my arse."

"Well why bother – unless you do a lot of mooning."

"Very funny. It's embarrassing."

"Aha, it's Edgar you're worried about." Silence. "What is it?"

"It's just a few words."

"Uh huh."

"Kind of pessimistic.. And I don't feel like that now with you and Edgar."

"That's sweet."

"It says: 'life is like eating sugar – sweet at first – then turns to shit'."

"Subtle." I winked at Roxy and patted her shoulder. "So, what about Edgar and you?"

She sighed. "Can you imagine Edgar and me having sex?"

"Please, Roxy..."

"Seriously. I like him, he's kinder to me than anyone I've stumbled across in my fucked up life."

"But?"

"But... I don't know. We have fun... but he doesn't..."

"Boot up your hard drive?"

"That's ridiculous!"

"Defrost your refrigerator?"

"Now you sound like an idiot."

"Mayonnaise your sandwich?"

That cracked us both up and almost ran my car off the road. It also caused me to notice in the rear vision mirror, a silver Lexus that had been behind us when we left the parking station at the shopping centre. "I think someone is following us," I told Roxy calmly.

"What? Why would someone be following us?"

"Long story."

"Are they likely to be friendly?"

"Aahh.. no. They are likely to kill us."

"Jesus, Frankie... I hope you have life insurance for your employees," Roxy said, as she looked at me and grinned.

"I think they're after a USB drive..."

"A what?"

"It's in my bag – a thumb-sized computer drive."

Roxy reached into my bag and located the drive. "This?"

"Uh-huh."

"Why would they kill us for this? Why wouldn't we just give it to them? Hey, I'll even buy you another one."

"I was intending to return it when you and Edgar arrived."

I put my foot down and squeezed through a red light at a busy intersection and watched the Lexus rocket through on my tail. It was no longer pretending it wasn't following me. The Annandale police station was about five minutes away and I figured to pull up there and confront them. Traffic was slow on the highway but it was a safer choice than one of the side streets. Up ahead the traffic ground to a halt.

"Shit!" I cursed, as I hit the brakes.

"Don't worry, they can't do anything here," Roxy said.

I pulled up with the Lexus close behind and thought about leaping out and putting a shot through their windscreen.

To my surprise, I watched gob smacked, as a tall, completely bald guy jumped out of the passenger side of the Lexus, ran forward, ripped open the rear door of the Falcon and jumped into the back seat.

"Before you get excited and do something silly," he said calmly, "We just want to talk."

I restrained Roxy, who looked as if she was about to leap into the back of the car and tear his throat out.

"Okay, talk," I said.

"Not me... and not here. There's a parking lot for the fish markets up ahead – turn in there."

That sounded reasonable to me – there were plenty of people around. I also had my baby Glock primed and sitting on my lap.

I pulled into the entry bay and drove to a corner of the parking lot as far away from the stench of dead fish as possible. The Lexus pulled up alongside and the driver got out and beckoned to us to get into the car.

"No way," Roxy said.

I tucked the gun into my front jeans pocket, grabbed my bag and got out. "Stay here," I told Roxy. Roxy immediately got out. "You are not the most obedient employee," I said.

"Divide and conquer," Roxy said. "We should stay together."

Baldie remained in the Falcon. "Okay," I said, touched by her loyalty. "No dividing – no conquering." I peered into the back seat of the Lexus and took a few seconds to recognize the expensive suit guy with the lunch bag who met Heyden Ericsson in the park.

"Please... get in, Ms Bennetti," he said, politely.

I hesitated. It unnerved me that he knew my name. He had an upper-class British accent. "Why?" I asked.

"It would be to the benefit of us both."

I slid into the leather seat and Roxy pushed in behind me. The driver shut the door on us and I heard the locks click.

"To come directly to the point, Ms Bennetti – I would like you to return what you took from Mr Ericsson, and it would save time for both of us if you had the grace and intelligence not to deny the theft."

Through the side window, I watched Baldie in my Falcon, searching through the shopping bags and glove compartment and under the seats. "It would help if I knew your name – you obviously know mine, and also what exactly you are missing, and why it is so important to you."

"An hour ago, your apartment was thoroughly searched..." expensive suit said.

"What?" Roxy said, sitting up aggressively. I frowned at her not to say anything about Edgar.

"Yes, there was a large gentleman there," he said with a smile.

"Did you do anything to him?" Roxy looked seriously pre-violent.

The bald guy had finished searching the Falcon and got back into the front seat. He shook his head at Mr Expensive suit.

"So, not in your car. Now, if I may peruse your bag, Ms Bennetti?"

When I failed to respond, the driver emphatically placed his hand on it. "No, you may not," I said, refusing to let go.

"I assure you we will return it to you unharmed and if that is a gun in your pocket – and we assume you are not pleased to see me, I would recommend that you proceed with caution."

"Okay go ahead." As I passed the bag to him, I actually felt relieved to be getting rid of the USB drive.

He carefully ran his fingers over slightly sticky make up stuff, keys, credit cards, a couple of unpaid bills, business cards and other flotsam and jetsam I wasn't even sure of myself. I waited for his aha! – and smiled encouragement at Roxy that everything was okay. She looked angry still about Edgar. No *aha* from expensive suit. He tipped the contents of my bag onto his lap and picked through it carefully. Then he stopped and looked at me.

"This is the last time I will ask you in a civilized way, Ms Bennetti."

I kept looking as he dropped my stuff item by item back into my bag. I couldn't believe the drive wasn't there. I had seen Roxy put it back in and zip it up.

"Take off your clothes," he said.

"That's not going to happen," I said, as I snatched my bag back.

"In your dreams, shithead," Roxy said as she looked ready to lunge at him. Baldie leaned over from the front seat with a silenced .38mm.

"I am not interested in you sexually, but I will have what I'm looking for – take off your clothes," expensive suit said.

"You might draw a bit of attention shooting two women here don't you think?"

"That is a risk I am willing to take. Please undress."

"It's okay," I said to Roxy, thinking it wasn't okay at all. Roxy looked like she was about to be sick, she doubled over with her hand to her mouth.

"I'm not taking my clothes off for this guy," Roxy said, looking pale and queasy. "And if he's done anything to Edgar..."

"He just wants to see we don't have this thing he wants."

"I'm thinking we have exactly what he wants," Roxy said glaring at him. "Now unlock this door!"

The door wasn't going to be unlocked. I pulled my T-shirt over my head and was grateful I had one of my better bras on – which immediately made me think I was loopy, worrying whether my corpse would look sexy. Roxy followed suit and we squirmed around in the small space pulling off our jeans.

As Mr Expensive suit examined our clothes, I saw through the side window, to my horror, my worst nightmare: Karl's unmarked police car heading straight for us. For a second or two I was frozen. How could he know where I was – and then I remembered the satellite tracker. I had forgotten to take it off the Falcon. Happy as I was to see Karl, I wasn't happy for Karl to see me.

"So, how much do you want?" Expensive suit asked.

"More than you could afford," Roxy said.

He saw that I was staring at Karl's car. "A friend of yours?" He asked as Karl pulled up on the other side of the Falcon.

"If you look on the dashboard of his car you will see a portable blue flasher light – I know him as Detective Muntz." He immediately sat up, covered the bald guy's gun with his hand and unlocked the doors.

"Get out..." he said, as he signalled the driver to start the car.

"Why don't we invite the detective over?" I said, smiling with some of my mother's venom.

He looked at me evenly. "Do you think we would have a problem with two semi-naked women in our expensive car?"

"Fuck you!" Roxy said, eloquently.

As we got out of the car he held out a small card to me. "Here is a phone number to call to return what is ours Ms Bennetti – last chance. If you involve your friend, the detective – we will also involve the detective. Is that clear?"

The Lexus drove off smoothly, as the driver and Baldie made a showy display of waving cheerily to us.

And then there was Karl. He lent against his car, staring at two women standing in their underwear in the fish market car park, clutching their clothes.

"So, girls," Karl said, shaking his head. "Business good?"

"Hey, dickhead, we're not on the game."

"He knows that, Roxy – he's teasing us."

"He's a cop – they know nothing."

"Best lunch break I've had in two years," Karl said, enjoying himself at our expense. "And I think those jeans might be a size too small, Frankie."

"Ha ha very funny."

"I know what might be too small around here," Roxy said, which cracked me up and made Karl laugh as well.

"It was too hot," I said to him, as Roxy and I started pulling on our jeans.

"Who's your too hot friend?" Karl asked.

"Roxy, she...ah...works for me."

"Wo, you can afford employees?"

"Did he say I was hot?" Roxy said to me under her breath.

"Too hot, he said actually."

It's the haircut...it's a very sweet haircut," she whispered. "And he is one very hot cop."

"Back in your cage, girl – he and me, we're about to date – tonight actually."

"So.. Frankie," Karl said. "Here's what's going to happen. I'm going to follow you to your place and then you are going to invite me in and tell me everything, and I mean everything. Deal?"

"Deal."

"I also have some bad news about our date tonight," he called out to me as he got into his car.

On the drive back to my apartment with Karl following behind, I worried what his bad news was. Roxy called Edgar and got voice mail, she seemed much more concerned than just a friend. I suddenly remembered the USB drive.

"Roxy, what the hell happened to the drive – I saw you put it back in my bag."

"Yeah, bit of a problem that."

"What do you mean?"

"When you said that the reason they were following us was for the USB drive, I took it with me into the Lexus tucked in my bra, and when he told us to strip, I knew he'd find it."

"And...?"

"Remember in the Lexus how I almost threw up? Academy Award stuff – that's when I swallowed it."

"You're kidding?"

Roxy grinned. "I'd have given fifty bucks for a glass of water."

#

As soon as I unlocked the door, Roxy pushed past me at a gallop.

"Edgar!" She called out.

"Hey, Roxy," Edgar called back.

Roxy and I started breathing normally again.

"Come and see this guy."

I stiffened and stepped carefully into the living room to see Edgar glued to the television watching Jamie Oliver chopping onions and coriander.

"This guy is amazing," he said, enthralled.

"Hey Edgar, did anyone come while we were out?" I asked, casually.

"Yeah, your cleaning guys. Frankie, girl you got the most thorough cleaning service I've ever seen, those guys cleaned everything – like inside drawers and cupboards, even your clothes. Man, they must charge a fortune."

Roxy and I looked at each other with horror before the funny side kicked in.

I bit my lip and said, "yeah, very thorough...did they have much equipment?"

"I don't know, I was watching this kitchen genius cooking wild salmon."

Karl came through the door and I introduced him to

Edgar who held out his hand.

"Is that Jamie Oliver?" Karl asked.

Edgar patted the couch. "Sit down," he said, making room for Karl. "This guy's gonna do a casserole thing with black garlic and lamb shanks..."

"He does this pizza with goats cheese and seaweed ..." Karl said, sitting alongside Edgar.

"Man's gifted," said Edgar.

Roxy and I looked at each other. "We'll be in the real kitchen, guys," I said, as I dragged Roxy off.

In the kitchen I pulled open cupboards with the delusional idea there might be something that could be described as edible.

"Roxy, do you feel okay?...you know with the..." I touched her stomach, "with the USB drive in there?"

"Should get it back early tomorrow," Roxy said, with a grin. "You gonna tell the cop?"

"I can't tell him, you heard that guy in the car – if we involve him, they'll involve him."

"He's a cop for Christ's sake!"

"Yes, but he's a special cop. He'll see it as too dangerous for me – he's very protective."

"Kill me, god! The guy is good enough to eat, watches cooking shows, and he cares about you! Throw yourself at him, girl." Roxy shook her head in disbelief and then squinted at me. "He's not gay is he?"

#

After takeaway pizza which apparently wasn't in the same universe as Jamie Oliver's goat cheese job, Karl took me aside.

"You're not going to tell me, like why you were naked at the fish markets, or anything meaningful, are you? Just a bunch of fake crap."

"Honestly?"

"Why not give honesty a whirl..."

"No."

He shook his head. "Thought I'd try anyway. Just tell me this, are you in any danger or risk or whatever?"

"No."

"I can't even tell if you're lying."

"What's the bad news about our date tonight?" I asked, not wanting to hear any bad news but wanting to change the subject.

Karl's expression sank a little. "I'm not on your dead guy's case anymore. I've been assigned to police security for the British Prime Minister as he travels the country."

"That's good isn't it – kind of a promotion?"

"I don't like security work."

"How long for?"

"Oh, five or six days."

"Okay, that's not long."

Karl took hold of me by the shoulders and I could feel the heat of his hands through my T-shirt.

"Listen, Frankie I've got to pack and get to the airport tonight. I just wanted to say... I was looking forward to our date... like a lot."

"Me too," I said and I wondered whether Detective Karl Muntz could read in my face the fact that he could have tasered and strip-searched me for two hours with no sign of protest. In fact the image of that happening was so delicious I almost asked did he have handcuffs on him.

#

After a restless night hearing, but not being able to make out the words of Edgar and Roxy, who slept apart, tucked up in their swags in the sitting-room, I called Heyden Ericsson and finally got him.

"Before we talk about your missing package," I said, with fake authority. "Did you send someone after me – to my apartment?"

"Why would I send someone to your apartment – I

don't know you, or where you live?" He said, without emotion.

I didn't want to give Phillipa and Travis away so I didn't mention letters or jealousy. Surprisingly, his answer had the feel of being more truthful than not.

"Do you know who would?"

"What?"

"Send someone after me... someone who specializes in... let's say, violence?"

He went silent for longer than he should have. I attacked. "You do, don't you – you know who might have done that, don't you? And today – the guy you met in the park and two thugs came after us and threatened us."

"I know nothing about what you're talking about..."

This time he had a slightly higher pitch and it sounded like a lie. "Listen, let's say if I had a strong idea where your package is and I could deliver it..."

"Ms Bennetti, it doesn't matter now – you can keep it."

This threw me – his tone was flat and defeated. "What do you mean?"

"It was just business data – a project that has now been shut down."

"Shut down... what does that mean?"

"Unfortunately it's not good news."

"Okay, not good news for whom?"

"Me, particularly.. and probably you"

"Why?"

"Aahh.. Ms Bennetti..you have no idea what you've done."

He sounded sad and tired. "Well, explain it to me.. maybe I can fix it."

"Goodbye Ms Bennetti."

"Wait... wait," I appealed. "I need to take Carol back to her mother, you know it's the right thing..." But I was already talking to myself.

I debated in my head whether I should call expensive suit – and as usual, 'doing' rather than 'not doing' won out.

I noticed my finger was sweating on the phone's screen as I tapped in the number and waited.

"The number you have called is no longer connected..." came the recorded voice.

#

After insisting Roxy and Edgar go climb the Harbour Bridge and visit Taronga zoo, I intended to go back to bed. I wondered how Edgar's relationship plan was working out – 'to know him is to love him', as the song says. For me, the more I've gotten to know most people – the less likely I am to even like them, but hey, I'm impossible to please – so I'm told.

I had nothing left in the tank, I shut all light off in the room, stripped off and just managed to pull a sheet over me as I crashed onto the bed.

#

There is no confusing the feeling of a steel blade pressing against the sensitive part of the throat. Waking was like rising from the bottom of a cold, dark lagoon. I kept my eyes shut, feigning sleep. I knew I was one breath away from bleeding to death. My head was between his knees, and his weight pressed into both sides of my pillow, making it impossible for me to move without being decapitated. As always when I am terrified, I felt a surge of anger. My gun was in the bedside table drawer – not in the specially designed safe it was supposed to be. There was no way I could reach for it without pumping arterial blood all over my pillow. I felt his body lean forward and the heat from his face on mine. I struggled to keep my panic from breaking out. His breath smelt of toothpaste as he began sliding the sheet down from my body. I didn't care – in fact I was more likely to remain alive if he was after sex. His free hand moved gently across my breasts. Would he

85

become distracted enough for me to bring my arm up under the knife – take a gash to my arm, roll out of bed and reach my gun? Probably not. His face was touching mine – his mouth slowly brushed the side of my face and stopped at my left ear. He whispered something so softly I couldn't make it out at first: 'don't…. go …..the ….. does it..' I knew the softness of his whispering was so that his voice would not be recognizable. Was this someone I knew? What was he saying – don't go…where? I felt him reach down between my legs. Okay, death or dishonour. No contest. Go ahead – if he started getting excited down there it would get very difficult to keep holding a knife to my throat. Maybe it was time to wake up. I opened my eyes to pitch black.

"Don't go where?" I said, as calmly as I could.

His body registered a slight shock, his free hand rose upwards from between my legs and clutched my throat, the knife resting across the bridge of my nose. He leaned forward into my ear again and whispered. "The desert… don't go to the desert."

"Okay," I whispered obediently.

"Or I'll kill you."

"Okay."

His weight shifted off the bed and the knife came away from my face and trailed down the length of my body. Okay, this is where I get stabbed or cut or something. The knife lifted and I waited without moving – without breathing. Nothing. Had he gone? I heard nothing. I lay there motionless and counted by threes to make me concentrate on anything other than my fear which I knew was coming because I felt safe enough to let it exist. At 291, I stopped counting, rolled out of bed and grabbed from the bedside drawer my baby Glock. No stabbing. No blood. No pain. I switched on the light and searched the apartment – the Glock at arm's length in front of me. He was gone. The front door was wide open. I slammed it shut and locked it. Roxy and Edgar must have left it unlocked. I wrapped the sheet around me and noticed how it was shaking. A dull pain seeped through the back of my head towards my eyes. I felt weak. I needed sugar. I found some dark cooking chocolate in the kitchen and a half jar of Manuka honey I ate with my fingers. I allowed myself to cry but only for two minutes. I made coffee and checked in the bathroom mirror – the knife had left a thin red line across my throat. Was it the brother of the curtain rod guy? Was it someone I knew? From now on I would sleep with my gun under my pillow.

I sat on my balcony sipping coffee and feeling sorry for myself until the fear was replaced by a cold anger. From my bedroom my phone rang. I felt groggy but better as I answered it. It was Carol and she sounded upset.

"Dad hasn't come home," she said. "I called him a dozen times and there's no answer."

The bravado was gone and the frightened little kid was talking to me. "Okay, has he been late before?"

"Never – not this late – and he always calls..."

"How late is he?"

"Four or five hours."

"Have you called your mother?"

"No."

"Maybe you should."

"It'll just prove she's right... like, everything she keeps telling me about dad..."

"Maybe she *is* right."

"She's not! She thinks she's right about everything... She doesn't care about dad or me..." The tears were coming. I could also hear pain and fear and disappointment in her voice.

"Would you like me to call your mother?"

"No. I won't talk to her."

"I'll come around. Give me half an hour or so." This opened the floodgates, I could hear her sobbing. I couldn't help feeling that whether she was right or wrong, spoilt teenager or whatever, Carol Ericsson was hurting. I'd been to enough shrinks to spot a fellow sufferer. Although in the parent stakes, Carol looked like a winner compared to me. But you could never be sure. I had learned over the years that the most fucked up people often came from the family with the sweetest Christmas photos.

"Hey, Carol..." I said.

The crying slowed, so she could talk.

"What?" She sniffled.

"I'm sorry."

"What for... you haven't done anything?"

"I'm sorry that stuff happened to you. The stuff that's making you cry – it shouldn't have happened to a kid." I could hear her struggling not to fall apart completely. "I'll see you soon, hang tight."

After I hung up, I noticed Roxy had left me a note to say that the USB drive had arrived on the 8:45am express and had been cleansed and dried and was on my bedside table. Using plastic gloves and a set of kitchen tongs, I took it into the shower with me. If it failed to work later – I didn't care.

8

Carol opened the door only a few inches after I knocked several times. "Are you okay?" I asked, a little puzzled at her reticence.

"Oh, yeah... I'm fine." She was pink faced and slightly nervous.

"So, are you going to open the door?"

"Ahh... look... Mrs Bennetti..."

"Miss Bennetti."

"I'm okay now, I was just a little upset before. I'm sure everything is okay with my dad."

"Okay. Why don't you let me in and we can have a talk."

"Well... I'm going to... to have a shower now and then I've got homework."

"Hey, Carol is there some reason you're not wanting me to come in?"

"No... no..."

"Well, let me in." I began to push on the door and was surprised at how strong Carol was in holding me back. But not strong enough. Slowly her feet started to slip as I forced the door open.

"You're not allowed to do this." She said angrily.

"Neither are you," I said, not knowing what I meant.

"I could phone the police..."

I held out my phone. "Here, you want to use mine?" I bluffed. She wasn't truly angry and I couldn't help seeing there was a shadow of relief on her face. "Have you got a coke?" I asked, as I walked past her towards the sitting room with the odd sense that there was someone else in the house. Carol trotted behind me.

"I'll get you a coke," she said. "And then I'll be okay, and you can go."

The sitting room was empty. I turned to her. "Carol, is there someone else in the house?"

"What? Of course not," she said, her voice rising at the end from tension like all poor liars.

I pushed past her and headed deeper into the house and down the hallway. About halfway down, the bathroom door opened, letting out a waft of steam, and a wet haired semi-naked man in a wheelchair.

"Hello, Frankie," he said cheerfully. "How are you doing?"

"Travis!" I said, as he wheeled up to me with his hand out. Even in my surprise, I couldn't help noticing his beautifully muscled upper body.

"Let me get dressed, and I'll be right out," he said wheeling past me.

I followed Carol into the kitchen. "Why didn't you want me to come in... " I started to say, and then I saw her face which was full of longing, embarrassment, and confusion – she had a crush on the captain.

We sat in silence in the sitting room, until Travis emerged fully clothed and chirpy. "Phillipa asked me to come and help out," he said. "In case Carol wasn't happy coming back with someone she didn't know."

"Is that right?" I said, unsure whether I believed him. "Well she knows me now." I turned to Carol who forced a smile.

"It's all right, Miss Bennetti, I'll go back with Captain Travis."

"Hey, Carol I'm not in the army any more – you can drop the captain rubbish."

I turned to Travis. "I thought you said to call you if I found Carol and you could talk to her."

"You never called, and Phillipa was worried."

"I'm going to pack..." Carol said, as she darted off down the hallway.

I waited until I heard her door close before looking hard at Travis. "She's got a huge crush on you."

"I know. Listen, I don't encourage her and I don't cross boundaries," he said, looking directly back at me. "She's a child."

"Okay, fair enough. So, her father...is he normally irresponsible like this – leaving her alone?"

"Not that I'm aware of, although he could get absorbed in his work."

"Can I ask you something about him? Seeing as you used to work with him."

"Sure."

"Could he be someone who is mixed up with something dodgy...or illegal?"

"Like what?"

"I don't know – business espionage or something?" I said.

He laughed. "Business espionage? Heyden Ericsson? I doubt it... he's not the type. He's a workaholic financial guy. Why do you ask?"

"Oh, doesn't matter really."

"Something made you ask?"

"I don't think he sent that...that guy after me, but I think he might be involved in something financially not good."

"Well, who knows...he does do some creative tax stuff for various companies."

"I've left three messages on his phone about taking Carol back – and he hasn't responded."

"Yeah, I've left a couple myself. Listen Frankie, I don't

want to cut you out of your fee by bringing Carol back, so you tell me what Phillipa owes you and I'll fix you up." He reached into a bag hanging off the side of his wheelchair.

"That's okay Travis, she already gave me a heap of cash – which, by the way, I was happy to take, considering it was almost my last job."

"Are you sure?

"Positive."

"I believe you've got your old car back?" Travis said, smiling.

"Better than ever."

"So you don't need to go back to the land of promise."

"Can I ask you something personal?"

"Sure."

"Were you and Phillipa sleeping together *before* she asked her husband to leave?"

"Why do you ask?"

"I'm not sure. I guess I'd like to understand who exactly it is I'm working with...or for?"

Something was wrong. Travis was focused beyond me with a look of horror on his face. I turned to see Carol – white faced, clutching her backpack to her chest with both hands, staring back at Travis. She had obviously heard the potent bits.

"Carol..." Travis was lost for words.

Carol wheeled around and took off back to her room, slamming the door so hard the vibrations could be felt through the timber floor. I followed Travis down the hall to Carol's room. He tried to open it, but it was locked.

"Carol? Hear me out," Travis said. "Your mother was disconnected emotionally from your father long before I came along. Carol? Can you hear me?"

Through the door, I could hear Carol sobbing. I turned to Travis. "Maybe we should leave her for a little while..."

"Carol? Please come out," Travis asked gently. "Let me take you home to your mother. We can talk about it on the way."

"I think we should back off, Travis," I said.

The lock on the door started rattling and I stepped back as the door was flung open. Carol stood in the doorway, swollen eyes and puffy face – an expression of cold composure.

"I want you to get out of my father's house," she said to Travis, softly but with conviction.

"Carol, I'm sorry," Travis said earnestly.

"I don't want to ever see you or talk to you again."

"You're right to be angry..." Travis started to say, "but it's not..." his voice trailed away, confronted by the child's hurt face. "I'll wait in the sitting room," he said. "When you want to come talk about it, I'll be here."

Carol looked at Travis and then turned to me. "Can I borrow your phone, please?" She asked me. "My battery is flat."

"Do you want me to open it?" I said. She nodded and I punched in my password and handed the phone to her.

"I'm dialling the emergency number," she said to Travis. "In five seconds if you are not out the front door and gone, I'm telling them I have an intruder in my house."

Travis was truly shocked. He looked at me and back at Carol – there was no doubt she meant it. He wheeled away in reverse down the hallway, spun around, and rolled up to and out the front door. Carol handed the phone back to me.

"Are you okay?" I asked.

She looked at me so mournfully and I put my arms around her which opened the floodgates. She sagged in my arms with deep racking sobs. This was a lot more pain than being disappointed by a misplaced crush. It was more like years of hurt or misery.

When I was a child, I remember my brother and I discovering a comfort drink: a large spoonful of Vegemite in a mug of boiling water with torn up pieces of bread tossed in. Incredibly salty, bitter and hot. It completely overwhelmed the hurt. I made this for Carol and watched her sip and grimace, curled up in a lounge chair.

"I don't want to stay here by myself," she said.

"That's okay, you can stay at my place." She smiled at me over the rim of the mug. "I have a couple of guests staying at the moment, you may know them – from the Promised Land."

"I don't think dad's going to come home tonight..."

"I'd like to take you back to your mum, what do you think?"

"This drink is horrible...but I kind of like it."

"I'll take that as a yes."

She smiled at me. "So, are you some kind of like person for hire?"

"Nah... I'm nothing like a person.."

"You're funny."

"But I'm kind of for hire. Are you ready to go?"

She got to her feet. "I need to have a shower first and finish packing, is that okay, can you wait for me?"

"No problemo," I said. This made her chuckle and repeat 'no problemo' down the hallway and into her room.

I called Phillipa, who was overjoyed Carol was coming home. I warned her that Carol was a bit upset over accidentally hearing about Travis and her. She was silent for a few seconds, and then said it was probably for the best, which is what I thought myself. I don't like secrets – 'don't tell this to them' kind of bullshit. Always ends in someone being more hurt.

I paced through the house – an unfortunate habit I have when talking on the phone – it helps me to concentrate. When I returned to the sitting room after exploring Heyden Ericsson's tastefully, 'decorated by professionals' house, I had a visitor sitting in a lounge chair: the bald guy pal of Mr Expensive suit from the fish markets.

"How did you get in?" I said, covering my shock and fear as best I could.

"It wasn't locked," he said, shaking his head at man's stupidity.

"I called your friend..."

"Yes, I know."

"He said he didn't want it any more."

"I know."

"There are other people in the house..." I said, lamely.

"Heyden Ericsson's daughter, Carol. She's having a shower," he said, evenly. He took out a packet of cigarettes and offered me one.

"Last request cigarette?" I said, trying for humour. He didn't answer. He looked at me for a full two minutes without saying anything.

"Sit down," he said, gesturing to the lounge chair opposite him. I sat.

"They'll kill you," I said, with my most charming voice. "The cigarettes, I mean."

He smiled, looked at the cigarette in his hand and back at me. "They already have," he said. I couldn't think of a response. He blew smoke and watched it. "Cancer of the oesophagus – spread to the lungs and pancreas."

"Seriously?" I asked.

"Seriously."

"I'm sorry."

"If your sorry were true Miss Bennetti you would be the only person on the planet who was."

"I'm sure that's not..." I stopped. There was a raw bitterness to his expression that wouldn't allow me to bullshit him. I looked for some way out, something I could get behind, something I could use as a weapon, anything. "I'm Frankie, by the way..."

"Girard.."

"I'm sorry, I didn't quite catch it.."

"Girard… they use to call me Giraffe at school.."

"Girard.. I like it.."

"Please don't try to get out your little gun, Frankie."

"Okay," I said, holding up my open palms. I knew that

I would be dead long before I got anywhere near it.

"Why did you get mixed up in this?" He asked, sounding genuinely interested.

"I don't even know what 'this' is," I said.

He sighed. "The guy you killed – I knew him."

"He was trying to kill me."

"Either you are very skilled or very lucky."

"Could I be both?" I said, still trying for humour. He laughed. That had to be good, I thought.

"Skill can fail you, Frankie and luck can run out."

"Has my luck run out?" I asked. I heard the sounds of Carol coming from the bathroom, walking down the hall and back to her room and closing her bedroom door. "Are you waiting for her... for Carol?" He was too experienced to respond in any way. All I could think of was to engage him in conversation – stall for time – try to connect. There was little doubt he was here to silence us both "Can I ask you about your...illness?"

"Go ahead."

"Have they given you a...an idea of how long?"

"Best case twelve months – worst, three months," he said, without emotion.

"Are you scared?"

"I was, in the beginning." Several seconds ticked by. "Do you know what's beyond scared?"

"No."

"Disappointment," he said.

I was about to be shot and yet I found this really interesting. "Disappointment?"

"Disappointment."

"With...?"

"Life."

"Okay, that's pretty comprehensive – pretty much everything."

"Aah...Frankie, I didn't know it, but I used to live with the idea that the good thing – the good life – the moment when everything became great, was up ahead – was about to arrive. I just had to make a little more money, get that fabulous girl, be really good at something and voilà, there it was – the great life. Now, when you've been given your use-by date, you realize that it's not going to happen – nothing good is going to arrive – and it slowly sinks in.. that it was never going to."

"Depressing," I said, meaning it.

"Disappointing," he corrected me.

I decided to try a different tack. "Are you going to kill me?" I asked. To his credit, he didn't look away. "Why?" I asked, hanging on to fear – not wishing to arrive at disappointment. "I'm not going to the police, and anyway I don't have anything to tell them other than a strip search in a car – and anyway I stole the USB drive, so I'd hardly report that."

"Its work, Frankie. It's what I do. The only thing I've ever been good at."

"Well, maybe it's what's making you... disappointed," I said. He was thinking. That was good. I was hoping Carol would take a long time. "I have an idea – will you listen?"

"Go ahead."

"What if you just walked away this time, instead of doing what you've been told? This one time you could make a different choice..."

"Kind of you to think of me."

"I'm not trying to bullshit you. I don't want a bullet in my head – but seriously, what have you got to lose?"

"What have I got to gain?"

"I don't know."

We sat in silence for a minute or so. Was he considering what I was saying? There was no way I could tell.

"Are you married or with someone?" He asked.

"No. You looking for some speed dating?"

He couldn't help laughing. This was good. My sense of humour to the rescue.

"It's been quite a while since I laughed."

"What if I disappeared – like I moved to Perth or New York – changed my name. You could say you did your job – for all intents and purposes, I'd be erased."

"Do you know the difference between amateur and professional, Frankie?"

"Maybe."

"Amateurs care about how they appear, what others are thinking of them – they get emotionally involved which lets doubt creep in, and they lose. Professionals care about two things – technique and outcome. They usually win."

"So you're going to do what you've been told, whoever it is told you – you must really think a lot of them."

"They disgust me, actually."

"Not enough, obviously."

He shook his head and laughed again and his cell phone rang. As he reached inside his coat for it, I sprang out of the lounge chair and without even glancing at him, raced down the hall to Carol's bedroom, my shoulders hunched, waiting for sharp pain. I flung the door open, which was, thank God, unlocked. I leapt inside, shutting and locking it behind me.

"What do you think you're doing?" Carol yelled, clutching a T-shirt and jeans to her chest. "Get out!"

"There's a guy out there, Carol..."

"What do you mean?"

"He's a... kind of violent..."

"Well call the police..."

"Here, you do it," I handed her my phone. I knew the cops, at best, would take ten minutes – more like forty-five which would be useless but at least it would keep Carol occupied.

I listened at the door as Girard's footsteps came down the hall in no hurry and stopped outside Carol's door.

"There are steel bars on the windows, Frankie," he said calmly, on the other side of the door.

I realized I had done exactly what he wanted me to. He was a professional. He hadn't taken my gun which was rule number one – he wanted me to have the gun and lock myself in with Carol. Why? Outside the door I could hear him moving about and the faint smell of something chemical – maybe something inflammable. He was going to burn the house down! Starting outside Carol's door! I tried to see through the keyhole but it was too dark in the hallway and all I could see was a blurred shape moving in and out of my vision. I considered whether I could shoot through the door and if the bullet could make it through, maybe I could get lucky. I knew I could more likely just make him angry.

"Listen...please...don't do this," I called out.

The sounds outside the door stopped and a different smell wafted in under the door – burning newspaper smoke. I grabbed an armful of Carol's clothes from her bed and packed them along the bottom of the door. I heard Girard's phone ringing. Behind me Carol was talking to some idiot person from the emergency centre.

"No!" Carol said. "Someone is trying to burn our house down. No... I can't get out!... I don't care which...the police or the fire brigade!"

With nothing to lose, I took out my Glock and fired through the door, keeping three shots in the magazine.

"... I'm sorry," Carol said into the phone, her eyes wide with shock. "Send them both then...that sound you heard was my friend firing her gun...no, she's not firing at me, you stupid woman... yes, I am a teenager... no, this is not a prank call..."

On the other side of the door, there was no sound. I knew he would wait long enough for the fire to be big enough to trap us which could be in a matter of seconds. I figured we had nothing to lose. I grabbed Carol's hand and told her to hold on to my belt and stay close to me. I unlocked the door. Still nothing.

"We're coming out!" I called out as loudly as I could.

In my mind, being shot was way more attractive than being roasted alive. I made Carol lie down on the floor and

I crouched beside her. With the gun out in front of me and Carol holding on to my belt, I flung the door open. I fired two shots immediately into the smoke that filled the hallway – that left one in the magazine. He was nowhere in sight. I waved away at the smoke and gradually in the doorway I could see a pile of smouldering stuff that looked like it had been stomped out. There was a pool of water on the floor around it as if someone had thrown water onto it.

"Are you there?" I called out. Nothing. Was this another trap? I signalled Carol to be still and quiet while I listened. Nothing. I waited, counting to one hundred to keep my mind focused. I told Carol to stay on the floor while I went to have a look. She refused to let go of my belt – which reminded me of myself.

"I'm going with you," she said.

"Okay," I said to her. "If he's anywhere, he'll be in the sitting room."

We inched our way down the hall, the gun in my shaking, outstretched hand. The sitting room was empty. I quickly checked out the other rooms. Nothing. He was gone. It didn't make sense. What had happened? What was he doing? It wasn't all just to scare us – because he would have at least extracted promises from us to shut up – there was no sense in just scaring us. Maybe he listened to me – maybe he made a different choice. Maybe he figured he'd get a week off for good behaviour when he went to hell?

The sound of sirens coming closer, jolted me back to reality. "Grab your stuff, as fast as you can," I told Carol. "I don't want to try and explain things to the cops, okay?"

"Okay," she said, obediently, taking off for her room.

We made it safely into the car and pulled away just as the fire brigade arrived.

Without warning, I was suddenly shaking – my whole body. Carol, beside me didn't seem to notice. Behind us I heard police cars arriving at the house, another one sped past us, lights flashing.

"That was fully insane," she said.

"Yeah, that about sums it up."

"What is it you do – like your job?"

"Being fully insane."

She laughed. "I think I want to do what you do when I finish school."

"Are you crazy – we were nearly killed back there!"

"Yeah, it was scary brilliant wasn't it?"

I asked Carol not to mention anything about what happened to us to Roxy and Edgar. They would both want to go to the cops and I still wasn't ready for that. There was no sense in worrying them for nothing.

9

By the time we reached my apartment, I had stopped shaking. Roxy and Edgar were cozied up on the couch – closer than I would have expected. I was glad they were home when we got there, they had started to feel like a real family – not that I'd know what that was like mind you. Carol recognized them both and they knew her – the joys of a small town. Edgar had spent the day preparing Jamie Oliver inspired dishes of seafood – muscles, scallops, barramundi and whitebait – brilliant. He looked more attractive after every course and I couldn't help noticing Roxy was developing a new appetite too.

Carol chose to sleep in a spare swag Edgar had rather than share the bed with me. I was grateful, I never liked sharing my bed even with a lover. I was always delighted when they chose to go after the exciting part. One of my friends said it was because they weren't the right ones for me. Romantic twaddle, I told them – why the hell would I want some wriggling, blanket-hogging, possibly snoring, probably farting, lump of annoyance alongside me all night, right? Okay, so maybe none of them were 'the one' but ask yourself, would 'the one' be any different? Probably.

On the television, some current affairs program was

covering the British Prime Minister's visit. I grabbed the remote, turned up the volume and hit record.

"My friend, Karl is part of the security team looking after this guy," I said, proudly.

Carol glanced up from her iPhone for half a second and Roxy and Edgar, who were playing poker, ignored me. I kept my eyes glued to the screen for Karl's easily recognizable body. The camera moved in on the Prime Minister and tracked around the stage. I couldn't see Karl. The Prime Minister was spouting the usual political, sucky nonsense and there were obvious security guys behind and around him – but Karl wasn't one of them. I watched closely as they changed camera angles and went to a wide shot of the stage: Karl wasn't there.

I was disappointed. He was probably watching nearby in a room with security screens. The report ended and I switched off the television and went to brush my teeth. I wondered whether Karl was thinking of me as I checked out my teeth in the mirror.

"Frankie?" Roxy called from the other side of the door.

"What?" I answered, with a mouthful of foam.

"There's someone at the door."

I moved my gun to my jeans pocket, there was still one shot in the magazine. "Who is it?"

"She says she's your mother."

I was more than stunned – maybe poleaxed. Not possible, I thought to myself. I hadn't seen or heard from her in seventeen years. She wouldn't know where I was. A thousand thoughts exploded in my mind: do I ask Roxy to make her go away? Do I slam the door in her face? How about a clean shot between the eyes?

"Frankie?" Roxy called out again. "Did you hear me?"

I strode out of the bathroom, headed straight to the front door and ripped it open.

"What do you want?" I said to my mother.

"Diane? It's me..."

"I know *who* you are – I don't know *why* you are?" Too

many feelings, like greasy little cockroaches were crawling inside my brain. Out of the corner of my eye I could see Roxy and Edgar and Carol, staring open-mouthed. I wanted to tell them who we were dealing with here.

"You have toothpaste on your face..." my mother said. "Can I come in?"

Roxy pushed me out of the way. "Come in," she said, taking my mother's arm. "Frankie's not feeling well."

"Who?" My mother said, as she stepped inside and Roxy shut the door. "Diane, did you change your name?" She said, staring at me.

"Sure did," I said, enjoying myself.

"Good for you," she said.

I almost fell over with shock. My mother saying something encouraging to me that didn't involve sharp instruments. Roxy led her over to a lounge chair. "Sit here, I'm Roxy.. would you like a drink?"

"That's very kind, Roxy, a glass of water will do nicely."

I watched Roxy signal Edgar and Carol to leave the room with her. They followed obediently.

"How did you find me?" I asked my mother.

"Your brother has kept in touch," she said.

Okay, implied criticism – that felt more like my real mother. "So why are you here, what do you want?"

"I've been wanting to come for a long time."

"Uh huh," I said.

"I wanted to say sorry."

"Sorry?"

"I'm sorry, Diane for how I was with you...particularly when your father left."

Okay, now I wanted to know what this woman had done with my real mother.

"Okay, you're sorry."

"Do you forgive me?"

"I don't know."

She looked around my apartment. "You're doing well, that's good, I always knew you would."

"And that's why you were so rotten to me?"

She smiled. "And you were always very funny."

"You're not... like terminally ill or something, are you?"

"Good heavens, no... strong as an ox."

"Are you short of money?"

"Why are you being cruel to me?"

"I was trained by an expert."

"You're quick-witted, just like me." She smiled. "Diane, I thought we might try and have a kind of... closer relationship. I mean now you're grown up."

"I've been grown up for two decades, mum."

"I know dear."

"What would that look like, you and me having a close relationship?"

"Well, we could do some things together – like have lunch and...and..." She stopped talking and rummaged in her bag. "I brought something for you." She held out a package wrapped in silver paper and tied with a neat little bow. "Here, unwrap it."

I slipped off the ribbon and peeled the silver paper away and there it was: a dog-chewed, tear stained, ear missing, furry, grey stuffed koala. My koala bear from when I was five. Given to me by Auntie Jayne.

"Piggy!" I squealed. Piggy was the best half of my five-year-old world – I called him Piggy, I figured years later, from hearing the teacher read from a picture book 'this little piggy went to market...' and the Piggy in the picture was amazingly happy.

"I found it in some old boxes," my mother said.

I remembered the pain when it disappeared. I stopped speaking for weeks.

"You were very attached to him," my mother said, encouraging me to become emotional. There was no way I was opening that Pandora's box of pain in front of her.

"Auntie Jayne gave him to me," I said.

Auntie Jayne was my mother's younger sister – she got all the kind genes – and all the fat genes. *Moon River*, my brother and I called her when we were teens, and we'd sing the punch line, 'wider than a mile'. Maybe my brother and I missed getting the kind genes too.

"That's right," my mother said. "What a good memory you have." Then she frowned and shuffled in her chair. "You probably don't know, Diane – about Jayne."

"I haven't heard from her in the last couple of years or so," I said. "Why? Is she okay?"

"No. I'm afraid she passed away a few weeks ago."

"Oh, God, I didn't know... I should have stayed in touch. Did she die okay...you know...without suffering?"

"They found her at her kitchen table, slumped over a plate of spaghetti carbonara." For some reason that made me smile. That was so right for Auntie Jayne – face forward into a pile of pasta and kaput – lights out! "It's good you can smile," my mother said.

"I'm not...it's not that it's funny...it's like we used to do...laugh at things. It's like sharing a joke with her..."

"She had quite a bit of money, you know."

"I didn't know... She didn't seem to have much stuff."

"Do you know who she left it to?"

"Freedom from Hunger?" I said, knowing that if she was listening, Auntie Jayne would find this very funny.

"No, she left it to you."

"Bullshit!"

"Close to half a million dollars."

"What?! Auntie Jayne had half a million bucks?"

"She did. I don't think she was quite right in the last years – like in her mind."

"I thought you two hadn't spoken since I was a kid?" I said.

"Yes, that's true but that wasn't my choice, Diane. I always cared about her, she was family and family is what matters in the end."

"You told me you were ashamed of her from the time she started school...and she told me you used to lead the bullies that tormented her half to death."

"That's silly."

"Is that why you're here? Auntie Jayne's money?"

"No, it isn't."

"Yes it is, I can see it in your eyes... And that's why you brought piggy..."

"No, that's not true. Although I do think Jayne was probably Alzheimic in the last few years and wasn't clear on what she was doing and I know she would have wanted..."

"Wow, you nearly had me, Ma..."

"Diane, you're letting your emotions run away – you know how you do that..."

"Have emotions?"

"Exaggerate everything... make me into the...the... bad person."

"You *are* the bad person!" That started me out and out laughing. "You have always been the bad person – which is why dad left – to save himself...from you."

"I just want my share... I don't want the lot... what's so wrong about that?"

"Nothing, except Auntie Jayne didn't want you to have any of it obviously, and it's her money."

"She was a greedy, selfish woman, Diane."

"No, that's you."

"I believe I am entitled to at least a third share with you and your brother – she was my sister..."

"Who you treated like shit."

"You can say what you like but I'm not leaving here, until you..."

Probably, the Glock whipped out of my pocket and sitting an inch from her forehead, interrupted her flow of thought. "Are you sure?" I said.

She stood up, her top lip actually quivering with rage and contempt. Now my real mother had returned.

"It doesn't surprise me you have a gun, you were always like your father – scum. He didn't want you and I never wanted you. I tried to get rid of you even before you were born."

It didn't hurt any more. In her eyes, in her face, her whole body, there was an emptiness and isolation that was, at the same time, both sad and frightening.

"Thanks for piggy," I said, as I pushed her towards the door and opened it. "You know, Ma – Auntie Jayne, dad and me – we all have one thing in common – we escaped you."

I slammed the door in her face knowing the second wave of bile was about to break on her tongue.

"You'll be sorry...you wait... you'll be sorry..." She shouted through the door. And then her tone changed to a phony sweetness. "There's something else. Something I never told you. Your little piggy koala – it never got lost. When you were little, I took it and hid it..."

I swung the door open, blood rushing to my head, fury erupting, and aimed the Glock at her face with my two hands extended. She screamed and tried to run and duck at the same time, tripping over and sprawling across the hallway. She sat up on the floor and held her bag up for protection in front of her face.

"Don't... don't..." She begged.

She sat there, frail and finally powerless – an old woman I was no longer afraid of. My anger lifted its wings and flapped away. No need for revenge – the revenge was there in front of me – it was her – an unloved, empty life. I realized I no longer felt the endless yearning to be wanted – no longing for approval – no love at all. Nothing.

"Goodbye, Ma," I said, and slowly shut the door.

10

Driving through the desert was great therapy, with so little to distract the eyes it allowed my mind to wander. Still and flat landscape with a weird kind of timelessness that encouraged introspection. Carol slept soundly in the passenger seat of the Falcon, flopping forward and back against the seatbelt with the motion of the car. She had taken an instant liking to piggy and he was squashed under her arm. Roxy and Edgar had gone ahead in the camel car and I noticed that maybe Edgar was beginning to defrost Roxy's refrigerator, boot up her hard drive – and could be the mayonnaise on her sandwich after all. I called Karl and got the police information desk which happens when his phone is off.

"Detective Karl Muntz is on leave," the bored woman's voice said.

I figured they weren't going to tell me he was on security detail for the Prime Minister of England. I left a message for Karl that I was taking a runaway teenager back to her mother.

Several hours ago, before getting onto the desert highway, I drove a little out of my way to visit Auntie Jayne's grave site. I apologized for not visiting enough when she was alive and I thanked her again for Piggy – and for the money, half of which I promised to give to an appropriate charity like *Meals on Wheels* which made me start laughing till the tears came. Carol watched me from the car and must have wondered who the hell she was travelling with.

I thought about my mother – what made her the way she was? I knew she had loved my father – at least until he left – but she was the cause of him leaving. I think even then I knew that she was the reason he left us – to save himself. Why did she hurt everyone around her, including herself? There weren't any answers, some people were just like that. The slightly crazy Fred Nietzsche said something like: 'We hurt those we want to feel our power, because pain is a much more efficient means to that end than pleasure.'

My thoughts drifted from pain to Karl – and his handcuffs and thick leather belts and police batons and that almost ran me off the road.

#

As we drove through the main street of the Promised Land, I saw my least favourite cop – Hugo Ravic, about to get into his car. He saw me heading towards him and waved at me to pull over. I wasn't concerned this time, in the middle of town and with Carol on board. I pulled in behind him and waited till he stood directly outside my window before rolling it down. His whole demeanour was different.

"Miss Bennetti," he said with a massive smile. "Nice to see you again." He had my name right this time which meant someone had filled him in.

"Hi, Mr Ravic," Carol said.

"Well, hi Carol," he said, dipping his head to see into the car.

"Is there a problem?" I asked, with enough heartfelt innocence to free a convicted genocidal maniac.

"I'd like to apologize, mam for our misunderstanding before."

"What misunderstanding?" Carol asked with genuine innocence.

"Oh, nothing," I said. "Officer Ravic was being extra protective of his township, that's all – just doing his job." Ravic's eyes softened and he took off his hat.

"The detective said you were a high-quality woman...and I can see he was right."

When I took off my revenge glasses, I could see an okay cop who probably did love and protect his community. I could also see a cop on the receiving end of Karl Muntz's aggression.

"Why, thank you, officer," I said with a little flirty smile. He nodded respectfully to us both and walked back towards his car, stopped and called out.

"You call me, Miss Bennetti, if you need anything now, I mean that, do you hear?"

"Thank you, officer – I'll do that," I said, as we pulled slowly away down the street thinking, I'll do that Officer Ravic when hell freezes over and I'm ice skating on it.

"I'm not going to speak to my mother," Carol said. "I might have to live with her, but I don't have to like her."

"But you do have to love her," I said, which was a weird thing for me to say.

"Well, you might love yours..." she said. Okay, She had me there.

"Your mother cares about you," I said. "She hired me to get you back, and I'm not cheap and she was going nuts when you left."

"Hmmmph." Unconvincing.

The main street of the town was quiet except for a couple of shoppers wheeling trolleys and two kids arguing in front of the Paradise Cafe.

"See that bank?" Carol said proudly, pointing to the side window. "We have a special account in there – dad and I set it up together."

"What's a special account?"

"Oh...dad had the bank install special equipment so it could be extra secure."

"Really?"

"I'm not supposed to tell anyone, not even my mum knows, but you're like a lawyer aren't you? Like you're not allowed to tell anyone stuff about your work or anything..."

"That's right. My lips are zipped." I said. Carol laughed and held up her pinkie finger.

" That's the only thing that will open it."

"Your finger?"

"Plus dad's pinkie. We have to go into this private booth..."

"Wow, it must have some seriously sweet honey in it."

"I don't know. I can't use it without dad and anyway I don't need it, dad sends me money all the time."

"Sends you money?"

"He's away a lot...he works really hard."

I wanted to tell Carol that maybe the parent that's gone always looks better than the one that's there. And then I remembered my own disappeared father. Carol and I maybe had something in common. "You wanna adopt Piggy for a while?" I asked.

"Can I?"

"Well you'll have to ask him, he's pernickety about who he sleeps with."

Carol shrieked with laughter.

#

Phillipa ran out to meet us as we drove up to Billabong. She had circles under her eyes and looked like she had lost weight. Carol allowed her mother's hug with arms dangling by her sides, and then ran into the house and off to her bedroom without saying anything. Phillipa grabbed my hand, she wasn't going to try for another hug rejection.

"Thank you, Ms Bennetti... Frankie... I can't believe you've managed to bring her back from Heyden so easily and quickly...it means everything to me."

"More luck than anything," I said, honesty keeping me honest.

"I don't care, you did it... I haven't been able to sleep."

"Have you heard from your husband?"

"No, but that's not surprising, he regularly goes out of contact." Inside the house it was cool, with high ceilings and large fans ticking over. "I asked Travis to stay in town until I can explain things to Carol," Phillipa said, passing me an icy glass of lemon with sugar and mint leaves. "You're welcome to stay – I'm sure Carol would love it – she would never have come back with you if she didn't really like you."

"She's a lovely kid... I like her," I said, truthfully. "It'd be nice to stay – it's a beautiful house but I've promised a friend that I'd stay in town. She's on work release from the correctional institution and I've signed on as her employer."

"That's wonderful," Phillipa said, her face lighting up. "I'm on the welfare board there – well, I'm the chairperson actually and it's almost impossible to find enough employers to take the eligible work release inmates – the town is so small. That's a lovely thing you've done."

I felt a bit uncomfortable hearing Phillipa tell me I'd done something lovely – but hey, compliments in my life are in short supply. "Well, Roxy... that's her name has been exceedingly good at her job. She is also trying to help Edgar, the camel guy to revive his late wife's business."

"That's so good to hear – many of the townspeople are not happy about having inmates in their town."

"There's something I meant to ask you, Phillipa, how did you find me in the first place, to hire me? I mean no one else seemed to find me."

"Oh, Travis had an old friend of his recommend you."

"Really? His old friend knew me?"

"I don't know, Travis just said someone who did military training with him."

"An army guy?"

"I think Travis said he's not in the army any more, that he's a policeman now."

"A cop?"

"I think so."

#

Inside Edgar's dating agency, Roxy made me sit in front of her computer. She was excited. Edgar flip-flopped around her like a lost puppy.

"Like I was telling you," she said. "We can totally revive this place. I think we should call it...are you ready? The Outback Introduction Agency." Roxy stared at me with anticipation.

I felt pressured for some kind of positive response. "Okay, that's better than Desert Dating for Dummies..." I said.

Edgar burst out laughing and Roxy squinted at him.

"I'm serious here."

"Ya gotta admit, it's funny – desert dating for..." Edgar started to say.

"Shut up both of you and look at this, I made our first client video," Roxy said. "She's in for fraud.." She clicked on the computer mouse and on the screen a wobbly video popped up showing an attractive woman smiling and talking into the camera:

'Hi, my name is Stacey, I'm thirty-one years of age and I come from Adelaide. I'm very single at the moment and I like a man who knows how to treat a lady.. I'm interested in shopping, collecting dolls, money and sex.'

The camera slowly pulled out to show a full-length shot of Stacey – completely naked. Roxy paused the video.

"What do you think?"

"Aah ... interesting," I said. "So, are you aiming for

takeaway lap dancing or out and out whorehouse?"

"Don't be prudish, Frankie – she has a nice body."

"She has," Edgar agreed.

"Be quiet, Edgar I want a woman's opinion."

I realized Roxy was in earnest and was really trying. "She has got a nice body," I said. "But showing it all at once like that might give the wrong impression."

"You heard her," Roxy said. "She said she was interested in sex...I think the right thing to do is to be up front about it."

"Yep, she's up front," I agreed.

"She's got a good point there, Frankie," Edgar said. "She wants me to video every miner, farmworker, and single male out of high school in the district... I think she's a genius."

"I have seventy-four eligible female prisoners," Roxy said, proudly. "I have no idea how I'm going to manage it with the prison...to film them all. And anyway, I think we should have this great big dance and invite everyone we've filmed and everyone in the district."

I took a large, deep breath and asked the gods for forgiveness in advance. "I know someone who might be able to help with getting the girls out for a night, and the filming," I said.

"Really?" Roxy said.

"Chairperson of the prison welfare board, actually."

"I knew it... I knew it would work," Roxy said, excitedly.

"Isn't she amazing?" Edgar said to me, beaming at Roxy.

"Well, it was you who thought of filming them," Roxy said to Edgar, with a flutter of eyelashes.

"Yeah, but you thought of the girls from the prison – I never would have come up with that."

"But you've kept the place going all by yourself..."

"Please, people...get a room," I joked. Roxy actually blushed, and Edgar walked rapidly off and disappeared down the end of the room.

"Funny you should say that," Roxy said. "I won't need to share your hotel room, Frankie. I'm gonna stay here tonight, Edgar has a lovely old room set up for visitors and we'll get some sandwiches from the Paradise..."

"Oh, okay...will you need any mayonnaise with your sandwiches?" I asked, with mock innocence. For a second, Roxy didn't get it, then her mouth dropped open with delighted shock and she threw a pile of notepaper at me and laughed.

On the way back to the hotel, my phone rang. It was Karl and my heart fluttered.

"Hey babe," he said.

I was caught off balance, he'd never called me a flirty name before. "Babe? I'm babe, now?"

"Is that a problem?"

"Of course it's not a problem, unless you're thinking of that pig movie?"

"Come to think of it..."

"Don't go there, remember I have my own gun."

He laughed. "I'm nearly finished here, and I've got some time off. I thought I might come out to the desert and check out – how hot you are..."

That got me laughing and certainly raised my temperature. I still hadn't taken the satellite tracker off the Falcon and even I could see that was no accident – a Psych 101 student could recognize an unconscious wish that obvious – for Karl to find me, or worse, rescue me. I promised myself to take the tracker off, just in case I ever, even unconsciously, allowed myself to want to be rescued.

"I won't be out here much longer," I said.

"Okay, maybe stay a little longer. I can get a ride up with a delivery truck or something and we can spend a few days in the dunes and drive back together."

"I could probably get you a free camel ride."

"Wo, I'm sold."

"They make me vomit."

"Okay, we probably shouldn't tell the camels that."

"Hey Karl, I saw the British Prime Minister on television but I couldn't see you anywhere..."

"Yeah, I was around – sitting in the control van most of the time."

"That's what I figured."

"I've got to go, I'll see you soon... I'll call you..."

"Wait, Karl...did you ever recommend me to someone... for a job.. You know as an investigator?"

"Possibly."

"Can't you remember?"

"I mentioned you to a couple of people."

"Was one of them an old buddy?"

"Why are you asking this, Frankie?"

"I just wanted to know."

"One of them was an old buddy. We did army training together a million years ago."

"Is his name Travis and is he in a wheelchair?"

"Yes.. Frankie, I've really got to go."

"Sorry."

"I'll see you soon, babe... I'll call you, okay?"

"Okay."

11

Something was tapping my head and shouting at me from a long way away. I sat up in bed, my brain, usually quick to wake was thick and slow to figure where I was. The tapping started again, only it wasn't on my head, it was outside my hotel room.

"Miss Bennetti..." Tap, tap, tap. "Miss Bennetti..." Tap, tap, tap.

Sleeping naked has its disadvantages. I occasionally wondered whether in a burning building, I would rush naked into the street or scrabble around in the billowing flames looking for something flattering to wear. Ridiculous I know, but hey, I'm a very private person. I stumbled around in the dark for the bedside lamp and called out. "Who is it?"

"It's Officer Ravic, Miss Bennetti."

What the hell! I thought to myself. "Officer Ravic, hang on a moment..." What could he possibly want in the middle of the night? I pulled on jeans and something I hoped was one of my T-shirts and not the hotel's cleaning cloth and opened the door.

"I know it's late..." Ravic said, apologetically, his hat held nervously in both hands across his chest. "It's not good news."

"Do you want to come in?" I asked, with half of my brain still under the bed sheet.

"Nah... I won't come in, thanks. Look I need you to come with me...over to the station..."

"The police station?" I say stupidly. Okay, now I was awake.

"There's been a...an incident, we've got a body... it's Heyden Ericsson."

"Oh, fuck!" I said. Ravic looked surprised. "Sorry, I can be foul-mouthed when I get shocked."

"Mam, I understand – I'm feeling shocked myself. Mrs Ericsson found...er...the body in the back of her car."

"My god, is she okay?"

"Yeah, she's fine...well not really fine, I mean she's not harmed or anything...but... she's a long way from fine."

"And Carol...?"

"She's okay, just very, very upset."

I grabbed my bag, checked it for my gun, money, and make-up. Funny how the mind works – even under stress – make up for Christ's sake!

Ravic walked rapidly down the street as I trotted alongside, my mind trying to catch up. Did Heyden Ericsson climb into the back of his wife's car and kill himself?

"Do you know what happened?" I asked.

Ravic stopped walking and grabbed my arm as if he needed support. He took a deep breath, looked me in the eye and said quietly, "He was all cut up... in a box...with parts of him missing..."

"Jesus!"

He took off again and I kept up. "Mrs Ericsson asked me to get you... I'm sorry... she didn't want to wait until the morning."

"That's okay, I'm glad you did."

Ravic seemed to be getting more upset the closer we got to the police station. He slowed his pace and when the station was in sight, he stopped again and shook his head at me. "Listen, I have to tell you something before we get there. I had to arrest her... Mrs Ericsson, we found one of her knives...it was sewn into her mattress. I only found it by accident, because I had this metal detector left behind by one of those weekend hobby miners... I don't believe for a minute she did it, but I had to arrest her. The detectives from Region ordered me to. I've never had anything like this happen out here...ever."

I began to feel the stress chemicals flood my brain – alerting, calming and helping to focus. "I don't believe she killed her husband – she doesn't have that in her – and why would she do it anyway – and she'd never chop him into pieces..."

"We found a letter from her husband's lawyer, threatening to get custody of Carol and to cut off any financial support," Ravic said, ruefully.

#

The police station smelled of dust and eucalyptus cleaning fluid. It consisted of two rooms – an office with stacks of cardboard boxes filled with papers and junk and a makeshift cell with barred windows and a steel barred door. Phillipa sat in the office on one of the two plastic chairs with Carol at her feet clutching her mother's hand. No sign of teenage anger anywhere. They both looked pale and frightened and alone. My heart went out to them both as they saw me and got to their feet. Carol grabbed me around the waist – a little girl again.

"Frankie," she said, her voice muffled in my clothes.

"Hey, Carol," I said, hugging her.

"Thank you for coming," Phillipa said.

I could see she was just holding together, probably for Carol's sake. "No problem," I said.

"Officer Ravic has told you everything?" Phillipa asked me earnestly.

"Yes, I'm sorry," I said, giving Carol an extra hard

squeeze.

"I'm not putting her in the cell," Ravic said, angrily, completely out of his depth – his hands passing his hat rim around and around like someone letting out rope.

"Officer, do you think you could take Carol for a little walk while I have a chat with Ms Bennetti?" Phillipa asked, mustering her self-control to ever be the lady.

"Ahh, sure, Mrs Ericsson... I'm sure it's okay, it's kind of like time with your lawyer really isn't it?"

"That's exactly right," Phillipa said.

He turned to Carol. "Is that okay with you, Carol?"

"I want to stay, I want to hear everything," Carol said.

"Do you know, Carol...sometimes you have to do things you don't want," Phillipa said. "Because someone who loves you wants you to."

Carol looked at me and I winked at her. "Are you going to stay around?" She asked me so earnestly I would have stayed around even if I had a free flight to Paris waiting on the tarmac.

"Yes, I am," I told her. Carol looked at her mother with concern.

"I'll be fine," Phillipa said to her with a little smile. "It'll be good for me to talk to Ms Bennetti."

Ravic rummaged around in his desk drawer. "Carol, I have the keys to the Paradise here...we can go make ourselves one of my special triple flavour shakes... that's one of my rewards for keeping an eye on the cafe." Carol headed to the door and Ravic was relieved. He put his hand reassuringly on her shoulder as they left. I realized again how I'd been wrong about him – he was just a simple cop doing what he thought was the right thing.

"Sit down, please, Frankie," Phillipa said to me. I sat obediently.

"How are you really doing?" I asked.

"Not good," she said. "If it wasn't for Carol..."

"She's holding together for you too."

"Ironical isn't it, that it takes something like this to

bring us close together again."

"If it means anything – I don't believe you killed your husband."

"Thank you. No, I didn't." She couldn't hold back the tears any longer, they streamed down her face soundlessly. Without thinking, I squatted down alongside her chair and held her as best I could.

"Do you know what surprised me?" She said, between breaths. "How sorry I felt for Heyden – he didn't deserve this, no matter what... He must have suffered, and he must have felt alone, and frightened and regretful..."

I couldn't think of anything useful to say. "Have you spoken to Travis?" I asked.

She blew her nose on a tissue and shook her head. "Carol begged me not to... I so need his support... he's so strong."

"She's just angry, it'll pass."

"I hope so. I wanted Travis to look after Carol, while I'm... while I.. can't be at home but she said if he came near our house she would run away."

"That's just teenage..."

"You don't know Carol. She's more determined and strong minded than I've ever been." Phillipa stopped crying and took hold of my arm. "Frankie, I need you to take care of her... I don't know how long they intend to hold me in here but I need to know she's okay and that she's safe. It was her idea to ask you."

"Good God, Phillipa, there must be someone...like... more appropriate than me...what about your relatives?"

"My parents and sister went back to England ten years ago, and there is no one here I trust enough – and certainly no one that Carol would accept."

"Phillipa, I'm not really a... child minding type of person..."

"Carol thinks you are and I've seen how capable you are – you got her to come back from the city."

"I'm sorry Phillipa, but I think I'd be a shitty mother.

I'm actually not that responsible..."

"I don't want to offend you but I can offer you..."

"It's not the money, I think I wouldn't be good for her – my life is... is.. Well it's certainly not what you'd want your child exposed to." I heard footsteps approaching from outside. "The police or the court will find a social worker or something," I said, quickly.

"Hey, you two," Ravic called out with fake cheerfulness as he came through the door. "Carol and I just had a chocolate strawberry banana milkshake." Carol moved straight to her mother.

"Are you okay, darling?" Phillipa asked her.

"I just want you to come home," Carol said.

I turned up my charm meter and smiled at Ravic, keeping a lid on my frustration. "Surely, Officer Ravic, she can go home for the night – I personally guarantee there is no helicopter waiting out there."

"The regional detectives will be here in the morning, and if she wasn't here my job would be gone and it wouldn't help Mrs Ericsson any bit either."

Carol turned to me with her swollen eyes. "Are you going to stay with me?" She asked.

I looked at her mother and Officer Ravic for a way out. A picture of my mother's face full of selfish spite leapt into my head.

"Hey," I said. "You have a swimming pool and a ten foot television, who'd pass that up?" Carol grabbed my hand and Phillipa smiled and mouthed, 'thank you' at me.

"My lawyer should be here tomorrow," Phillipa said. "He thinks I have a good chance for bail."

Ravic followed me out and asked Carol to give us a moment. Carol walked on ahead.

"Are you two gonna be okay out there by yourselves?" He asked, glancing towards Carol.

"I have a gun," I said.

"I know...I've seen it...would you like me to find someone to stay with you?"

"Nah, would be just another person for me to look after," I said, trying to sound tough and hoping to convince both him and me.

"I could give you a bigger gun – a rifle maybe?"

"That's very thoughtful," I said, "but we'll be fine."

"We could have some kind of psycho..."

"I don't think so, whoever it was must have hidden the knife to deliberately implicate Mrs Ericsson and they must have had access to the house – probably rules out strangers and means it was no spur of the moment thing."

"Right. Good thinking," Ravic said.

12

Billabong was much nicer than the hotel, at least that was some compensation for becoming a child minder. Carol told me she wasn't worried about her mother because they would soon find out she didn't do it.

The farm had been shut down and the workmen sent on paid leave which made it like a private upmarket resort. Animals, birds and insects were drawn to the impossible bubble of green foliage and water in a dry, red desert. It was just what I needed.

I slept uneasily, tossing and turning throughout the night in the very comfortable guest room bed. As soon as the yellow morning light showed shapes in the room, I gratefully got up and squeezed into a one-piece swimsuit of Phillipa's and plunged into her gigantic swimming pool. I was a terrible swimmer – all thrashing and gasping for air but I ploughed up and down watching the bottom of the pool and letting the thoughts come. I remembered what Heyden Ericsson looked like, and the word ordinary popped up. He seemed just an average, business type guy – a mother's pride – probably clever at math. Why would it ever be necessary to do that to another human being – kill them, and cut them up? Anger? Revenge? Psychopathy? Carol would never be quite the same person: the world would be darker, more treacherous, more unloving. Not surprisingly, my mother's watery face followed me up the pool. Did she choose to be like she was? Some smart person, I don't know who, said, *'we become the choices we make'*. I thought about my own choices – some smart, plenty not so smart. The confusing thing was that the choices made by my heart, rather than my head, were often the most costly and eventually painful, but at the same time, the best things I did. Go figure.

I thought of Phillipa and Carol, they didn't deserve this to happen to them – and Travis with his busted legs – so unfair. I swam harder and harder, my lungs hurting, limbs aching. Faster and angrier – thrashing and smashing the chlorinated water. And then I couldn't swim any more. I latched onto the tiles at the end of the pool, sucking in air, my head dizzy, a shape taking form in front of me, a dark blurry thing making a breathing sound. Pointed ears and flashing white teeth – head cocked to one side – a beautiful black kelpie – tail wagging as I reached for him.

"Hello, beautiful," I said, immediately wondering why I always talked to animals. The dog inched closer in the crouched position. I lifted myself out of the pool which totally delighted him. He spun around joyfully and did a lap around the pool to show how fast he was. "Clever boy," I said and he sat in front of me totally still as if to say – 'see, I can be totally still too'.

#

The kitchen was big enough to need a tour guide, with a pantry that could have supplied an African village for a month. The Black dog seemed to believe that one of us owned the other, as he trotted around with me wherever I went. He liked chicken breast and scotch fillet I discovered as he sat obediently and stared at me every time I fed him.

"Just like a guy," I said to him, "feed you well, and you're mine." He wagged his tail in agreement. "This relationship is already off to a better start than most of the dates I've been on," I told him. He cocked his head to one side as if I would make sense if he could just hear me properly.

"Who are you talking to?" Carol's voice came from the next room.

"Your beautiful dog," I called back.

"Great, except we don't have a dog," she said.

"Well you do now," I called back cheerily.

Carol burst into the kitchen. "Oh my God! He's beautiful!" Black dog wagged agreement at Carol and turned back to continue looking at me.

"If he's not yours, whose is he?" I asked.

"I've never seen him before," Carol said. "Maybe some tourist or something lost him."

The doorbell rang and Carol and I looked at each other.

"Did you invite anyone over?" I asked Carol.

"No."

"Any deliveries or workmen or anyone likely to be calling?"

"I don't know."

"Okay, come with me."

I took Carol's arm and led her to the front door. The bell sounded again. She looked through the peephole.

"They're standing too close – I can't see properly," she whispered to me.

"Listen to me, when I reach five, I want you to pull the door open hard and fast and get out of the way, okay?" She nodded. "One...two...three... four... five.."

The door flew open and I swung into the opening, the gun pointed into the face of whoever was there.

"Ms Bennetti, nice to see you again," he said.

My jaw literally dropped. Standing in front of me was Mr Expensive suit from the Fish Markets. I kept the gun pointed between his neatly trimmed eyebrows.

"What the hell are you doing here..." I said.

131

"Please, Ms Bennetti the gun isn't necessary," he said. Carol peeped around the corner of the door. "Oh, hi Mr Worland," she said.

"Hello Carol, can I come in?" He asked.

Carol put her hand on my arm holding the gun and smiled at me. "It's okay, he's our lawyer."

I lowered my arm, my mind racing.

"Thank you," expensive suit said, as he stepped forward.

Squeezed between my ankles, I could feel the dog beginning to growl. I reached down and patted his head. "It's okay, it's okay.. but feel free to bite a chunk out of him if he bothers you."

Carol giggled and whispered to me. "My God, you're worse than me."

"Carol, would you mind if I spoke to Ms Bennetti privately for a few minutes?" Worland said.

"Is mum going to be all right? Will they let her out? She didn't do it...it's ridiculous."

"It's a bit early to say, Carol. I have to talk to the police and make some applications to the court."

"But she will be coming home, won't she...when they find out it wasn't her?"

"That's the plan," he said with a smile to both of us.

"Okay, good, you two can talk, I'm going for a swim."

Carol disappeared into the house and I returned to the kitchen with Worland and the dog following. I kept hold of my Glock and made sure he could see it as I waved it around as I spoke. "So your name's Worland?"

"That's right." He sat in a kitchen chair and the dog stayed near me, his eyes fixed on the man in the chair who was not yet considered safe by either of us.

"So, did you kill Heyden Ericsson?"

"Rather silly question, don't you think? If I did, I'd be unlikely to tell you – and if I didn't, you wouldn't believe me anyway."

"Yep, you're a lawyer all right." The dog picked up on

my tone and became alert.

"What's his name?" Worland said, smiling at the dog with fake pleasantry.

"Beautiful," I said, without thinking.

"Oh...really," Worland said with mild distaste.

"Before you say anything, did you send your bald-headed friend after Carol and me in the city?"

"Yes."

I pointed the gun at his chest. "I should shoot you, you fuck and tell the police what you did."

"Put the gun away and sit down. Shooting me would just get you locked up – and you're not a killer anyway."

He was smart and right, but I was angry. I took two quick steps towards him and clipped him on the point of his nose with the butt of my gun. He fell out of the chair to the floor, spraying blood across the table. The dog leapt at him to join the attack. I just managed to grab him by the scruff of his neck and hold on to him as he barked and snapped. It shouldn't – but it did – feel good.

Worland got to his feet, holding his nose to stem the bleeding. For a moment he was unsure what to do. If he reached for a gun it would have been exactly the mistake I needed for my angry side to be let loose.

"Do you feel better now?" He asked.

The dog had quieted to a low growl. "Sit!" I told him. He sat immediately, obviously well-trained. I turned to Worland. "Yes, I do feel better," I lied. I didn't feel better. Sometimes I think that being angry just makes you angrier. "So why did he walk away – Baldie, when he had us trapped and was about to finish the job?"

"Perhaps you should ask him."

"What? He's here with you?"

"Nearby."

"Jesus!"

"I had no wish to alarm you."

The dog sensed my sudden increase in tension and pricked up its ears. "So how do you think the police are going to react to me telling them that Mr City lawyer followed us, made us strip, threatened us – and actually almost burnt us alive?"

"Do I look like a fool to you, Ms Bennetti?" He opened his jacket. "May I?" He asked, as he reached in and brought out his cell phone. He tapped quickly on the screen and held it up to me. "Look closely."

I peered at the tiny screen and took a few seconds to recognize a video of myself and Roxy, half naked in the back of the Lexus. The sound was scratchy but understandable it was Worland's voice: *'How much do you want?'* Then came Roxy's reply: *'More than you can afford.'* The video then cut out.

"I have several copies," he said.

Now I truly wanted to shoot his smug little face. Roxy and I looked like prostitutes and I knew there was no way we could link Baldie and him to preparing to barbecue us – we would sound like idiots or blackmailers.

"If you put the gun away and sit down, there is something I want to say to you," he said.

I made myself breathe slowly, which helps me with the anger thing. I wanted to hear whatever he had to say – maybe it could make some sense out of everything. I sat in the chair opposite him with the gun in my hand resting on the table between us.

"Okay, talk away."

"Heyden Ericsson was responsible for...let's say.. looking after a special account for us – an account involving a serious amount of money. Recently, we discovered that what we thought was in that account was in fact, not there. That left us surprised to say the least but with the need to locate those funds, whose whereabouts were known only to Heyden Ericsson. Are you following me, Ms Bennetti?"

"Uh-huh."

"Good. When we tried to locate Mr Ericsson, he was in fact nowhere to be found. Now the people I represent were most unhappy and felt Mr Ericsson should be held to account and persuaded to return the funds. Further to our misfortune, Mr Ericsson has now turned up in a cardboard box, in pieces – and we are forced to explore other means of retrieval."

"And you think I might know something about where this money might be?"

"No. If you had any knowledge, you would have acted on it by now. We've watched you quite closely."

"So why are you talking to me?"

"Because we believe someone close to Ericsson may have the information we want."

"Why don't you just ask them, then?"

"Because they may be reluctant to tell a... stranger."

"But not someone they trust – like me?"

"Isn't that what you do – debt collection?"

"You could beat and threaten it out of them, isn't that your style?"

"We do not like attracting attention, we are businessmen, but as a last resort..."

"I should hit you again."

"That would not be in your best interests and would put Mrs Ericsson at greater risk of remaining locked up – I am her lawyer, and she trusts me."

"You shithead."

"If you strike me again – or approach anyone about our discussion, including your detective friend – I assure you, your young charge who is swimming right now will remain in the pool a very long time." He paused to let this sink in. "What we are asking of you is to find out and tell us the whereabouts of our own money. Not so unreasonable, not so unfair – it *is* our money and we are happy to hire you as our debt collector if you like, to recover it. We can offer a special finder's fee."

"And if I say, shove it?"

"Then we will risk using the attention attracting method." He stood up and tested whether his nose had stopped bleeding. "I'm going to wash up now and go see my client. I suggest you and Carol visit Mrs Ericsson later today and have a long chat." He handed me a card with a phone number on it. "You will get an answer this time. One more thing," he said. "We understand Mrs Ericsson is having a relationship with a man in a wheelchair – an ex-army captain..."

"Travis."

"Good, you know him then. Apparently he worked for Ericsson in Paris, we don't believe he was close to Ericsson but we would appreciate your opinion."

"So you can chop him up too?"

"Goodbye, Ms Bennetti."

After Worland left, I sat and watched Carol do laps of the pool. Unlike me, she was graceful and precise in her strokes. As usual, I was trembling but clear headed. I thought about telling Karl the whole story from go to whoa. I knew he would believe me which might ease my stress levels, but it would put him in the firing line – even if he is a cop. I wasn't sure how big or powerful or punishing Worland and his friends were. My best and most reliable instinct was telling me to keep my mouth shut. I wondered whether Worland was telling the truth – that he wasn't responsible for killing Heyden Ericsson. And then there was Baldie – he was capable of it. The tiniest doubt sat on the edge of my mind about Phillipa. She seemed way too smart to hide the knife in her mattress – which led me to wonder was that a way to look innocent? Do something so stupid when you are obviously very smart. And chop the body up when you're a refined lady and have no reason to.

Carol was still moving like a dolphin in the pool. I remembered what she told me about her special bank account. Was the money Worland was after sitting in the bank here in the promised land? In the account Carol and her father went to so much trouble to open? It must have been very important to him. If the money they were after was in that account, do I tell Worland and let them take it and go? But what if they got their money and decided they needed to tidy up loose ends that could unravel their obviously illegal business.. whatever it was? Loose ends like me, or Phillipa or Carol. Enough thinking.

"Hey, Carol," I called out. "Let's go see your mum."

13

Beautiful liked his new name and refused to be more than five steps away from me. He sat in the back seat, his eyes fixed on the road ahead. As we approached the police station, I could see Travis's van parked out front. I knew Carol could see it as well.

"Do you want me to go in ahead of you?" I asked her.

"No," she said, as she strode out in front of me and pushed through the door.

Inside, Travis was sitting in the cell with Phillipa, holding both her hands. Ravic sat at his desk. As we entered, Phillipa dropped Travis's hands and beamed at Carol.

"Why is he here?" Carol said to her mother, refusing to look at Travis.

"I want him here, Carol."

Ravic shifted uncomfortably. "Hi Carol... Miss Bennetti," he said and indicated Travis. "I can't see any harm in him being in there for a while." He gave Beautiful a pat and turned to Carol. Is this your dog, Carol... what's his name?

"No, he just... arrived and attached himself to Frankie."

"Beautiful," I said. Three puzzled faces stared back at me. "The dog, I called him Beautiful."

"Oh, right," Ravic said, doubtfully. "He should wait outside."

"If you can convince him of that, go right ahead," I said. Ravic and the dog looked at each other and decided to let very awake dogs lie.

"Frankie, would you do me a favour?" Phillipa asked.

"Sure," I said.

"Could you take Travis to lunch while I talk to Carol?"

"Frankie doesn't need to take me to lunch, I'll take her," Travis said. "I'm always happy to watch a newbie try the Paradise menu." Ravic unlocked the cell and Travis wheeled out.

"Can I go inside?" Carol asked.

"Can't see why not," Ravic said. "Little boy detectives are gone for the day."

Beautiful sniffed the wheelchair and then Travis.

"Hello, Beautiful," Travis said. The dog wagged his tail and moved alongside the wheelchair so Travis could pat him.

"I'll be back soon," I said to Carol, as Travis and Beautiful followed me out.

We sat at the outside table of the Paradise under the tattered umbrella, rather than attempt to convince Beautiful that he wasn't welcome inside. I ordered beefsteak, rare as hell as Edgar had taught me. Travis laughed as the waitress left.

"You're a quick learner, Frankie."

"Maybe. How is Phillipa handling it?" I asked.

"With her usual classy courage."

"Carol will get over being angry with you."

"It had to come out. We got along so well... before...in the beginning."

"Travis, can I ask you something difficult?"

"Difficult? Story of my life, go ahead."

"Do you think Phillipa could possibly have done this?"

Travis took a deep breath, looked away and back at me

again. "No possibility whatsoever."

"Good, that's my instinct. Problem is, my instinct is occasionally completely wrong."

"The only thing she would kill for, in my opinion, is Carol."

"Well, Carol was being taken away by her father...?"

"Not really. You've seen Carol with her mother, she adores her."

"I can't imagine what Heyden Ericsson could have done that would have made anyone angry enough to kill him and cut him up?"

"There are a lot of strange people out there, Frankie."

"Do you think it was someone connected to his business dealings – someone he owed money to or took money from?"

"Maybe. He was very secretive about his business dealings, Phillipa said she knew virtually nothing. I told the detectives it could have been me. I had access to the house, and I was seeing his wife so getting him out of the way was good for me." Travis's expression changed. "You know I can do most things – I can drive my van, I cook for myself, I work out at the gym... I could have killed him and cut him up. They said it was heart-warming to hear someone supporting their friends."

I could see the hurt in his eyes and I could feel what it must be like to be considered not dangerous.. not man enough to be a suspect. "I'm sorry," I said.

"Ah Frankie, you get it, don't you? Most people don't."

"It would make me angry."

"I tried that – it just gave me a headache."

The food arrived and held no surprises, huge servings, cooked to death. "You know most of Carol's anger is because of her crush on you."

"Aah that'll pass, she's a good kid.. and smart."

"Do you know anything about Phillipa's lawyer, Worland?"

"Not much, he's supposed to be very good at his job.

Personally, I don't like him."

The waitress was hovering, waiting for a moment to intrude. "Pardon," she said to me. "You're with the camel man, Edgar?"

"Excuse me?"

"The introduction agency?"

"Oh, yes well...kind of...not really."

"I've got a list of names for him."

"Okay – a list of names?"

"For him to video – you know – that want a..." She glanced at Travis and back to me with a shy smile. "Like a.. match."

"They want a match?" Travis asked, completely puzzled.

"A partner..." She said.

"Oh, right."

The waitress continued. "Edgar said he was organizing a big dance and there would be over a hundred people. Anyway I had this idea that he could do along with the dance, you know, to get people to come."

"Great...what idea?"

A talent quest!" She got very excited now as she spoke. "They did it years ago and a lot of people came from hundreds of miles around. Listen to this." She stepped back from the table, took a deep breath, pursed her lips and made a piercing whistle that ended in a cracking sound. Beautiful leapt up in shock, his ears pointed, his head cocked to one side in disbelief. "It's a whip bird!" She said.

"I know whip birds – that is definitely a whip bird," Travis said generously. "You'd swear it was sitting on your shoulder."

"I've won two talent quests – one when I was sixteen... I can do a crow and a kookaburra..."

"I think that's a brilliant idea," I said. "I'll tell Edgar as soon as I see him."

"My name is Edith," she said. "I'm going to tell

everyone... And you can have the big serve next time at the small serve price," she grinned ear to ear as she left.

"Now there's something to look forward to." Travis said, laughing. "You're going to be a big hit with the people in this town."

"What can I say – I've thrown up on their camels, become a business advisor to a dating agency, hired a prisoner, cornered their agoraphobic mechanic, been threatened by their cop, employed by their wealthiest resident – what's not to like?"

Travis laughed. "Absolutely nothing."

#

After I picked up Carol and she had eaten a hamburger at the Paradise that resembled a hat left out in the rain, an idea struck. "Hey Carol," I said. "You know the account at the bank you opened with your father, why don't we go find out what's in it?"

"Why?" Carol asked, reasonably.

"Because I'm an investigator, Carol and that's what I do – investigate."

"But why does it matter about a bank account? It'll only be money."

"Because your father went to a lot of trouble setting it up and because it might tell us something – maybe something about what happened to him."

"Do you think?"

"I don't know, but it can't hurt."

"Okay."

Outside the bank I decided to test Beautiful's training, he obviously had some. "Sit," I said, with authority. "And stay." Beautiful sat obediently and I immediately wanted to take him with me.

In the bank, Carol was obviously an A grade customer. The two female tellers greeted her warmly and then became awkward as they remembered what had happened to her parents.

"Could we talk to Mr Curlewis, please?" She asked the younger of the two.

"I'll just go and see if he's busy, Carol... I won't be a minute."

I couldn't imagine Mr Curlewis being busy. There were no customers, and the whole place looked like it still lived in the 1880's gold rush era with ornate ceilings and stone pillars – except for the modern plastic teller protection barriers.

"Hello Carol." The manager greeted her with his hand out, opening the counter doorway, trying to adjust his hastily put on jacket around his shoulders. "Come in..." he said, as he led us behind the counter into his office and shut the door.

"This is Miss Bennetti," Carol said. "From the city – she's looking after me... since mum... can't... you know..."

"Nice to meet you, Miss Bennetti," he said as he shook my hand and turned back to Carol. "Yes, we all heard Carol, I'm so sorry... if there is anything we can do... or the bank can do for you... or your mother, you know you just have to ask."

"Thanks," Carol said. "Mum is going to be home soon... It's kind of like a legal formality thing... our lawyer said."

"Of course... the whole thing of locking her up... even for legal formality is ridiculous to anyone who knows your mother."

I turned on my charm generator. "Mr Curlewis," I said. "Carol wanted to access her account here – the one she set up with her father."

"Oh, right, that's actually a joint account, Carol," he said looking from me to Carol and back again. I raised my eyebrows pointedly until he got the message. "Oh, I see, of course... I'm really sorry about your father, Carol he was a good man – and very generous to this town, we are all going to miss him." He turned to me. "Mr Ericsson asked us to set up a private security space off our safety deposit room with special fingerprint recognition technology – it's been an excellent investment for us, we gained a number of very good accounts because of the extra security."

"Good for you – keeping up with the latest technology," I said, nodding and smiling shamelessly. "So how do we access the account now?"

"Oh, you can't... I'm sorry, we need the death certificate, beneficiary and probate statements and a few other things."

"But you know Carol...and you know the circumstances."

"It's a legal requirement, Miss Bennetti, there's nothing I can do."

"What if we only wanted to check the balance – like you could make it so we can't withdraw anything?"

He blinked several times at me. "Do you know, I'm not sure with this kind of account, we don't have anything to do with it here at our branch – it's all done by head office – we don't even know the balance. Anyway, let me make a call to head office." He left the room and I got up to check on Beautiful through the window behind his desk.

"Hey, Carol come and look at this," I said.

Outside, on the street, Beautiful was sitting near the doorway facing a young couple trying to get into the bank. Each time they took a step towards the door, Beautiful came out with a low, rumbling growl and displayed a set of impressive white teeth. The couple had no idea what to do. "Beautiful must think I meant him to guard the place," I said. Carol thought it was hilarious as I tried to get Beautiful's attention by waving my arms.

"Is everything alright?" Mr Curlewis said, as he came back into the room.

I felt like an idiot. "I was just waving to a... friend," I said lamely.

"Well, I spoke to head office and they said they

145

understand the circumstances but they can't allow you to access the account. They can however, permit a balance check if Carol logs on – they said they would only program that access for the next fifteen minutes."

"Well done, Mr Curlewis," I said, meaning it.

"I did point out to them that they might lose the account if they didn't cooperate – that seemed to galvanize them into action ha ha..." He got up. "Come with me."

He led us through a safety deposit vault to a tiny room with a computer terminal, chair, desk and a large wall screen. "You know how to use it, Carol – you don't have long, so I'll leave you to it. Come and get me in my office if you have any problems."

Carol tapped away at the keyboard, answered a few onscreen questions and then stuck her little finger into a hollow above the keyboard that looked like the neck of a black plastic bottle. An online banking homepage opened on the screen. Carol scrolled down and clicked on the account with her and her father's name. The balance displayed clearly on the bottom of the screen: $174,624,211.

14

Back in the street, after relieving Beautiful of guard duty, Carol and I were both still in shock. It was an amount of money that didn't seem real to either of us. I figured I now knew where to find what Worland was after. Beautiful was unimpressed with Carol's bank account and panted along in front of us in the dry heat. Across the street as two teenage girls waved at Carol and headed towards us, a text message sounded on my phone. It was Roxy: *where r u – cum we need u.* The two girls grabbed Carol's hands and hugged her as I replied: *on my way,* to Roxy. Carol looked at me with an expression I recognized: 'please don't embarrass me in front of my friends'.

"These are my friends, Mandy and Ursula, they want to get a Coke at the Paradise – is that okay?" The implication was, 'without the old lady'.

"If you promise to stay in the Paradise until I come and get you."

"Thanks, Frankie," she said – half to impress her friends she could use my first name.

"I won't be long..." I called as she took off. Beautiful watched her go. "You could go with her if you want," I said to him. He lowered his ears and wagged his tail twice as if to say, 'hey, I go with the one who has no friends –

147

and dishes out the food'.

At the agency, Roxy and Edgar stood in front of the computer with a tall man in a suit facing them. Roxy saw me and turned to the man.

"Oh good, here she is now." The man turned and I could see he was obviously a cop. "This is Frankie Bennetti... Detective Ross," she said. "Frankie he's here because some townspeople are concerned about us – what we're doing here. I told him you were like a part owner, and a registered legal investigator and that you'd explain... and... Frankie there's a dog behind you!"

"Oh that's Beautiful, he's adopted me."

The detective extended his hand. "Region asked me to investigate a complaint while I'm here on another investigation," he said.

"Who complained? What's the complaint?"

"In a nutshell, that you're running an illegal establishment here. The complainant is confidential as I'm sure you'd appreciate."

"What do you mean... illegal establishment?"

"Prostitution."

"You must be kidding..."

"Afraid not. The complaint involves filming of clients."

"This is ridiculous, we film prospective clients to help find a date for them," Roxy said.

"I'd like to look at your computer files if you don't mind?"

"Nothing to hide here, Inspector," Edgar said.

"Detective sergeant," he corrected.

Roxy opened the folder labelled, *Client Videos* as he watched the screen. There was only one file, titled, *Stacey*. "We only have one client on video as yet," Roxy said defensively. "But we have a lot lined up."

"Sergeant, are you married?" Edgar asked.

The detective looked surprised. "Divorced."

"Ah that's sad," Edgar said. "We might have someone

here for you."

"Can you play that Stacey file," he said, ignoring Edgar. Roxy hesitated. "We haven't edited that one yet, sergeant," she said.

"That's okay, play it anyway."

I shrugged at Roxy and rolled my eyes. She hit the play button and Stacey lit up the screen and told us she was thirty-one, from Adelaide, interested in shopping, collecting dolls and sex. I gritted my teeth and watched the detective's face for the next part. The camera did a lingering tilt, from Stacey's pretty face all the way down her very nice, naked body and all the way back to her pretty face.

"It's not how it looks," Roxy said quickly.

"It was our first recording," I complained.

"I'll take a copy of the file, if you don't mind," the detective said.

"I'm sorry," I said, with exaggerated authority borrowed from television cop shows. "You'll have to get a court order."

The detective looked embarrassed. "No, I mean for myself..." he said. "I'd like to arrange a date with... ahh... Stacey."

"Maybe you'd like to wait till we have more on our files?" Roxy said, cheering up.

"No, I like her."

"Ah," Edgar said, nodding wisely. "The man who knows what he wants is the man who will want what he gets."

"What?" The detective said, puzzled.

"Don't take any notice of him sergeant," Roxy said. "He spends a lot of time in the sun riding camels."

Edgar laughed. "She is so funny..."

"You know sergeant," Roxy said, enjoying herself. " I'm not surprised you like Stacey – you're exactly the kind of man she likes to have chasing after her."

I managed to turn my laugh into a coughing fit as Roxy

copied the file onto a thumb drive and handed it to the delighted sergeant.

"We're having a dance, you know sergeant – to introduce a whole lot of clients at the one time, you should come – Stacey will be there," Edgar said. The detective reached into his wallet and took out a business card.

"Give me a call," he said with a smile.

"So you've finished with investigating us?" I asked.

"Look, if you don't mind," he said, glancing up and down the room to make sure no one was listening. "I'll keep the file open as a current investigation, that way no one else will bother you and I can stay in touch."

"It's no wonder you're a detective," Edgar said, shaking his head in admiration.

After he left, I told Roxy and Edgar about Edith the bird calling waitress and her talent quest idea. They were enthusiastic.

"Listen Frankie," Roxy said. "Can you help us with the filming? We need someone... like an interviewer to get them talking – someone with class. And they won't let me film at the prison without you as my employer being present, and Edgar can't get the guys to talk at all. What do you say? You can fit us in around your work."

Heading towards the Paradise, I realized I had a problem saying no to people I liked. Maybe it wasn't a bad thing – I certainly liked Roxy and Edgar. To see love begin to lift its wings between them was somehow life affirming, encouraging – maybe love *was* possible.

Carol was seated at the back of the Paradise by herself – she seemed glad to see me and stood up as soon as she saw me.

"Are you okay?" I asked.

"Yeah," she said unconvincingly.

"What's the matter?"

"Nothing...really..."

"You want to tell me?"

"It's nothing. It's my fault... I just lost it with my friends..."

"Uh huh."

"It wasn't their fault, I'm just very... I don't know..."

"Sometimes losing it with people is the right thing to do."

Carol looked at me with shock. "That is so not what my mother would say."

"Well your mother is probably right. I'm not big on the right thing...or politeness – and that's cost me at times."

"They wanted to take pictures of me with themselves to post on their Facebook pages."

"Uh huh."

"Because now I'm like famous..." She refused to let the tears come.

"And what did you say?"

"I didn't say anything."

"Well that was very mature."

"I tipped my can of Coke over them."

I couldn't help it, I squealed with delight. Carol was shocked and Beautiful barked just to be included. "You know, Carol that was even more mature."

"Really?" She said, a tiny smile appearing.

"Yep. The world is full of insensitive, little people with heads up their asses – and every now and then we get to tell them who they are. Well done, you struck a blow for our side."

"And then this guy came up to me and asked me about the bank and did I think it was a good one and did I have an account there..."

"What? What guy? Did you know him?"

"No, I've never seen him before – he was well dressed but he had no hair."

There was no way to stop the angry hornet buzzing inside me. I phoned Ravic and asked him to do me a favour. "Hugo, I need to find a bald-headed, city guy who is staying around here – probably driving an expensive car, can you do that for me?"

"Give me a few minutes," he said.

I put my arm around Carol's shoulder, patted Beautiful, and headed towards the police station.

"Are you okay?" Carol asked.

"Absolutely," I said.

By the time we arrived, Ravic was standing in the doorway beaming. "Only took two phone calls," he said, pleased with himself. "He's at the Riverside Caravan Park near the bridge, south of town."

"*Riverside* Caravan Park?" I said, wondering why I'd never seen any river.

"Well it does rain here, you know, about every thirty or forty years we get like a monsoon and then it's a river for a little while."

"Hugo, could Carol and Beautiful stay here with you while I have a quick chat with this guy?"

"Sure, I can lock them in with Mrs Ericsson."

"Is that okay, Carol? I'll be as quick as I can."

"Great – I want mum to get to see Beautiful."

#

The Riverside Caravan park hadn't been alongside a river since Armstrong walked on the moon. Most of the trailers had long ago lost their wheels and been jacked onto blocks. It wasn't difficult to find Baldie's trailer – the Lexus was parked in front of the largest and best looking one. I stopped the car and stared at it. A philosophy guy with a long German name, said: 'the fly that doesn't want to be swatted is most secure when it lights on the flyswatter.' So I was going to light on my flyswatter.

I accelerated towards the trailer and slid to a grinding halt in the gravel, dust rising in the air. I leapt out of the Falcon, my Glock extended in both hands in front of me pointed at the van door, my heart racing.

"You ugly, bald piece of shit – are you in there?" I

shouted.

Nothing.

"This might look like a little gun – but it has handmade ammunition that will go through both sides of your trailer and you – and possibly through a couple of trees on the other side..."

The door opened and Baldie stood there smiling at me. He looked thinner with dark half-moons under his eyes.

"You're looking well, Frankie," he said.

"You're not," I snapped back.

His smile widened. "Ah, you're so refreshing – everyone tells me I'm looking better all the time."

"Did you speak to Carol Ericsson at the Paradise?"

"Yes, I did – I'm investigating, like you."

"You're not like me."

"Perhaps."

My anger was slipping away. "Why did you let us go – back at Heyden Ericsson's home – what stopped you burning the place down?"

"Why? Do you think I had a change of heart – an epiphany – facing death in a few months, I could find salvation – do some last redeeming act?"

"You tell me."

"We don't change, Frankie – none of us. We may want to – we even try, and lots of us talk, talk, talk about it. But in the end the cat will torture the mouse and the dog will bite the cat."

"You might be an animal – but I'm not." As I considered just how much animal I was, my phone rang – I ignored it. Baldie just smiled a tired smile. "If you say so – I mean you're the one with the gun pointed at my head."

"So why didn't you do your animal thing and finish us off?"

He sighed. "Perhaps I just wanted to scare you."

"Bullshit! You know what I think? I think your boss discovered Heyden Ericsson was missing – and that we were your best chance of tracking him."

He laughed. "Smart and beautiful – with a cute gun – you are the complete package, Frankie."

"Okay, so here's the deal. You don't go anywhere near Carol, you don't speak to her or threaten her or do anything else that will make me angry – or I will shoot you. And believe me I am best pals with the local cop – all I have to do is tear a bit of my T-shirt and you're a dead rapist – and I'm the girl who defended herself. You following me?"

"Every word," he said, smiling at me as if I was a cute child performing at a family get-together.

"As a matter of fact," I said, wanting to wipe the smile off his face. "Why don't you reach for your gun and I'll save you from dying of cancer, and if you're right that we are what we are, then I'm an angry and violent person."

"Ah, Frankie – another time..." he said, laughing and shaking his head.

"There won't be another time – I'll shoot you on sight – and you can tell that to Worland."

"We almost have what we want."

"What do you mean?"

"You're over reaction to me speaking to Carol tells me that she is the one we need to focus on."

The blood pounded in my head. Without thinking, I fired three shots at the Lexus, shattering the windscreen and blowing out both front tires. I ripped my T-shirt open at the front and aimed the Glock just above his nose. With surprising speed, he flipped backwards into the van, kicking the door shut as he moved. I emptied the magazine through the door of the van and as the holes appeared, some sanity returned. I knew I'd be dead if he came out the door.

"Go away, Frankie. I don't want to hurt you," he shouted from inside the van.

I clipped a new magazine into the Glock. "That's how we're different... I do want to hurt you."

"Frankie, let us get what we want from Carol and you'll

never hear from us again."

"You're a liar – there's no way Worland and whoever he works for are going to leave us alive after this. We can bring them down, and you know it."

Across the park I could see the manager, an old white-haired man open the door to a van and look towards us. I put the Glock to bed and got back into the Falcon. Before I took off, I called out to Baldie. "Tell Worland – he's next – if he doesn't leave us alone."

As I took off out of the park, I stopped in front of the old man. "Lover's quarrel," I said, with a slightly insane grin and handed him $100 which probably would've bought me the whole trailer. I figured the guy would never report the crazy lady with a gun and risk the chance of me coming back.

15

On my way to pick up Carol, I wondered whether it was time to talk to the police and Karl. To explain the whole thing and let them handle it. Immediately I could see the drawbacks – Ravic was way out of his depth and the city cops would take days with lots of talk and form filling before they would take any action. Carol and I could be bleached bones in the desert by the time they actually did anything and who knows what power and influence Worland and those above him would have on the police department – they obviously had enough money to employ the entire state force. The other worry was that Karl might act on his own – out of anger or chivalry or whatever and get himself killed. Telling the police how much was in the account would give Phillipa a bigger motive and she would appear even more guilty. Thinking of Phillipa, a scary thought arose – what if she was involved – what if she knew about the money in the account – that she was working with Worland. What if she did kill her husband or was involved in it. She did lie convincingly right from the beginning – on the first day I met her.

Okay. No police, and no Karl. Question mark re Phillipa. Could I make a deal with Worland? If he got his money would he leave us alone? Instinct told me – no. The money involved was too much. We'd be loose ends and they couldn't risk one of us going to the police or media or trying our hand at blackmail. So what to do? Two options left – the most appealing one – shoot Baldie and Worland, which doesn't even work as a fantasy, even if I could manage it – puts me in prison – and anyway they were unlikely to be top of the food chain. The sort of money involved means there is a major player or set of players at an impressive height somewhere. Okay, last possibility – going into hiding. Problem is, Phillipa is in jail – how long could Carol and her mother be out of contact, even if they could handle it? And hide where? For how long? Years? It might take forever – these guys aren't going to walk away. Worland could also use Phillipa as a bargaining chip – 'come back, Carol and give us the money or your mother will be found hanging in a cell'

I had never felt so trapped. Not a feeling I could tolerate for long. Sun Tzu, the ancient Chinese war genius said when faced with the enemy – 'pretend inferiority and encourage his arrogance'. Actually, I was feeling inferior without pretending – and their arrogance didn't need any encouragement. Okay, I'll think about old Sun Tzu.

With the jail in sight, I remembered the phone call that came when I was thinking of shooting Baldie in his trailer. I pulled out my phone – there was a voice message from Karl:

'Hey, Babe... I've got a ride to the Promised Land... Ha ha.. sorry, the name always makes me laugh. I found an off-road nut case who wants to try out his new four-wheel-drive monster in the desert... Should see you the day after tomorrow... looking forward to catching up with all that heat and sweat... Kiss Kiss'.

I played it again with a silly grin on my face – mostly for the end part. I called him back and left a message: 'hurry up'.

Carol was quiet on the drive back to Billabong. She told

me her mother was the closest to falling apart she had ever seen her. Sitting in the back, Beautiful occasionally rested his head on her shoulder then mine. Whenever I stroked him he dropped his ears and wagged his tail – he was definitely my kind of guy.

As we approached the homestead, Travis's van was parked in the circular driveway. I looked at Carol to see her reaction.

"It's okay," she said, as she saw the van. "I can be polite – for mum's sake but he's not staying in my dad's house."

"Good, I'd hate to have to shoot him."

Carol grinned. "Hey, Frankie," she said, looking away from me. "I'm really, really glad you're here."

I had to stop myself from tearing up. "Hey, Carol," I said. "So am I." Beautiful tried to climb into the front to get in on the love fest.

Inside the house, Carol went straight to her room as Beautiful and I searched for Travis. I could see he'd been in the main bedroom and the kitchen because things were moved but he wasn't anywhere inside the house. I looked through a rear window and scanned the outbuildings – nothing.

I headed out the back door, past the swimming pool and pulled up with surprise. Travis's wheelchair flag was lying on the timber decking. The flag was a black and white skull and cross bones which I remembered fitted into a slot on his wheelchair. My heart lurched and I ran to the edge of the pool. There he was, clinging to the side of the pool, his mouth bobbing above and below the waterline. I wanted to scream but I always hated women who did that in the movies. I jumped in, shoes and all and saw Beautiful leap in behind me. I quickly discovered the reason Travis hadn't climbed out of the pool – his legs seemed to be stuck to the wheelchair which gave a watery, silver twinkle on the bottom of the pool. I lifted his head above the water line and could feel his breath on the back of my hand. He was alive! I was energized. Beautiful licked

Travis's face and swam around in excitement at this new game.

"Travis, can you hear me?" I said, treading water and shaking his head to wake him up.

"Hey, Frankie," he said. A strong whiff of alcohol made me blink.

"Jesus, you're drunk!" I said.

"As a skunk..." he said.

I dived underwater to the wheelchair and saw how the strap normally around his legs which kept his legs from flopping out of the chair, had snagged on the footplate. I came up for air and lifted his head up.

"Carol!" I shouted as loud as I could. "Carol!" Beautiful gave a watery bark.

"Wow, you have a big voice, Frankie," Travis said.

"You're an idiot."

"I think your dog is trying to save me."

"Shut up."

Carol came running to the edge of the pool and knelt down. "Oh my God," she said, her eyes wide with shock.

"Hold his head up above the water while I try and unhook the wheelchair... It's caught around his legs."

Carol immediately grabbed Travis's head and lifted as I dived down to the wheelchair. With my feet firmly on the bottom of the pool I lifted the chair upwards, unhooking it from Travis's leg strap. He immediately rose in the water as I surfaced. "Can you lift yourself out?" I asked him.

"Sure," Travis said, as he spread his hands on the pool edge and lifted himself up and out in one movement.

I climbed out and sat beside him as he stretched out on the decking. "Thank you very, very much," he said to us both.

"You're drunk!" Carol said, shocked.

"I demand a breath test," Travis joked.

"What happened?" I asked him.

"I drank too much...?" he said with a grin.

"How did you fall into the pool?" Carol said.

"Ah well... that my two beautiful girls is a mystery to me as well."

With Carol's help I lifted the wheelchair out of the pool and dried it with Phillipa's hairdryer. Travis had a second, smaller, non-motorized chair in his van which I was grateful for as I imagined carting him around in a wheelbarrow.

Dried off and full of coffee, Travis and I sat in the kitchen with Beautiful trying to get us to play the game in the pool again as he looked from me to the pool and back again. Carol deliberately played loud music in her room.

"So, how did you end up in the pool?"

"I don't know... I must have fallen asleep... I had a few drinks..."

"A few?

"I thought I had the brakes on the chair..."

"You don't strike me as the suicidal type."

"Ah, Frankie... you don't know me."

"Was there anyone else here?"

"One of the workmen, the guy who maintains the pool and gardens, dropped off some pool cleaning stuff... that's all. Why? You think there's a homicidal maniac around here?" He laughed.

"You know what, Travis – I do, actually."

"Because of Heyden Ericsson?"

"Yes."

"I think he got himself mixed up with the wrong people on some financial deal or something."

"Maybe."

"It's all gone to shit, Frankie... I wasn't trying to kill myself but I wouldn't have tried too hard not to either."

"Ahh, self-pity avenue... that's where you're going down?"

"I live there."

"Rubbish."

"Frankie, can I confess something to you... just between us?"

"Confess?"

"About Phillipa and me."

"Is it going to be something you regret telling me later?"

"Make me another coffee," he said, as he patted Beautiful.

I rose and read the instructions on Phillipa's Italian coffee making machine for the tenth time. "This thing looks like it came from NASA," I said, hoping he wouldn't do his confessing thing. People's confessions rarely made me happy.

"Before Phillipa asked Heyden to move out, even before she came to see you, I was trying to find a way... or to be more honest, find the courage to end it between us."

I turned towards him in shock. "Holy crap, Travis!"

"Exactly."

"Does she have any idea about this?"

"I don't know. When she threw Heyden out... and Carol turned against her, I couldn't do it. I couldn't tell her, I felt... guilty and selfish. I tried to get it back... you know... what we'd felt in Paris... and in the letters..."

"Well you can't tell her now. Not until she's out of jail at least."

"I know."

"Jesus, Travis..."

"Yeah, I know... I know."

We sat there in silence as the minutes ticked by and the coffee machine made noises. I felt sorry for Phillipa whose life was unravelling – but I wasn't going to judge Travis. Sometimes love just leaves... and there's nothing you can do. I knew it wasn't a good time to ask but hey, Travis had introduced the personal between us and it now seemed relevant. "Travis, this is personal – and you don't have to answer it if you don't want to, but are you able to have sex with Phillipa?"

"Yep... It's only my legs that don't work properly. Why are you asking?"

"I'm sorry, it's not any of my business... I'm just really a curious person... about some things."

"It's cool, Frankie... I get that."

"By the way, an old friend of yours is coming here in a day or two."

"Who?"

"Karl Muntz."

"The cop? He's coming here?"

"Well, we have... we have a... not sure what we have yet. We're still trying to have a first date."

Travis seemed to be more surprised than pleased.

After Travis left, Carol insisted on dragging her mattress into the guest bedroom where I slept. I would have wanted to do the same thing at her age. A lot of scary, insane stuff had happened. Beautiful bounded around on the mattress as if he had died and gone to heaven – a soft place to sleep and two people who were obviously in love with him – could life get any better?

I knew both Carol and I would feel better if we kept busy so I told her she would have to come filming with me and Roxy and Edgar because we needed at least one competent person to use the camera. She brightened up and told me she had a camera the size of her hand that was brilliant and she loved filming people. I went to sleep feeling like a TV sitcom mommy.

16

Roxy and Edgar arrived at the crack of dawn. Fortunately, Beautiful had bounced around on my bed and licked my face awake an hour earlier. We piled into Edgar's camel car and headed towards a tiny little outpost called, Wandabeyer, two hours' drive into the desert. Wandabeyer, consisted of a one hundred year old hotel, a disused schoolhouse, a closed general store, a dozen empty, rotting, rusting, boom time houses and a large compound with a massive barn and yards with two dozen of Edgar's camels. Edgar pointed it out to Roxy proudly.

"Can we go see the camels?" Carol asked. "I can film them."

"Good idea," Roxy said. "From some of the farmers I've seen around here, it'll be easier to match a few of the better looking camels,". Carol and Edgar laughed.

The coolest meeting place was the pub which had large ceiling fans, tiles everywhere, and lots of empty space – not to mention ice-cold drinks.

Waiting for us at a table in the corner was our first victim – an embarrassed looking, enormous-shouldered man of about thirty with dark, leathery skin and the stoop peculiar to those who had been working on the land since they were four years old. Carol had the camera up and running as soon as we had shaken his gnarled hands.

"I'm Vivian," he mumbled.

"Vivian?" Edgar said, surprised.

"Me mum wanted a girl."

"I'd say you were quite a disappointment," Roxy said.

"Yeah, I think Mum was disappointed – I've got six brothers."

"Wow," Edgar said. "That's seven brides for seven brothers."

I had a quick flash of how this would look on video and stepped in. "Ah, Vivian... Could you look into the camera and tell us... err... something about your life out here. This is so we can show prospective... err... ladies looking for a... err... partner."

Edgar was impressed. "I knew you'd be good at this, Frankie."

"My life out here?" Vivian thought for a second or two and shuffled uncomfortably. "Well, I've lived here all my life. My grandfather got the property as a soldier's settlement lease after the war, it was just scrub them, he cleared it by hand with my grandmother pulling stumps alongside him. They didn't have enough money for a tractor then so he rigged up a system of like ropes and pulleys and the two of them would hitch themselves up like draught horses..."

Roxy was making a knife across the throat sign to me.

"Aah...that sounds very interesting Vivian..." I interrupted. "Ahh.. tell us what sort of girl are you looking for?"

"I haven't thought about that, really. I think she'd have to like...sheep."

"Sheep?" I asked.

Vivian noticed my concerned look. "Well, not so much the sheep themselves...but being around sheep. You know what I mean? And being alone, she'd have to be able to stand being alone a lot. The nearest neighbour is a couple of hours away."

"Ahh...good Vivian," I said, trying to think of the question that might actually help Vivian to win a heart. "Ahh.. What do you think you could offer someone... I mean what would her life be like?"

"Her life?" Vivian asked, as if it was an odd question. He pushed his hat back on his head and thought. "Well, she'd have to get up about five every morning, that's when I get back from milking and have breakfast. There's the fire to light, chooks to feed, the dogs, firewood, the washing – once a week, there's two calves being hand fed, and the vegetable garden. Mondays I bake bread and bring up the week's meat from the cool room. She could help out with the sheep – crutching, dagging, dipping, shearing, drenching – lambing time it gets busy – and when I have to spread super, or plough, or cut lucerne down the bottom paddock..."

"I think we've got the picture, Vivian," I said, feeling like I needed to lie down.

Edgar whispered to Roxy. "He doesn't need a partner, he needs a boat load of slaves."

"What about interests, Vivian...you know things you like doing when you've got the work done?" I asked.

"Never got the work done," he said, matter-of-factly.

"Well how do you relax?" Roxy asked.

"I'm always relaxed," Vivian said.

"I mean what do you do besides work? And don't tell me sleep." I was beginning to question my new career as an interviewer.

Vivian looked down at the floor as if pondering whether he would answer or not. He looked up suddenly. "I play the violin."

Even Carol, holding the camera, wobbled.

"I like Bach best," Vivian continued to a stunned audience. "He seems to understand the nuances about loss and loneliness."

Roxy's head shot forward. "Shuut upp," she said.

167

After Vivian left, we all agreed that you should never, ever judge a book by its cover. The publican was our next subject and he looked to be a bigger challenge. A pudgy, little man with a white shirt buttoned to the neck, comb-over hair and a habit of absentmindedly picking at various scaly patches on his cheeks. Okay, I was determined to look inside the cover this time and asked him how he came to be here – in a pub in the desert.

"Jesus sent me," he said, looking confidently into the camera.

Edgar and Roxy looked at each other with concern.

"Who is going to see this video?" the publican asked.

"Only special ladies we carefully choose," Roxy answered.

"The Lord sent me here as punishment.. for my redemption. I've already saved two souls," he said proudly.

"From the demon drink?" Edgar asked.

"No, I'd go out of business. Fornicators...a man and a woman, unmarried, in my hotel.. I saved them from the sufferings of hell."

"They not using condoms?" Edgar said.

"I prayed over them...while they were coupling. They were shamed in front of God."

I shut my eyes and wondered if we could edit the video down to the two lines about him saving two souls.

"So, you'd like a church girl?" Roxy asked.

"No, I want to do God's work – I want a sinner."

"I think we got a few of them," Edgar said, pleased with himself.

After the hotel lunch, the publican drew me aside and asked in a hushed voice, looking towards Carol. "Is that Heyden Ericsson's girl?"

"Yes," I said.

"Terrible, evil thing. Poor little girl."

"Yes."

"He used to come out here."

"Heyden Ericsson?"

"He rented a little cottage from me back of the school house, used to be the mine manager's."

"Really?"

"He called it his music room. He told me he needed to be alone and quiet where he could listen in peace."

"So, he came by himself?"

"Don't know – kept to himself. He usually came late at night and left real early. Occasionally he bought some milk or had a meal."

"Have you told the police?"

"I'm not my brother's keeper, the bible says."

"Fair enough. Do you think I could have a quick look?"

"Why?"

"I'm like.. private security for the family – you know her mother's been arrested? Maybe there's something that could help clear her."

"Maybe she did it. Satan works in mysterious ways."

"Okay. Yep... Satan, I can see that. What about I rent it from you for a day?"

"I only rent by the week."

"All right, how about a week's rent?"

"That's expensive."

"How much?"

"Four hundred...plus a deposit on the key."

"Okay, I don't mind, seeing as how the money is probably going to do the church's work."

"Don't believe in churches – just believe in God the Prophet."

"Can never have too much profit," I said.

He squinted suspiciously at me and I smiled back my innocent love of mankind.

I asked Roxy and Edgar to take Carol and Beautiful to see Edgar's camels, and before either of them could ask me why – I told them 'don't ask me why and tell Carol the publican wants to show me his collection of bibles, okay?'

#

Heyden Ericsson's secret music room was tucked away down a small hill behind the old school house. From the outside it looked like it had been abandoned fifty years ago. Inside was a neat, three room cottage with very few furnishings other than a large reclining leather lounge chair in the middle of the main room and a top of the line multispeaker sound system. Three walls had been filled from top to bottom with shelves that now contained literally hundreds and hundreds of books. The power was still on as a small freezer hummed away in one of the other rooms. I felt I had opened a door on someone's very private and personal world.

All three rooms were spotlessly clean which surprised me, as fine dust blew in from the desert non-stop. The place had been cleaned recently – I couldn't imagine the publican either doing or paying for a cleaning job this good. My phone rang – it was Karl.

"Hey, Babe – we're lost!" He said.

"What?"

"The guy's sat nav must be wrong – we've been driving around the dunes in circles."

"Oh, crap – are you okay?"

"Got plenty of water and food but the car has ground to a halt. We've called an emergency number and they said it could be up to eight to ten hours or so before they get to us."

"Ten hours!"

"Worst part is this four-wheel-drive idiot who won't shut up telling me how this has never happened to him...anyway how are you doing?"

"Oh...okay... I'm doing okay. I'm at a little place called Wondabeyer making videos for Roxy and Edgar's dating agency."

"Won't get into much trouble in Wondabeyer..."

"What? You know this place?"

"My battery is flashing red, Babe... I'm gonna have to go I'll call you after the cavalry arrives... kiss kiss."

"Bye."

I was disappointed Karl was close by but not within touching distance. I also wanted to know how he knew about this tiny little place. I kept running my fingers over the objects in the room, testing for dust. I squatted down, flattened my hand and wiped it across the floor. Clean. Too clean. Why would someone scrub this place so meticulously? Then, like a plane out of the blue, the thought landed: because this is where Heyden Ericsson was killed and cut up and it had to be hospital cleaned afterwards.

The little house suddenly lost its charm and my survival instincts kicked in. I felt the Glock for reassurance and went through the rooms again. There were no bloodstains – no signs of a struggle or fight – no clothes, and hardly any food. I sat in Heyden Ericsson's cosy music chair and wondered what it would be like to be him – wife leaving you – business in some kind of dangerous mess – the only person who cared about you, your daughter. No wonder he opened the account with Carol.

I stood up and checked the rooms again. I pulled sections of the books away and checked behind the shelves. Nothing. Many of the books were self-help types which surprised me – the poor guy was trying to improve himself. I looked in the tiny cupboard under the sink and lifted the lid on the little freezer. Inside there were frozen vegetables and meals of chicken and pasta. I lifted a handful of them out – nothing too gourmet here. At the bottom, amongst the old hardened ice, I noticed an object about the size of a drinking glass wrapped in plastic. I leaned in and lifted it out, shaking the ice away. I dropped the frozen food back into the freezer and shut the lid. The packet had been wrapped in bubble wrap and carefully and tightly sealed with masking tape. I picked at the tape with my fingernail and peeled it back. The bubble wrap was stiff from the cold and crackled as I unwound it. It kept unravelling until there was a pile like snakeskin on the floor. What was left was a small, tight, aluminium foil wrapped object. The foil had become frozen tight to whatever it contained. I picked at it – feeling the cold bite through my skin. And then I could see a tiny patch of pink. To my horror, I knew exactly what it was: Heyden Ericsson's index finger. Automatically, I dropped it and leapt back. Fortunately I didn't scream. My mind raced. Oh God, oh God – that was why he was cut in pieces, so no one would notice a missing finger. Whoever killed him knows about the bank account with Carol – how it operates. Oh God. Okay, I need to think. Calmly. I picked the finger up off the floor and peeled back a layer of foil to make sure it really was a finger. It was. I sealed it back tightly in the foil and wrapped the bubble wrap around layer by layer and reattached the tape. Now what? Should I get rid of it? Give it to the police? The security bank account would be uncovered and Phillipa would look like she had even more reason to kill him. And it wouldn't stop Worland and Baldie from silencing me.

I grabbed the bag of frozen peas from the freezer, emptied half of them out and shoved the wrapped finger deep inside. Hopefully it would keep the flesh from rotting for a while. With the frozen peas jammed into my bag, I had a panicky thought: Carol was in serious danger – she was obviously the other half of the equation for whoever chopped off Heyden Ericsson's finger.

I ran from the cottage, slamming the door behind me, my heart racing. My god, I'd sent her off with Roxy and Edgar – she was totally exposed. It had been a long time since I'd run as hard as my body would let me – up the hill, past the schoolhouse and down the short walkway towards Edgar's camel compound. My lungs hurt and the heat was pressing from the inside and outside, as I saw Roxy up ahead at the camel yards. And no Carol. As I drew closer, I shouted. "Where's Carol?"

"What?" Roxy called back.

"Carol – where is she?" I said breathlessly, as I reached Roxy.

"She took off on a camel," Roxy said. I almost collapsed into Roxy's arms.

"She what?"

"I'm kidding, she's here."

"Oh God... Oh God." I sucked in air gratefully. Beautiful came running directly at me – crazy with excitement. "My man," I said, as he leapt and wagged and licked all at once.

"You look like you're about to die," Roxy said.

Inside the barn attached to the yard, I could see Carol feeding a camel with Edgar explaining patiently to her. I immediately felt ten years younger. Carol saw me and came running excitedly.

"Hey Frankie, come and see...there's this cutest baby camel you've ever seen... she's white and fluffy-looking and she hasn't got her hump yet."

"Calf... she's a calf, Carol not a baby camel," Edgar said shaking his head.

Carol grabbed my hand and dragged me into the barn and down to a pen. "Wow, you're all sweaty," she said. "What have you been doing?"

"Oh...just running..."

"You need to exercise more...we have a little gym at home...you should use it... anyway look at her, she's so gorgeous... Edgar said he's going to name her Carol..."

"Carol the camel?" I said. "I like it."

I returned the key to the publican and asked him to call me if anyone came to the cottage for any reason. It required another donation to the work of the Lord for him to keep an eye out – and the promise of an even bigger deposit if he actually called me with information. Fortunately Jesus was okay with MasterCard.

On the way back in the rear of Edgar's camel car, I didn't want to talk and was grateful Carol fell asleep. Roxy and Edgar chatted away to each other in the front. I had no idea what to do next – telling Carol would only terrify her. I called Karl and got voice mail. I couldn't think of what to say, so I hung up.

17

After Roxy and Edgar left and Carol went to her room to change into her swimsuit, I buried the packet of frozen peas with Heyden Ericsson's finger at the bottom of Phillipa's freezer. My now very wet bag, I dropped in the bin – the idea of a finger melting into it was too much.

Alongside the pool, I threw sticks for Beautiful who leapt in and eagerly brought them back to me. I swam a couple of laps in the warm water to clear my thoughts and then climbed out and rested in the deckchair alongside Carol with Beautiful dropping sticks at our feet, puzzled why anyone would stop such an insanely wonderful game.

"Carol, this is important...we can't stay here any longer," I said.

"What? Why? What do you mean?"

"I can't explain, but we have to go somewhere...where it's hard to find us."

"Find us? Who wants to find us?"

"You have to trust me."

"But mum will be coming home soon... Mr Worland will get her out of jail..."

"It doesn't matter, we have to go.. now...today."

"Go where?"

"I don't know yet."

"I'm not going anywhere until mum comes home."

"It's not a request..."

"Frankie, I don't want to disobey you – you're my favourite person ever – besides my mum but I'm not leaving here till mum comes home."

I looked at Carol and saw my twelve year-old, determined and innocent self staring back. I thought she'd long since died from people poison – but no, seeing Carol's hopeful face that assumed everything would work out okay, wakened that younger, sweeter Frankie. My heart and face softened.

"You know what, Carol? You're right. We shouldn't let anyone drive us out of our home... well your home. Especially since it has a big pool and a gym."

Carol laughed and leaned over and hugged me as my phone rang.

"Miss Bennetti, it's Officer Ravic here. I thought I needed to tell you some not so good news. Mrs Ericsson has been formally charged – the detectives found some e-mails on Mr Ericsson's computer that don't look so good for her."

I walked further away from Carol. "What was in the e-mails?"

"Oh, just angry stuff about how she would never let him take Carol away... they wouldn't show them all to me."

"But that doesn't mean anything. She was just worried and frightened..."

"The Regionals just want to wrap up quickly so they can go home. Anyway the reason I called is because they've transferred her to the women's prison."

"Here? The prison here?"

"Yeah... look it's way more comfortable for her..except her lawyer said she won't let Carol visit her in the prison."

"That's bullshit!"

"I'm just the messenger..."

"I'm sorry Officer Ravic..."

"Hugo."

"Hugo, it's just that Carol needs to see her mum – she needs to know she's okay." There was a short silence. "You're a good person, Miss Bennetti."

"Frankie."

"Frankie. I think her lawyer guy...is really calling the shots. I don't really like him."

"Me either, Hugo. And by the way, I think you're a good cop."

After I hung up I thought about what to do. I needed to talk to Phillipa, to ask her about Heyden Ericsson's secret cottage at Wandabeyer – did she know? I wanted to ask her about Worland – how much did she know about him? If she lied to me, I'd know it – I'd see it in her eyes. I needed to see her face while I asked the questions. I had an idea. I called Roxy.

"Have you arranged to film the eligible women at the prison yet?" I asked Roxy.

"Long as I've got my employer with me and it's part of the job, there's no problem. I did suggest to the social worker and the warden that we had a couple of gorgeous farmers on our books before they agreed."

"Great, I'll pick you up in an hour."

"Now?"

"Is that a problem?"

"Ah, no... Just Edgar and I planned..."

"Don't...too much information," I joked.

Roxy laughed. "Yeah, who would have thought I'd fall for a guy that smells like a camel..."

"He's adorable."

"Yeah, he is isn't he." Roxy actually giggled.

"I'm on my way."

I didn't care that Phillipa wanted Carol to stay away. I was hired to look after Carol and that was what I was going to do. And Carol needed to see her mother – and that's what was going to happen. Hopefully.

When Carol and I arrived to pick up Roxy, I asked her

could she make Carol look older as they wouldn't allow a minor into the prison.

"How old?" Roxy asked. "Like...a granny?"

"No, idiot... about nineteen or twenty... is it possible?

"Well, I'm used to trying to make my face go in the other direction...so this should be easy. Come on Carol." Roxy dragged a delighted Carol off into the back rooms of the agency.

Edgar came up to me with a big grin on his face. "Don't worry, Frankie... Roxy can do it...look how she's aged me."

I laughed. "Edgar, you look ten years younger."

"I'm gonna marry that woman, Frankie."

"Make an honest woman of her," I joked.

"Naah, I'm not magic..."

I laughed again. "Edgar, you are single-handedly restoring my faith in the male animal."

He looked at me seriously. "You know Frankie, there's not one corner of my life that isn't brighter because of her."

One of the ways you know you really like someone is when you feel joy when you see they are happy. It was nice to feel joyous.

When Carol finally emerged, she had one of Roxy's short skirts pinned at the back to reduce the size, a bra full of Edgar's socks, hair pulled forward to half cover her face, way too much make up, and a pair of thick rimmed glasses.

"Wo hoh, Carol – you look like my brain injured older sister..."

Carol looked concerned. "Have you got a brain injured older sister?"

"Ah no, sweetie... I was just saying you look a lot older...which is good."

"Too much make up, you think?" Roxy asked.

"Nah... don't want any of that twelve year-old skin showing."

"I can hardly see through these glasses," Carol said.

"Good," I said. "Best way to look at the world."

I asked Edgar to hold onto my Glock until we came back. He had to be convinced that it was a real gun and shot real bullets. In his gigantic hand, it did look more like a water pistol.

#

At the prison checkpoints, no one took the slightest notice of any of us. We were on the permissions list and went straight through. Getting to Phillipa was another matter. The assistant social worker, Beryl was less easily fooled and immediately recognized Carol. She didn't blow the whistle on us but refused Carol entry to see her mother. Carol was disappointed, but cheered up when I sent her off with Roxy to do the filming. When they were gone, I took Beryl's arm.

"I need to see Mrs Ericsson," I said, with my most convincing look.

"She's on the 'no visitors' list, I'm sorry."

"Okay, fine – but if I can just slip in and speak to her for five minutes. It's important. I tell you what, I know you're interested in finding a partner, you can have first look and choice of all the farmers and miners on our books..."

She considered for a beat or two, chewing her lip. "Five minutes," she said. "I'll come and get you... and you tell no one, is that clear?"

"Perfectly."

"Your friend tells me she has quite a lot of very nice men on her books, is that true?"

"Beryl, you would not believe the guys we have..."

With a new bounce in her step, Beryl led me off to a more secure looking wing of the prison, down a long, tiled corridor and stopped outside a locked steel door.

"I'll be back in exactly five minutes," she said, as she

unlocked the door.

"Okay, thank you," I said, as I slipped inside.

Phillipa was sitting at a tiny desk under a barred window, she was writing carefully on a sheet of unlined prison paper and spun around as I entered. "Frankie!"

"Hi Phillipa, how are you doing?"

"Okay," she said, struggling to put on a brave face. I felt sad. This person was a long way from the classy, designer label woman who first came to my office.

"I only have five minutes... they won't let Carol visit you."

"I was writing to Carol... It's me that won't let her. I don't want her to see me here... It's too... too... confronting for a child of her age."

"Uh-huh," I said, feeling guilty that I had smuggled Carol in to this confronting place.

"She's had enough to cope with."

"Phillipa, I need to ask you about a couple of things, okay?"

"Of course."

"Did you know your husband rented a little cottage at Wondabeyer?"

"Yes...his music room, he called it. He said he needed to be alone and quiet from time to time to escape from his work, otherwise he'd go crazy."

"Did you ever go there?"

"No. I felt he needed something that was his and his alone and I respected his privacy. He had a very hard childhood."

"That makes sense. What about your lawyer, Worland... What do you know about him?" I watched her eyes and her mouth as she spoke. I read once that when people are genuine – the tone, words, expression, body movement etc – all were in line – were saying the same thing.

"Heyden employed him to do our personal work after they did some big business deals together. About him personally, I know he is divorced, has no children – is very smart, and that's about it."

Phillipa appeared to be completely genuine, I could see nothing incongruent. "Did you know, or did you suspect, that your husband might be involved in something with his work that was... aah... risky, or possibly illegal?"

For the first time, she broke eye contact with me and clicked the retractable pen she was holding, in and out – in and out. "He never told me directly...and I never asked directly. Once, he got drunk and said he had made a mistake...a big one...he said he felt like a little insect stuck in a spiders web."

"What do you think he meant?"

"I asked him – what mistake? He wouldn't tell me anything. He said the most generous thing he could do for me was to tell me nothing, that way I would not be implicated or caught up in the mess."

"Have you told this to the detectives?"

"No."

"Why?"

"Because it wouldn't bring him back to life, and if some kind of corruption or fraud or whatever came out – the one who would be hurt most would be Carol."

I saw not a scintilla of anything about her that might suggest she was lying or even withholding. "Okay, thanks Phillipa... I really needed to hear that. If you'd said you had no suspicions about your husband's work, I probably wouldn't have believed you."

"Frankie, are you and Carol safe by yourselves – do you need to hire extra help, or anything – I have no problem with any expenses you think necessary."

There was a tapping on the door and I knew our time was up. "We're fine, Phillipa, I lied. "Carol is safe and well – and only worried about you."

"I wrote her a note. Could you give it to her?" She folded the paper she had been writing on and handed it to me.

"Sure," I said.

18

Back at Billabong, I sat with Carol watching the video she and Roxy took of the prison inmates. They were surprisingly compelling. One of the things that most struck me was the openness and honesty. Rather than oversell themselves they were more often harshly critical. I figured that prison was probably a great bullshit filter. It was obvious that Roxy's idea of giving the single, low security inmates the chance of a real relationship, was probably brilliant therapy. A tiny dot of hopeful colour on a grey canvas. My phone rang and I got up and walked away from Carol.

"It's Harvey," the voice said. "...From the Wandabeyer Hotel."

"Oh, Harvey..."

"You said to call you if anyone came to the cottage."

"Someone came?"

"Sure did."

"So, did you recognize them?"

"That money you offered...that still stand?"

"Absolutely."

"I didn't actually see him... or her."

"So you're just making it up?"

"Nope...they left a calling card...must have been pretty

fit and agile...strong too, 'cause they climbed onto the roof
and tore away a sheet of corrugated iron and climbed in
from there."

"When was this?"

"Must have been early this morning – in the dark. I'm
closing and cleaning up to around midnight and I'd have
heard it."

"So you have no idea who it was?"

"Nah. Smart, whoever it was – they must have parked a
ways away so no one would hear."

"Okay, thanks. You've got my credit card numbers, so
add it on."

"I'll do that. You want me to call you if anyone else
comes?"

"Yes, please."

"Okay, nice doing business – you go with God now."

I stopped myself just in time from saying something
smart mouth like, 'I could go with God, Harvey but I'd
rather he went with me'.

Late in the night, I checked Carol was sleeping and got
up to pace around and think in the still silence with
Beautiful tagging along trying to figure out the new game.
An idea was forming. Maybe I could take the initiative
rather than wait for Worland and Baldie to strike.

I checked out the house's security camera system. Carol
told me every large room had either two or three cameras
which were voice or motion activated and recorded by Wi-
Fi back to a large computer located in what must have
been Heyden Ericsson's office. I made a strong cup of
coffee to help get my head clear. The sitting room had
three cameras, two near the ceiling and one at head height
in the wall facing the lounge. Perfect. I sat in various chairs
in the room and moved about, talking softly, mumbling
and sitting still for minutes at a time – Beautiful watched
and seemed to happily accept that I was insane. When I
checked the recordings on Heyden Ericsson's computer,

the images of me moving and sitting were sharp and clear, the sound was understandable at half volume. Heyden Ericsson had spent a gazillion dollars on the house and hadn't skimped on the security system. The questions I couldn't answer with certainty were: would Worland come? Could I get him to incriminate himself and record it on camera – and would that be enough to stop him?

As the sun rose yellow across the desert, I took a deep breath and made the call.

"Worland?"

"Yes."

"It's Frankie Bennetti... I want to talk."

"Is that right?"

"You come here – alone – no bald-headed friend..."

"How do I know you won't shoot me?"

"I'd hardly ask you to come to where I live if I was going to shoot you – even though it does have a certain appeal."

"Ms Bennetti I need to tell you the patience of the people I work for has run out. This will definitely be the last time we talk."

"Suits me."

"I have to see Phillipa this morning at the prison but I can be there say... around two this afternoon?"

"I'll be waiting."

My heart was pounding when I hung up – I'd never ambushed anyone before – and I knew this guy was smart and not to be trusted.

I had time to make Carol and Beautiful a big hot breakfast. I couldn't eat myself – I knew things could go seriously wrong – that in so many ways I was out of my league.

"Frankie, I don't think you're supposed to feed dogs bacon and eggs on toast," Carol said.

"Tell him." I pointed to Beautiful who was sitting wagging his tail at a licked-shiny plate. Carol laughed and then noticed that I was staring at her.

"What? Why are you looking at me like that?"

"Because I need you to do something for me without asking why."

"What? What do you want me to do?"

"Will you promise to do it?"

"I can't promise something I don't know..."

"Yes, you can. If you don't, then I'm going to have to drop you off with Officer Ravic and leave the Promised Land," I said.

"Oh, you wouldn't do that. I know you now – you wouldn't abandon me."

I pulled my serious face, knowing Carol had to agree or my plan became impossible. "I would have to," I said. Carol got it.

"You're serious, aren't you?"

"Deadly."

"Okay, I'll do what you want."

"Without asking why..."

"Without asking why."

"Promise?"

"Promise."

I showered, drank more coffee, and tested that I could see the road into Billabong through the front window if I sat on the lounge, as I didn't trust Worland not to drop Baldie off on the road before he got here and have him sneak up while we talked.

From the veranda, I listened to the radio playing country and western music that didn't require me to think, as I trained a pair of Phillipa's expensive binoculars on the road from town. I estimated I would have seven or eight minutes from the time I could see Worland's tail of dust until he arrived at the house. I assumed that he would insist that I put the Glock away, so I found a 12 gauge shotgun in Heyden Ericsson's gigantic barn – a very nice, eight-shot Winchester which I shoved down behind the pillows on the lounge where I intended to sit. Old Lao Tzu said: 'an ant on the move does more than a dozing ox'. So I was on the move. I tested the cameras in various positions in case Worland moved about or was suspicious or chose an odd spot. I also went to the bathroom three times.

Through the binoculars, the heat rising off the desert floor made watery, wriggly distortions of the landscape. I thought of the craziness of my current moment – how did I get to be here – in the desert, caretaker of a twelve year-old and a dog – waiting for someone who was likely to have me killed? At least I wouldn't die of boredom – was the most positive thing I could come up with. And then I saw it. A tiny thread of red dust rising in the distance.

"Carol!" I yelled loudly, making Beautiful leap to his feet and growl at nothing. Carol came running, her face slightly flushed, carrying a bottle of water.

"I'm ready," she said.

"Turn off your phone..."

"It's already off."

"Good. Have you gone to the bathroom?"

"Yep...empty as."

"Okay," I said, noticing a bulge under her T-shirt at the waist. "What's that?"

"Don't make me put it back... Frankie, it's a kitchen knife... I just feel better with it."

There was no time to argue and I saw myself again. "Okay, are you sure you can keep Beautiful quiet?"

"Yes, we practiced – he's so clever, I just hold my fingers up to my lips and he doesn't hardly move or breathe."

"Now Carol, this is important – when you hide... And don't tell me where – I don't want to know, I want you not to come out – no matter what... unless I say 'Carol and Beautiful come out!' You got it?" Carol nodded but I wanted to make sure. "If I say 'Carol come out' or 'Carol, please come out', you stay put – okay? You've got to hear me say 'and Beautiful come out' – you don't hear 'and

187

Beautiful' – you don't come out."

"'Carol, come out' – I stay. 'Carol and Beautiful' – I come out. Got it."

"Good girl... and don't go past the outbuildings, okay?"

"Okay. Are you going to be alright, Frankie?"

"Yes, Carol – I'm a professional – this is what I do," I lied. "And you will be okay too."

"And Beautiful?"

"And Beautiful. Now go – and make it a really good hiding place."

"Oh it's great.."

"Don't tell me," I said quickly. Carol laughed and rushed up and hugged me. I kissed her forehead. "I can't wait till you come work for me."

Carol grinned with pleasure. "See you, Frankie... Come on Beautiful."

I watched them disappear through the house and heard the back door slam. In the distance, the approaching car was still a few minutes away, enough time for the fear to crawl from my belly up into my throat.

I kept the binoculars on the Lexus to make sure it didn't stop on the last three or four minutes towards Billabong. My hands were sweating and shaking which made the landscape wobble and blur even more in the haze.

As the Lexus pulled up, and before Worland got out, I strode to the car and checked that it had no one else inside. "Would you mind opening the trunk?" I asked, coolly.

Worland smiled his charming smile and tripped the lock. I opened it cautiously. It was empty and I watched Worland shake his head.

"Miss Bennetti, we need to develop some trust between us."

"I will," I said, marshalling my pretend confidence. "As soon as ducks walk on their heads." He laughed and I immediately thought, Christ, I even want to amuse someone who is likely to kill me – maybe I should give up investigating and become a comedian.

"Shall we go in and out of the heat?" He asked.

I led him into the kitchen and offered him a glass of water. "Sit down," I said.

He continued to stand. "Why don't we go into the sitting-room," he said. "And I'd feel more comfortable if you'd take your gun out and leave it here."

Bingo! I knew he wouldn't sit where he thought I wanted him to – and I knew I'd have to lose the Glock. My confidence rose – so far, so good. "Okay," I said, leaving my gun on the table and leading him into the sitting-room where I had placed a T-shirt of mine on the lounge where I wanted to sit. I was counting on the idea that no one likes to sit near someone's personal stuff. He sat in the chair opposite and I flopped on the lounge. I was feeling smarter by the minute. Now I needed to get him to say something incriminating.

"So, here I am Ms Bennetti, ready to listen."

"Can I ask you something?"

"Of course."

"You're obviously a very smart lawyer with lots of wealthy clients – you couldn't need the money – why are you involved in this...this risky, illegal... whatever it is?"

"You're appealing to my vanity – a good strategy."

"Are you just...greedy?"

"Provoking with an insult – also a useful technique."

"Seriously."

"You think it's all about money?"

"Isn't it? Isn't that why you almost burnt Carol and me to death?"

"But you're here."

"No thanks to you," I said and decided to change tack. "Look, I know you're not top of the food chain here..."

"If we wanted you gone, Miss Bennetti, you wouldn't be sitting here now talking to me."

I prayed the cameras were picking up the conversation.

"If I was able to get your money back, would you leave us alone – Carol and me and Phillipa?"

"Of course."

"I don't believe you."

"It doesn't matter whether you believe me. Are you aware I can get Phillipa off or get her convicted? And I can basically do what I like with both you and Carol. You are not in the strongest bargaining position."

Yess! Gotcha! I told myself as I continued. "But I'm guessing your boss or bosses don't want bodies and investigations and media attention."

"Smart girl," he said, as he looked at me with a tinge of respect.

"Perhaps."

"Here is the position. We know Carol is the key. We know she is the one person Heyden Ericsson trusted. I have spoken to the fool of a bank manager in town who chatted on about how Carol and her father started their fingerprint security account system."

"I don't know what you're talking about," I said, hoping my increased heart rate was not obvious.

"You do. We know you went to the bank with Carol."

"She has an account there," I said, lamely.

"Your face gives you away."

I cursed the fact that my emotions strutted nakedly around my face no matter how hard I tried to dress them. "And your face gives you away," I said with as much sarcasm as I could muster.

"Look, Frankie...we are happy to pay for a small service, just let me talk to Carol, that's all."

"Be warm and friendly – good strategy," I said, mocking him.

He smiled acknowledgement. "Touché." The smile disappeared. "As Phillipa's lawyer, I'd like to talk to Carol if I may."

"In your dreams."

"Where is Carol?"

"I took her away from here."

"No, we've been watching you."

Now the anger started to rise. "Here's the deal... I now have you on camera – everything you've said here is recorded on Heyden Ericsson's security system."

"Really," Worland said, still with his charming smile.

"Enough recorded to get you arrested and convicted and to start authorities after your boss..."

"Blackmail?"

"If you like."

"So you think... you now have leverage, and I'm a complete fool?"

"Your words."

"Perhaps we should ask Mr Girard?"

"Who?"

"Mr Girard – standing right behind you."

I turned, and at the same time, felt for the shotgun hidden down the lounge. Behind me, Baldie advanced – his arm extended with my own Glock pointed at my head. I let the shotgun lie, blood pounding in my ears.

"Hello, Frankie," Baldie said.

"So your name is Girard?" I said, struggling to keep composure. "Where did you come from?"

"He headed out here straight after your phone call to me," Worland said, pleased with himself. "And waited in the sand dunes."

I quickly tried to calculate whether Girard might have seen Carol and Beautiful when she went to hide. "You look sunburnt," I said.

"It was very uncomfortable out there, Frankie."

"Mr Girard, do you have the security recordings?" Worland asked. Girard held up what looked like a computer internal hard drive. My heart sank. Worland turned to me with mock graciousness. "So, Frankie if you would be so kind as to get Carol for us, we'd be most appreciative."

"I told you, she's not here."

191

"My guess is that she's probably not too far away – perhaps hiding somewhere? What do you think, Mr Girard? Should we go and have a look for her?"

"I left her in town with the family of one of her school friends."

"She's not in the house," Girard said to Worland.

"So let's try outside, shall we?" Worland stood up and smiled at me, enjoying himself. "After you, Frankie."

At the rear of the house, as I was about to open the door, Worland grabbed hold of my arm. "Here is what you will do," he said. "Open the door and call out as loudly as you can for Carol... that's all...if you warn her in any way, Mr Girard will seriously injure you."

"Sounds fair," I tried to joke, praying that Carol would follow my instructions. Worland opened the door and shoved me out onto the step.

"Call her," Worland whispered.

"I told you, she's not here."

"Then it won't hurt calling her," Girard said, giving me an odd smile.

"Okay," I said, shaking my head at the silly thing they were asking me to do. "Carol!" I called out. "Carol!"

"Louder," Worland said.

"Caarroolll!" I shouted. "Caarroolll..."

"Tell her to come back now...everything is fine," Worland said.

"Caarroolll...you can come back now...Caarroolll... everything is fine."

"Now let's wait," Worland said.

The seconds ticked by into minutes. I listened to my own breathing. Nothing. I turned to them. "I told you... she's not here."

Worland pushed out the door and took my arm. "Let's look in some of these buildings." Girard followed behind, my gun disappearing into his pocket.

The two of them searched through the stables, machinery and tractor sheds, lifting and moving anything that could possibly be used as a hiding place. Inside my head, I could hear a high-pitched scream, of hope and terror. They lifted the heavy wooden cover on the well and peered in. The hay barn was full – with nowhere to hide. Girard looked through the chicken shed and skirted through and around each of the buildings. No Carol. Worland was no longer smiling or charming. He was angry. For some reason this made me feel better. He grabbed my arm and pulled me out into the open courtyard.

"Mr Girard, would you see that she doesn't move," he said. Girard stood behind me and twisted my arm up my back. Worland cupped his hands around his mouth and shouted out loudly. "Carol! You need to come out now – we found out that Ms Bennetti here is the one who killed your father. Did you hear me? This is Detective Girard with me... he can explain everything. We are going to the correctional facility to get your mother out... We want you to come... your mother wants to see you..."

The high-pitched scream in my head went up a notch. I shut my eyes, praying that Carol wouldn't fall for Worland's clever line, as he continued. "Carol? Carol?" He shouted. "Did you hear me? Carol?" I made sure I looked at him as if he was totally wasting his time. Several minutes ticked by.

"Are you satisfied?" I asked, as calmly as I could. Worland stared at me, and for the first time I saw the ugliness of the real person – his meanness and cruelty.

"Mr Girard," Worland said. "Would you put Ms Bennetti's pistol to her head?" Girard tightened his grip and held the Glock to my temple. Fear and anger and stupid thoughts, raced through my brain. I was going to die.

"Don't run," Girard whispered. "It'll hurt more... you'll get shot in the body and it will be slow."

"Last chance," Worland said to me. "Tell us where Carol is?"

I thought about lunging forward and shoving my fingernails into Worland's eyes. They knew more than I thought – they knew they only needed Carol – I was never going to be allowed to walk away from this.

"I can take you to her in town," I said, with no conviction.

"If she *is* in town, we will be able to find her in... probably an hour," Worland said.

With nothing to lose, I thought I'd go down swinging. "I know why you do this," I said to him. "It isn't the money – it's the power, isn't it? You're trying to feel powerful because you're not. I think you're a powerless, little man – a weak, greedy, powerless, little man." Bull's-eye! At last I'd cracked his arrogant, suntanned, male-product-pampered image. His expression barely changed but around his eyes I could see my little knife had gone deep.

"Shoot her...up close," he said to Girard. "The right side of her head... It should look like suicide."

"Out here?" Girard questioned. "Not exactly where someone would choose to kill themselves."

"Doesn't matter, just do it."

"Tell you what," Girard said to him. "How about you do it?"

"What?" Worland said, surprised.

"You're the one who got insulted."

"Are you refusing?" Worland said. "You've become attached to her haven't you?"

"No, I was just considering whether you were a... " Girard turned to me. "What was it?".

"A weak, greedy, powerless, little man," I offered.

"That's it," Girard said.

"Give me the gun," Worland said, his face flushed, his breathing shallow and fast.

Girard passed him the Glock. I stopped breathing and shut my eyes. I could feel Worland's shaking hand through the cold barrel of the gun as he pressed it into the soft flesh of my temple. Wham! The explosion and pain hit at the same time. The world flashed red then white, the pain spiked through each temple like a spear shooting through my brain. As my legs buckled I felt the blood ooze down over my eyes and face. So this was dying. I toppled backwards and hit the ground, my chest collapsing as if pressed by a terrible weight. My eyes were full of blood and my ears were ringing. My breath wouldn't come. Panic charged through my whole body as I struggled not to die – not to die like this. The weight on my chest seemed to move, to slide away. My breath came back with a rush. I thought of Carol and Beautiful – they hadn't come out, they hadn't come out! I was shaking – something was shaking me.

"Get up." I heard Girard say.

I wiped and scraped and blinked away at the blood sticking to my eyes and opened them to see a blurry Girard standing above me. And alongside him, the bloody and smashed head of Mr Expensive suit, Worland.

"Get up," Girard said again. "There's nothing wrong with you...you can see who got the bullet."

I felt the side of my head for a hole or a wound which I knew must be there. I was dead and this was my last fantasy. My temple throbbed. "Aahhh," I called out, as I touched it.

"I clipped you on the side of the head with the butt as I removed Worland's life problems," Girard said.

"Whaa?"

Girard reached down and pulled me to my feet. My head was spinning – but life was coming back. I wasn't dead. A rush of joy flooded through me. Girard was leading me back to the house.

In the kitchen, he turned on the cold water, filled the sink and pushed my head under. The cold felt good – the water felt good – everything felt good – even Girard's hand on the back of my head. Life was good. Death was bad. I wasn't dead. Girard pulled out a length of paper towelling and dried my face and hair.

"Make us some coffee," he said.

I would have stripped naked and given him a lap dance if he'd asked. I took a few deep breaths and concentrated on the coffee making. I thanked the gods, or whoever was running the show, that Carol and Beautiful had remained in hiding the whole time. Did Carol see what happened? She must have heard it? It would have been very difficult to stay hidden. Good girl – stay hidden, not safe yet.

I sat opposite Girard sipping coffee, which tasted like heaven's nectar. "Why is Worland lying out there and not me?" I asked. Girard took his time answering, he was calm, even thoughtful.

"Orders," he said.

"I thought he was your boss?"

"He was up until ten minutes ago."

"Why did you tell him to shoot me?"

"That was personal. I was curious whether he'd be excited, frightened or sick to the gut."

"And?"

"He was all three."

The coffee had unsettled my stomach, I felt queasy and for a moment I thought I'd throw up. "Nice," I said.

"He was seen talking to a detective."

"That's why you shot him? He could have been just doing his job – he's a lawyer!"

"Wasn't my decision. He was also considered responsible for this whole mess."

"So what happens now?"

"I don't know what you did with Carol, but I'm impressed – very professional. You could do well, Frankie..."

"If I survive."

"If you survive."

"Am I going to survive?"

"If you do as I tell you."

"Which is?"

"Frankie, we know the money is in a joint account in the name of Carol and her father. To operate the account by herself, Carol needs the death certificate and a few other legal documents which the late Mr Worland has kindly procured with his usual efficiency." Girard took out a brown envelope from his jacket and passed it to me. He pulled from his pocket a small card. "This is the account number you need to get Carol to transfer the money to. All of it. We know how much is in the account. Do you understand everything I'm saying?"

"Yes."

"If Carol does that – transfers the money – you'll never hear from us again."

"And if she doesn't?"

"You will hear from us again."

For some reason I believed him. Perhaps I wanted to. Perhaps I wanted to believe there was a way out of the boggy quicksand my life was sinking into. "Okay, I'm going to believe you."

"You have good instincts."

"What about Worland's body?"

"I'll take it with me. It will only be found if you fail to do what we ask."

"What do you mean?"

"Aahh Frankie...much to learn. He was shot with your gun."

"But he was holding it to my head? How could you shoot him with it?"

"Unfortunately for Mr Worland, being an amateur, he closed his eyes before pulling the trigger."

I was so out of my depth. In the second or so Worland shut his eyes, Girard must have grabbed the Glock and turned it on him. They now had perfect evidence I was a murderer.

"Do what we ask and information will be found that Worland had massive gambling debts and was seeing a psychiatrist."

Oh my god, they knew exactly what they were doing every step of the way. "You're going to keep my gun aren't you?"

"Aah Frankie, wouldn't want to leave behind a vital piece of evidence, would we?"

I was perfectly trapped. Girard got up and placed his coffee cup in the sink.

"I may not see you again," he said.

I didn't ask whether he meant *I* would be dead or *he* would be dead from cancer – maybe that story was made up as part of his complete control of me and everything else.

I watched him wrap Worland in blue plastic and into a roll that looked like a camping tent or a giant cocoon and drag his body into the Lexus. He called me over to the car and lowered the window. "It probably doesn't mean anything to you, but I'm glad he's the one rolled up here and not you," he said.

"It means a lot to me that I'm not the one rolled up here, too," I said.

He laughed. "They've given you twenty-four hours... and they mean it."

"Okay," I said.

"Goodbye, Frankie Bennetti," he said. And then he paused, blew me a little lip kiss and drove away.

19

Through the binoculars, I watched Girard go until he was the tiniest wisp of dust in the distance and then I took off through the house and out the rear door.

"Carol!.. and Beautiful!...you can come out now..." I shouted as I headed to the outbuildings. "Carol!.. and Beautiful!...you can come out, everything is okay!" I ran through the stables and machinery sheds shouting as loudly as I could, stressing 'and Beautiful'. Nothing. I did a complete circuit of the courtyard, calling out as I went and finally stood still, listening for any movement. No Carol. Panic was beginning to rise – but it was a luxury I couldn't afford. I climbed up the bales in the hay shed for a higher view. Zero. I called Carol's phone which went to voice mail. I left a message saying 'Carol and Beautiful can come out now, Carol... it's Frankie, everything is okay'. I wanted to cry but that wasn't going to happen either. I needed to think. I tried to imagine the places where I might have hidden – where it was possible to hide. I couldn't think of a place that hadn't been searched. Perhaps she had gone to sleep? But surely Beautiful would have heard me calling?

I climbed down from the stacked bales and on the last bale resting on the ground, I noticed a splash of colour. Red. Blood. My heart lurched. The bale was slightly out of alignment with the rest of the stack. I touched my finger to the red patch, hoping it was dry and old – and not fresh. It stuck to my fingertip. I prayed it didn't belong to Carol or Beautiful. I remembered Carol had taken a kitchen knife with her. I pulled at the bale which came away easily from the stack. There seemed to be a hollow inside, but it was too dark to see clearly. I grabbed my phone, opened it, and hit the torch app. The hollow was a veritable cave about the size of a double bed. On the floor was Carol's full bottle of water and her phone. My blood turned to ice. This was the hiding place – why would she leave it? Where the hell were they? What had happened? Girard had no time to find her, and anyway he would have brought Carol into the house with him. It was a brilliant hiding place. Carol had done well. But where was she? Could she have run off into the desert? I asked her not to. I shone the torch around the tiny cell. Not a single clue. I turned towards the house and called again – so loud it hurt my chest. And waited. Silence.

I ran back to the house and straight to Carol's room. Was there anything here – anything that might help? It was a teenage girl's room – posters of pop groups, awards, clothes everywhere. I sat on her bed trying to think my way through the nightmare I had created. Check the house? Perhaps as Girard was leaving, she snuck back into the house. I ran through each room, opening cupboards and wardrobes and moving anything that could possibly provide a hiding place.

"Carol and Beautiful you can come out," I shouted in each room.

Frustration and fear and anger were jostling inside my head. Across the hall, at the door to the walk-in pantry off the kitchen, there was a small, moist patch on the floor. I hadn't noticed it before when I checked the pantry but it must have been there as it had my own footprint pointed in both directions stamped in it and recognizable from the *Runna* brand embedded on the sole of my sneakers. I must have walked through it when I first searched. I opened the door of the pantry and switched on the overhead light. Alongside the freezer there was a wet slick on the floor. I hadn't thought to look in the freezer – it hadn't occurred to me. Now, it stopped my breathing and set off a siren howl through my brain. I stood alongside the freezer, wanting to shut my eyes, and ripped the door upwards. Inside, everything had been rearranged – frozen vegetables and meat and other packages had been shoved to both sides. But no chopped up Carol or Beautiful. I slumped against the freezer with relief and the siren's howl stopped. I knew what had been taken. I leaned over and searched for the packet of frozen peas. It was gone. Someone had taken Heyden Ericsson's finger.

#

Outside again, I sat on the rear step and made my breathing become steady. I couldn't think who could have known Heyden Ericsson's finger was there. Then I remembered the security cameras always operating throughout the house. Someone could have watched everything I did – watched recordings of me putting the finger in the freezer – and they would have been recorded too – but now Girard had taken the recordings, I wouldn't know who it was. The only time anyone could have managed to slip into the house was when Worland, Girard and I were outside – which was fifteen minutes at the most. Long enough. I pushed it out of my mind, knowing I had to concentrate on finding Carol. The only place in the yard I hadn't completely searched was the well. It was unlikely as Worland and Girard had looked into it and seen nothing.

I got up quickly and strode to the edge of the well. It was sealed with two heavy, timber, hinged covers that looked like they had been there for fifty years. I lifted them one at a time. Inside, as far as I could see, the walls were lined with neatly laid curved bricks covered in a slimy green mould. It was too dark to see to the bottom. I lowered my head as far as I could into the opening and listened. There was a sound. Very faint – it could have been anything – moths, a bat, my imagination. I tapped on my phone torch but the battery was flat. I remembered seeing a rope and timber ladder rolled up in the machinery shed – it was probably used to climb onto high roofs or hay stacks.

The ladder was surprisingly heavy and I needed to feed it into a wheelbarrow to get it to the well. I had no idea how deep the well was as I lowered the ladder an arm's-length at a time until it eventually hit water. I hooked the top end over an old concrete pump platform and tested it for strength by climbing onto the first three rungs, gradually applying weight while holding the iron hinges of the well covers. It sagged and groaned a little but felt solid. I knew I couldn't allow myself to think about what would happen if the ladder broke or slipped off the pump platform. Breathe. Focus. One step at a time I moved down into the darkness. A sour, musty smell wafting off the wet bricks became stronger on each step. As my eyes adjusted a little to the blackness, I strained to see anything. Below me, a faint watery sound echoed off the walls. I continued on, noticing how the temperature had dropped – and then there was a clear whimper-like sound. My sneakers touched the water and the cold seeping through was icy. Something touched my foot and I squealed and pulled my leg away. Immediately I knew it was Beautiful. I climbed down two more rungs until the water was up to my waist, reached out and grabbed a handful of fur and pulled. Beautiful clawed at me trying to hang on but still hardly made a sound. I took hold of him around his middle, lifted him clear of the water and called out.

"Carol?... Carol? Are you here... Carol?" I strained to see in the darkness. There was no movement or sound anywhere and I could see enough to know there was nothing else floating in the water. There were scratch marks on the mould of the bricks all the way around the well – Beautiful's desperate attempts to stay afloat. Tears filled my eyes.

Beautiful hung limply in the crook of my arm which was beginning to ache. I climbed up three steps free of the water and took a rest. I tried swapping him to my left arm but it was too difficult – I had visions of falling into the water below and not being able to get out. The sooner I got to the top the better. I sucked in air, over-breathing to help my arm cope with supporting Beautiful as I hauled and pushed my way up the ladder.

Near the top, with the daylight reaching in, I could see why Beautiful hadn't made any noise. His jaws had been bound shut with packing tape. He looked at me lovingly and flopped his tail slowly from side to side. He was beyond exhaustion. The last steps were painful, my arm had cramped in position and I was at serious risk of dropping him. I half lifted, half dragged him onto the wooden covers and lay back sucking in air with Beautiful looking at me and occasionally trying to wag his tail. If Carol had been dumped in the well and weighted with something heavy, she would be at the bottom, dead.

Carefully, I peeled off the tape around his jaws as he lay there and watched me. He nuzzled me gratefully and I realized that in a short time I had come to care for this dog a lot. Somehow he had stayed afloat by half clinging to the wall and treading water. As I stroked him my hand opened the fur on a deep cut across his neck. It was no longer bleeding but he would have lost a lot of blood – no surprise he was now so weak.

"Carol?" I said to him. "Carol... where is Carol?" His ears pricked up and he tried to sit up but couldn't manage it. "Wait here, I'll be back." I had no idea whether he understood the words but I know he trusted me. He watched me get up and head for the house.

Inside, I grabbed a T-shirt of Carol's from the floor of

her room and from the kitchen a handful of minced meat and ran back to Beautiful. I offered him the meat which he ignored and then I held the T-shirt close to his nose. "Smell this...can you smell Carol? Carol?... where is Carol?" He sniffed at the T-shirt, looked at me, and wobbled to his feet. He stepped off the well cover, took two steps towards the hay barn, and slumped to the ground. Was he trying to go to Carol? He had nothing left. "Good boy," I said as I picked him up and placed him in the wheelbarrow.

"Carol... Show me where Carol is."

He looked from me to the hay shed. Perhaps he was just remembering where they were last together? I wheeled the barrow towards the hay shed and stopped at Carol's hiding place. Beautiful's nose was twitching as he tested the air. He looked out into the desert and back to me and to the desert again.

I began wheeling in the direction he looked. Could Carol have run away or been chased? Was the blood on the hay bale Carol's or Beautiful's? I followed Beautiful's nose as he pointed north-west into the scrubby, high dune area. On the horizon ahead, a massive dust storm was building and heading towards the Promised Land. I increased my pace and mentally thanked Heyden Ericsson for owning such a high-quality wheelbarrow with a large rubber wheel. There were no obvious footprints – the sand was too tightly packed. I hoped we really were following Carol's trail.

As the dunes grew larger, the going got harder. I wheeled around the largest ones and noticed Beautiful's nose held true as a compass needle.

"Carol!" I began calling. "Carol and Beautiful you can come out... Carol and Beautiful..."

I realized I should have taken a bottle of water with me as the sweat ran down my face and dropped off my nose. My jeans were only half dry and chafed on each step. My mind raced – settling on anger. If anything had happened to Carol – or if Beautiful didn't make it, I knew I would hunt down whoever did it. I also knew my fury had a function – a shrink had told me once that I got angry to avoid dealing with loss – that anger gave me the illusion of being in control – loss was always about something we couldn't control. I didn't care – I knew I would hurt whoever did this.

Using the anger like fuel, I pushed on harder and suddenly Beautiful gave a weak, throaty bark. I stopped and called in the direction he was looking.

"Carol? Carol and Beautiful you can come out... Carol and Beautiful can come out..." Beautiful was trying to sit up and his tail wagged once, twice.

"Frankie?"

The voice was weak and tentative. My heart leapt up. "Carol!" I shouted, as I ran towards the sound of her voice and Beautiful barked from the barrow.

As I rounded the dune and slid downwards on my bottom, I saw her. Just her face. It was pale and ghostly. The rest of her body was covered by sand. Pure joy ran through my entire body. I scrambled the last few steps and collapsed onto her, pulling her out of the sand and hugging her. As I rocked her backwards and forwards, the tears came.

"Frankie... Oh, Frankie... Oh Frankie..." She repeated over and over, as she sobbed and shook uncontrollably. On the back of her head I noticed a dried patch of blood.

"It's okay, Carol... It's all okay, you're safe... I've got you..."

"He took Beautiful... he took Beautiful, Frankie... and I ran... I ran when he took Beautiful... he tried to protect me... Beautiful.... he attacked him...and he hurt him... I heard Beautiful cry out and I just kept running... I was so scared..."

"Carol... he's okay... Beautiful is okay, he's just exhausted. He's going to be fine..."

Carol pulled back from me and threw up into the sand. I patted her back. The sobbing changed from its note of fear to a complete release of everything. Snot streamed from her nose and the full grief of things a twelve year-old should not have to face, flooded out. On my back, an odd wet patch seemed to stay where Carol's hand had been. I felt behind me for her wrists and pulled her arms around so I could see them. A blood and sand-caked lump at the base of her hand was all that remained of where her little finger should have been. It was gone. I took her hand and pressed it to my face.

"Oh God Carol... Oh God Carol..." I kept saying and my tears came, and I couldn't stop them. Painful, regretful, heartbroken tears for Carol and for everything.

"It's all right, Frankie, it doesn't hurt...it doesn't hurt..." Carol repeated. But it did hurt. She trusted me to protect her. "Take me to see Beautiful..." She said. "I want to see Beautiful..."

As we rounded the dune, Beautiful's head resting on the edge of the wheelbarrow lifted as he saw us. His ears shot up and his tail flopped up and down.

"Beautiful!" Carol squealed, as she ran towards him. She hugged him and stroked him. "Oh Beautiful... I'm sorry for running away... I'm sorry... I love you..." Carol said. "Oh look, Frankie, he's been hurt...it looks like a cut."

"It's okay, he'll be okay," I said.

"He saved me, Frankie... he actually saved me."

"Saved you from who, Carol? Who was it?"

"I couldn't see...we were hiding in the dark in the hay...when he pulled the bale away...the light was too bright...he was just like all dark...like a silhouette and then he hit me... and Beautiful attacked him... and I just lay there... I couldn't even move." Carol held tight to Beautiful, her whole body was shaking as she remembered. "It was like a dream... he held Beautiful by the throat and I tried to scream and nothing came out... and he took my knife and cut my finger and I must have passed out and he took Beautiful away...." She began crying again and I hugged and rocked her back and forth.

"It's all okay," I whispered. "You're both okay..."

"And when he was gone I could hardly stand... I was so giddy and I ran and ran... I was so scared... I shouldn't have left Beautiful but I was so scared..." She nuzzled her face into Beautiful's neck fur. "I'm sorry... I'm sorry..." She said over and over.

20

Back at the house, I cleaned the stump of Carol's finger, applied antiseptic, bandaged it as best I could and placed her in a cool bath. I thought about the possibility of finding her finger – tracking down whoever took it, and having it sewn back on. But even if I could find it, in this heat, it would have deteriorated considerably – and it was unlikely that anyone here could sew it back on. Beautiful's cut would need stitches and it got the remaining antiseptic. Thankfully, he ate some leftover ham and was beginning to walk around by himself.

I called Roxy and told her what had happened. Her anger had a calming effect on me – she swore violently and very creatively.

"I need you to do something for me, Roxy," I asked. "Could you get Carol into the prison hospital – the only doctor this place has comes once a week, and he's ninety-six?"

"No problem, the warden loves me... I showed her some pictures of our farmers with their shirts off, so she wants her own video."

"I want Beautiful to go with her... and the doctor to look at his cut... and do you think you could get Carol's mother in to see her?"

"Cheez, Frankie you must think I'm wearing a cape..."

"You know what, Roxy... I do think you are wearing a cape... It's just invisible to you."

"Aww, Frankie...that was nice."

"Okay, don't get carried away."

"I want to work for you when I get out, Frankie...is that going to be possible?"

"It's going to be inevitable," I said with conviction.

"Woo hoo!"

"I'll see you soon."

I called Karl again and got voice mail. If I was a drinker and a smoker this is when I would down a half bottle of Scotch and give myself lung cancer.

I forced some cereal down – for fuel rather than hunger and made a ham sandwich for Carol. In the sitting room, the shotgun was still in place down the back of the lounge. I pulled it out and sat it across my knees. Whoever cut off Carol's finger and took Heyden Ericsson's from the freezer would have headed straight for the bank. I called the bank and asked for the manager. He was at home sick. I asked the assistant politely whether anyone had come in to operate Carol's security account today. She told me it was against bank policy to give out customer information of any kind. Great. I knew it was a waste of time to argue. I thanked her as politely as I could and hung up.

Whoever it was, would have operated the account by now and cleaned it out anyway. So now there was no way I could transfer the money as Girard had ordered. If I told them someone had stolen it, would they believe me? Would they think that I was orchestrating the whole thing – taking the money for myself? They'd shoot me anyway and come for Carol. I realized I didn't have Girard's phone number which made it simple – no way to explain something he wouldn't believe anyway. If I had less than twenty-four hours to live, I was going to use it to find the bastard who cut Carol's finger off and threw Beautiful down the well. I called Hugo Ravic.

"Officer Ravic, its Frankie Bennetti here."

"Frankie...how are you doing...everything okay?"

There was no way I was going to tell him about Girard or about Worland's brains being blown out or of the attack on Carol. He would be lost – and I had no intention of being restricted or questioned or worse still, arrested. "Aahh...good, Hugo... look, I just wondered whether you've seen any new faces in town in the last couple of days?"

"Nope, can't say I have, except for detectives, all asking me to fill out forms...why? Are you worried?"

"No...no... I just wondered whether whoever killed Heyden Ericsson, perhaps they were after money... you know perhaps they tortured him for information... like his bank accounts or something..."

"Well, it's out of my hands, Frankie. Big city boys in their suits got it all under control...no offence now I know you're from the city, but they don't want to listen to a hick country cop."

"Maybe you could ask in the bank whether anyone new has come in...say in the last day or so?"

"I don't think that'd be much help Frankie."

"Could you do it as a favour to me, Hugo. Mrs Ericsson has hired me and I kind of feel I need to just check that out. It'd just be between you and me."

"I'll go and have a chat with them, it can't hurt."

"I really appreciate that Hugo, thanks."

The dust storm on the horizon was rolling towards the Promised Land like an advancing army. As I waited for Carol on the veranda, it billowed half a mile into the sky and would have been stunning if I hadn't known the destructive, blinding force of the monster. Beautiful sat at my feet, his head resting across my sneakers as Carol knelt down to stroke him.

"Frankie, I don't want you to go after whoever did this... I don't want you to get hurt. It's not worth it..."

"Uh-huh. You feeling okay, now?"

"Will you promise me you won't?"

"I could do that, Carol but I don't want to lie to you."

"It's just stupid money...and a little finger..."

"Not to me."

In that moment, I knew that it really was beyond my control. Nothing would stop me going after someone who could do what he had done to a child and a dog. Deep inside, I could feel the flow of a dark, cold river of violence fed by unfairness, injustice, cruelty and lack of love.

"There's a big dust storm coming," Carol said.

"You know, Carol they won't bother you again..."

"Because they think they got what they wanted?"

"What do you mean they think they got what they wanted?"

"He got the wrong finger, Frankie."

"What!?"

"I'm left-handed...he must have assumed I was right-handed. It won't operate the account."

"Jesus Christ! Carol, are you sure?"

"I tried it when we opened the account, it only worked with my left finger."

"Oh my God, we need to go...now!"

I found the brown envelope with Heyden Ericsson's death certificate that Girard left behind, stuffed it into one of Phillipa's nice clean Prada bags, snatched up the shotgun, and hurried Carol and Beautiful to the car. If we could make it to the bank before it closed we could transfer the money as Girard wanted and they'd leave us alone. With luck, we'd also beat the dust storm which would make it impossible to drive. I'd been told that in the worst storms around here, visibility was zero and it was difficult to breathe.

Carol nursed Beautiful in the passenger seat as I sped dangerously along the gravel road, muttering to the gods under my breath to be kind.

As we reached the edge of town, we had minutes left before the bank closed. I pulled into the main street and parked opposite the bank building.

"Stay," I said to Beautiful, who got back into the car and sat in the driver's seat. I told Carol to put her bandaged hand in her pocket to save answering questions.

The assistant manager, Mrs Eriani fussed over us at the enquiry counter until I lost patience. "We are actually in a hurry, Mrs Eriani could we go straight to the security account room?"

"Oh dear, I'm sorry, I wish Mr Curlewis was here but it's not working, someone seems to have pushed something... like a key or something into the fingerprint recognition terminal...and it won't work. We've called head office and they said they'd send someone out. But that could take another day or two."

For a second or two I didn't know how to respond. I quickly figured whoever tried to open Carol's account, failed and decided that the best course of action was to disable the thing – that way at least the money stayed put and they knew where it was. "Do you have any idea who might have used it today?" I asked as casually as I could.

"I'm sorry, but you know I can't give out information on our customers."

Carol chimed in. "What if it was really important, like life or death?"

"Not even then, Carol. I'm really sorry."

In my head, I wondered whether if I got the shotgun out of the car and shoved it under Mrs Eriani's nose whether we could bend a rule. Probably not – she looked like she would be ready to take one for the bank. "Okay, thanks anyway," I said and stopped Carol who was about to try one more time.

We drove to the agency where Roxy hugged Carol and demanded to see the wound.

"I worked as a nurse," Roxy said.

"I didn't know you were a nurse?" I said, as Edgar came over to see the damage.

"I didn't say I *was* a nurse..." Roxy smiled. "I just said I worked as a nurse." I decided not to go there. Roxy pulled off the bandage from Carol's hand and inspected the cut closely. "It's clean. It'll heal fine...does it hurt?" She asked Carol.

"Not much," Carol said. I could see the way Roxy looked at Carol – she would have adopted her on the spot. "Girl," Roxy said. "You are going to have the best story to tell...for the rest of your life. Makes me want to chop one of mine off." Carol laughed.

"I knew a guy born with only one ear," Edgar said. "Told everyone a pack of wild dogs attacked him and bit it off in a fight to the death – girls loved it."

"Ignore him, Carol... I haven't trained him yet," Roxy said.

"Carol, Roxy is going to take you and Beautiful to the prison hospital. She's also going to try to get your mum in to see you," I said.

At the mention of her mother, tears filled Carol's eyes and everyone struggled to avoid falling in a sobbing heap.

"Okay. Good...can the doctor look at Beautiful's cut too?" Carol asked Roxy.

"We have the warden under our spell," Roxy said to Carol with a grin. "I'm figuring we can have whatever we want."

#

I waited in the Falcon and followed Roxy and Carol in the camel car until they entered the prison. I was never taking a chance with Carol again. I sat in the car and tried to think like the person who disabled the bank terminal. What would he do now? Would he know that the reason the account wouldn't open was because he had the wrong finger? Probably not. Would he know that Carol would be able to access the account when she had her father's death certificate? Probably. Would he cut his losses and run? Would he hang around and try for Carol again? Who knows?

I drove to the police station and found Ravic filling out forms at his desk.

"Frankie. Come in, for God's sake save me from this dumb paperwork."

"Hi Hugo, did you have any luck over at the bank?"

"Nah, the manager is away and the others are too scared to tell me whether they had lunch or not."

"Do the detectives have anyone in their sights?"

"Now those guys wouldn't talk to their mother on her deathbed – they tell me nothing. I could be a suspect for all I know."

"So where were you, on the day in question?" I said.

"What?" He was genuinely surprised and then he realized I was teasing him. "Oh, good one...ha ha."

The desk phone rang and he picked it up. "Officer Ravic.." he said with his deeper, official voice. "Okay...yes...that sounds like the one... yes... give me the number." He wrote on his notepad. "Okay, thanks...yeah... yeah two guys apparently headed north west towards us...okay that's good. Dust storm hit there yet? Okay, you better put the pedal to the metal, Artie. Okay, bye."

"Problems?" I asked.

"Aahh.. a couple of city boys lost out in the desert – Artie just found their four-wheel-drive. Of course they don't have the brains to stay with their vehicle, do they?"

"Are they going to be okay?" I asked, knowing one of the idiots was my Karl.

"Oh yeah, kind of funny... they've only been a two hour walk from town the whole time – and their footprints, Artie said, go in opposite directions, one towards Wondabeyer, the other towards the middle of nowhere."

"So one of them should be in Wondabeyer soon?"

"Possibly, hard to tell how long the footprints have been there."

" Maybe they changed direction?"

"Could be. Anyway we won't be out looking for them now till that dust storm blows itself out."

I headed over to the Paradise and searched the menu for something that I could keep down. I ordered tea, and Edith, the waitress fussed over me. I called Roxy and got voice mail. If Karl had made it to Wondabeyer, there was really only one place he could be. I called Harvey at the hotel.

"It's Frankie Bennetti, Harvey."

"Miss Bennetti, what can I do for you?"

"Has anyone new...like a guy from the city come in recently?"

"Yep."

"Okay... aahh where is he now?"

"Sitting about ten feet away drinking iced water."

"Is his name Karl?"

"Haven't asked him."

"Right... ahh Harvey, can you ask him?"

"Not sure I want to do that."

"How about another donation?"

"At this rate, you might have to put me on your payroll... ha ha.. hang on." I crossed my fingers for it to be Karl. I felt alone and tired and sad.

"Babe?"

"Karl!"

"I was going to surprise you..."

"Well, you have."

"Harvey here, was going to drive me into town when he closed."

"What happened to your four-wheel-drive pal?"

"He insisted on following his sat nav which I lost

confidence in when it dumped us out in no man's land. We went opposite directions."

"You want me to pick you up?"

"Can you?"

"Could be there in thirty minutes."

"Great, I'll see if I can get cleaned up."

21

As I headed out to Wondabeyer, directly into the advancing dust storm, I was too excited to be worried. The dust was rising high and thick and was beginning to affect the light like a giant dimmer switch. My tiredness had disappeared since hearing Karl's voice. The fact that he'd gone to so much trouble – driving out to the desert to see me, made me feel all mushy inside. I wondered what it would be like in a serious relationship with Karl. I'd had only one live-in relationship before, which ended in such pain, I swore I'd never let anyone that close again. Yeah right. So here I was speeding through the desert towards my...what? Future? Or a new version of the past?

In the rear vision mirror there seemed to be a tail of rising dust behind me. It was difficult to be sure in the poor light as there was dust beginning to rise everywhere as the wind picked up. I didn't care anyway, I was going to see Karl.

The Wondabeyer Hotel sign was swinging wildly as I pulled up. Wow, how did they think of the name, I joked as a way of calming myself down. Humour had pulled me through lots of nerve racking, scary and sad moments since I was a kid. I figured all you needed to survive life was a sense of humour, good food, occasional sex and a gun. I was missing my little Glock, but I did have Heyden Ericsson's shotgun in the car. As I came through the front door, I shouted, "Harvey!", like he was my best friend.

"Miss Bennetti, not sure you should have come out with that whopper brewing..."

"Where's my friend?"

"He wanted a shower, so I gave him the keys to the Ericsson cottage – I figured you'd be happy to look after the rental."

"Harvey, you are a seriously good businessman – the Lord is lucky to have you as his investment adviser," I said, as I handed him my credit card.

"Heh heh.. that's kind of funny in an atheist sort of way," he said, as he swiped my credit card again.

On the veranda of the hotel, I looked back down the road to the Promised Land. There was no one in sight – no vehicle dust plume as far as I could tell. I breathed a grateful sigh, I could do with some uninterrupted Karl time. I grabbed the shotgun from the car and headed off to the cottage, trying to keep my hair from blowing into haystack style.

As I got closer to the front door, I could hear a man's voice, singing. I moved closer. It was Karl's voice all right. I was surprised how good it was – deep and pretty much on the right note – an old AC/DC number, with the joke line: *'it's a long way to the shop if you want a sausage roll'*. It made me smile. I stood outside listening for a few moments and then went inside. The singing was coming from the bathroom. I had a flash thought of surprising him in the shower – then lost my nerve. His voice made embarrassing twangy guitar solo noises.

Oh, hell – when did I stop taking risks? That's not who I wanted to be.

I propped the shotgun against Heyden Ericsson's lounge chair and peeled off my clothes, fast – so I had no time to think. May as well make a grand entrance –

something to tell the grandchildren – something crazy and sexy and scary. I checked my body out – yep, it was all there – maybe a little too much there. I took a yoga breath and pushed through the bathroom door.

"Jesus Christ!" Karl shouted, with what could have been horror. I stopped dead.

"Surprise..." I said, weakly.

"Frankie... Jesus, you scared the shit out of me..."

"Can I join you...? I'm feeling dirty..."

Karl laughed and swung the shower door open. "That is the best greeting I've ever had," he said, grinning widely.

I suddenly felt stupid and awkward. I realized I knew the Karl in my head way better than the Karl in the shower. I hugged him and held on – more to stop him looking at my nakedness than from passion.

In the movies – the music would be swelling – something operatic or with saxophones. We would have this... squelching kiss as the water streamed over our faces and the camera closed in on our beautiful bodies.

"Where's the soap?" I asked. Okay, that's a mood killer I admit – but I was seriously flustered and clinging to a very muscular, slightly hairy, wet stranger.

"You want me to wash your back or your front?" Karl asked, suggestively.

"Back," I said, wrenching around with the strength of a charging buffalo. He soaped up the sponge and started in on my shoulders.

"You have strong shoulders," he said.

Strong shoulders? What the hell? Was that good? I almost said the insane 'so do you', but stopped myself. "So, how was it out there?" I said, realizing I had swapped the insane for the inane.

"Dry and sandy," he teased.

Okay, I needed to get back a little power here. "I mean wasn't it a bit dopey to try inventing a shortcut through the desert of death?"

"Not when I had you waiting patiently for me..."

Kaching! He could soap anywhere now. I turned around, looped my arms around his neck and kissed him wetly on the mouth, directly under the shower stream. He lifted me off my feet easily which made me feel lighter than I was entitled to – and a little bit helpless. His skin smelt of steam and flesh and sweat. He pressed me backwards and I felt the porcelain soap holder press into the small of my back. His hands parted my legs, neither of which needed any encouragement. He leaned heavier against me, kissing my neck and lifting me higher to kiss down my body. The soap holder dug painfully into my back but I didn't care – there was no way I was interrupting this. Crack! The soap holder snapped in half and clattered to the floor of the shower.

The shock stopped us both. He dropped me immediately – perhaps a cop reaction to loud noises. We looked at the damage and then committed the mistake of making eye contact. Goodbye mood. The mortal enemy of romance and passion – reality – tapped us both on the shoulders saying: 'excuse me, you two hardly know each other, and you look ridiculous'.

"Aahh...sorry," he mumbled.

If reality is the enemy of passion – apology is its funeral director. "Not your fault... I should have...moved."

Mercifully, he grabbed me again and held on tightly. "Ah... I kind of missed you," he said.

"Yeah, me too... I mean you... I missed you too...not me...ha ha.." Oh lame, thy name is Frankie.

"So, are you nearly done out here?" he asked.

"Not sure...things have gotten sort of complicated..."

"Weren't you just hired to bring that teenager back to her mother?"

"Well, yeah..."

"So that's done?"

"Kind of... her mother is in a bit of trouble, so I'm kind of looking after the girl." I wished now I had told Karl more of everything that had happened. I reached for the soap. "Let me do your back," I said.

He turned obediently. "So where is she now – the teenager?"

"Oh, she's with Roxy and Edgar."

"Visiting her mother?"

That was odd. Why would Karl say 'visiting her mother'? I had never mentioned she was in prison or jail or somewhere requiring 'visiting'. Something was wrong.

"What's wrong?" Karl asked.

"What do you mean?"

"You've stopped washing my back."

I started scrubbing away again. "How did you know her mother needs visiting?" I asked. There was a slight pause.

"I just assumed... you said her mother was in trouble..."

"Turn around," I said. I needed to see his eyes. "Assumed what?"

"Why are you looking at me like that?" he said.

"Why are you not answering my question?"

He breathed a patient sigh. "I assumed if her mother was in trouble, and you had to look after her...then her mother must probably be locked up. I'm a cop for Christ's sake, Frankie."

Something wasn't right. I couldn't read his face clearly, perhaps he was off balance, after all we were naked in a shower. "In trouble could mean a lot of things," I said. "She could have been in trouble like... drugs, or illness, or a car accident..."

Karl's face was slipping towards annoyance. "Hey Frankie, what are you trying to say?"

"I don't know, Karl... I just... I don't know..."

"Because I guessed her mother was in prison...you think what?"

There it was again – 'prison'. He said 'prison', not jail – why would he think she went to prison – he was a cop, he would know jail isn't prison – people don't go directly to prison – Phillipa's circumstances are unusual, a one-off. How could he know that. His eyes weren't right, either.

"I'm going to hop out, Karl" I said, stepping out of the shower and grabbing a towel.

"What the hell, Frankie! Are you looking for an excuse to run away?"

I darted through to the living room and started pulling on my clothes without even bothering to dry myself. Water evaporated here in minutes anyway. I called out to Karl. "I'm not running away... I'm just a little tired...and I need time to think..."

"Come and think in here..."

As I picked up my socks and sneakers, a flash of light through the window at the front of the cottage signalled only one thing – the windscreen of a car parked outside. I dropped my sneakers and leapt towards the shotgun as the door flew open. For a second or two the light blinded me but I pointed the shotgun anyway.

"Wo, Frankie!" It was Travis – his wheelchair just squeezing through the doorway.

"What the hell, Travis! Did you follow me out here?"

Karl called from the bathroom. "What's going on out there, Frankie?"

"You're a popular girl, Frankie," Travis said, indicating the bathroom. "Do you mind pointing that shotgun somewhere else."

"Why the hell are you following me?" I said, trying to sound angry.

Karl came out of the bathroom with just a towel around his waist. "Travis!" He said, truly shocked.

"Karl!" Travis mocked his tone.

Karl looked at me with concern. "Frankie, what are you doing with a shotgun, put it down."

"He followed me out here..." I said.

Travis gave a little laugh. "You obviously haven't told her," he said to Karl.

I swung around to face Karl. "Told me what?"

"Jesus, Travis...just piss off," Karl said, angrily. "Frankie, give me the gun."

"No. What haven't you told me?" I said, pointing the shotgun at Karl.

"Travis, give us a minute..." Karl said, quietly.

"You might need me, Karl." Travis laughed.

"Karl!" I shouted, pointing the shotgun directly at him. "Tell me now!"

Karl drew a deep breath. I could see pain in his eyes. "I was going to tell you...you didn't give me much of a chance in there," he said, indicating the bathroom.

"Uh-huh," I said, my heart pounding. "Go on."

Karl stared back at me. Travis shook his head and grinned. "He was supposed to convince you to get Carol to the bank to transfer some money, Frankie...that's all."

My brain over revved for a moment and then became calm. "So, you're involved here Karl? Is that it? Tell me?"

"Hey, Travis just asked for my help..."

"From the beginning, Karl?" I asked. "When that maniac tried to kill me in my own apartment...were you part of that?"

"Don't be ridiculous, of course not!" Karl said. "Travis asked me to help right a wrong – take some stolen money back from some thieves..."

"It's true, Frankie," Travis said. "I didn't tell him anything until Phillipa was locked up and I couldn't get to Carol because of you."

I swung the shotgun back at Travis. "Did you kill Heyden Ericsson?" I said to him.

Karl was truly shocked. "Heyden Ericsson is dead?"

"Chopped up, actually..." I said, to emphasize the point.

Karl advanced on Travis. "You told me no one was going to be hurt..."

"Oh, calm down, Karl. How would I have been able to kill Ericsson – run over him in my wheelchair and then chop him up in my lap...and why would I?" He turned to me. "Listen, Frankie, here's the thing – you get Carol to come with me to the bank – we transfer the money from these thieving bastards, and I'm gone – out of your life forever."

My head was spinning – the pain of Karl's betrayal was on hold somewhere at the back of my heart – the angry hornet was in charge. I looked at Travis. "Were you working with Worland?"

"Phillipa's lawyer? Why would I be working with him? He seems to have given up on Phillipa and gone home."

"You idiot, he was working for the people you're trying to steal from..."

"Worland?"

"He had his brains blown out in front of me..."

"Jesus Christ, Frankie, why didn't you call me...?" Karl said, his face showing true concern.

"Good riddance," Travis said. "He was an arrogant shit."

"The guy that shot him...a bald guy called Girard, is still here. They want me to transfer the money Ericsson took and locked up in his security account back to them, or else I'm dead and Carol and Phillipa too, most likely."

"You piece of shit," Karl said to Travis. "I told you I was out if anyone.. even looked like getting hurt..."

"Ahh Karl, you're out of it anyway... I can't see you persuading Frankie to do very much at all." Travis indicated with a suggestive raise of his eyebrows towards the bathroom.

I turned to Travis. "You cut Carol's finger off, didn't you?"

"What the fuck!? You cut the kids finger off!?" Karl shouted at Travis as he stepped quickly towards me, snatched the shotgun from my hands and swung it at Travis.

As if in slow motion, I watched Travis reach under the blanket covering his legs and bring out a handgun and fire twice. Karl crumpled, spilling the shotgun across the floor. I leapt towards Travis who thrust himself forward, driving his head hard into my stomach. Down I went, gasping for air. I could see blood spreading from Karl who lay motionless alongside me, as I struggled to breathe.

"You're only winded, Frankie...but I will shoot you if you don't behave." He wheeled across the room and snatched up the shotgun. The air came back to my lungs with a rush and I crawled across to Karl and felt for a pulse. He'd taken a shot to the chest and one to the side of his hip. His chest was bleeding the most. I had nothing to stop the blood oozing out. "Get up, Frankie... we're going to pick up Carol."

"I will...let me stop the bleeding and call for a doctor or ambulance."

"You can get help for him after we've been to the bank with Carol."

"He'll have bled to death by then..."

"Life can be cruel, Frankie."

I grabbed one of my socks from the floor and figured infection was hopefully better than haemorrhaging to death. I placed the sock over the wound in Karl's chest and poked and stuffed it with my index finger into the hole. The bleeding was immediately slowed.

"Okay, Frankie... I know Carol is with your friends at the prison. I want you to call her to meet you at the bank."

"Or what? You shoot me? That's gonna make it tricky. The finger you cut off didn't work at the bank did it?" I waited for this to sink in. "You need Heyden Ericsson's death certificate and Carol – and it might look suspicious if you take Carol into the bank at gunpoint – because she's never gonna cooperate with you without me being there." He stared back at me with what I hoped was respect.

"There's another option here Frankie," Travis said, as he leaned towards me. "That account has a lot of money in it. I'm not greedy, you could have an amazing life... anywhere in the world..."

I paused to consider, with no idea what the hell I was going to do, hoping my brain would catch up to my racing pulse. "Do you know what, Travis that sounds good to me. Something good coming out of this... I don't mind having a bit of luxury. Can we get some help for Karl first?"

"You're a terrible liar, Frankie."

"And you're a prick, Travis." The hornet was buzzing, the pitch rising. "What sort of a man cuts a little girl's finger off? How did that feel, Travis...make you feel less of a cripple for a few minutes...and the dog...you stab a dog and throw it down a well, for Christ's sake!"

"The mongrel bit me," he said. "It's even infected..."

He held up his arm which had unmistakable teeth marks that were now red and swollen and yellow with infection. If I survived this, Beautiful was going to be made a partner. "You know that can kill you," I said. "Bacteria from animal teeth can be deadly..."

"Let's go, Frankie."

He opened the door and a huge blast of wind and dust blew through the doorway, catching us both unawares. The surprise was a godsend. I leapt forward crashing my weight hard against his shoulder, tipping the wheelchair sideways and spilling Travis head first onto the floor, the shotgun catching in the spokes of the wheelchair and flipping end over end across the room. As Travis struggled to right himself, I dived for the shotgun, the dust stinging my eyes. I snatched it up, swung around on my knees and shoved the barrel against Travis's throat.

"If I pull the trigger, I should be able to use your head as a football..." I said, as I kicked the door shut. "So why don't you put your gun on the floor..."

"Okay," Travis said, as he released his grip on the gun and placed it on the floor in front of him. I grabbed a handful of his hair and pulled him and the wheelchair back upright. With the shotgun aimed at his face, I sat on the floor in front of him, my heart racing, my head filled with fury and revenge and disappointment and fear.

"What the fuck, Travis..."

"Ah, Frankie... I thought you understood..."

"I thought I did too."

"You won't be able to shoot me."

"Is that a gamble you want to take?"

"It's not in you."

"The thing that's in you, you mean?"

"Not quite as simple as that."

As I felt around in Phillipa's bag for my phone without taking my eyes or the shotgun off him, he smiled, and then to my horror, he stood up! Out of shock I almost pulled the trigger. "Jesus!"

Travis laughed. "No, it's not down to Jesus. I've been able to walk for some time. Apparently the nerves weren't completely severed... only severely crushed"

"Sit the fuck down, Travis!"

He ignored me. "Feeling started to come back gradually a few months after it was damaged. Doesn't feel quite normal yet, but it's getting better all the time."

"I'll shoot you... I swear..."

"You have no idea, Frankie the special considerations you get in a wheelchair. Everyone feels so guilty."

"Sit down!"

Travis turned his back to me. "I'm going to leave now, Frankie which means if you want to stop me, you'll have to shoot me in the back."

"I will, Travis..."

"You won't, Frankie...you know why? Because that would make you the same as me." He opened the door and a blast of grit and wind flew through the doorway – and he was gone, disappearing into the blinding dust storm.

I slammed the door shut and opened my phone. I knew Roxy couldn't take calls while she was in the prison so I called Hugo Ravic as I checked Karl's pulse. He was still alive. I got Ravic's voice mail. "Hugo, listen I can't stop to explain but you need to get a doctor or ambulance or whatever you've got out to Wondabeyer – a cottage at the rear of the hotel – a detective has been shot in the chest and he's bleeding a lot – it's urgent, can you do that for me please? I'm fine, I'll explain it all later but I've got to go – please hurry, Hugo."

Outside, I heard Travis's van start up and drive off. I rifled through Karl's clothes and found his police issue 9 mm Smith and Wesson. I stuck it in my belt and immediately felt better. I wasn't a shotgun kind of girl – maybe Travis would be lying in a bullet riddled heap if I'd had the handgun. There was nothing more I could do for Karl. I patted his cheek. "I'll get the bastard," I told him.

I jammed my sneakers onto my feet and flung the door open. There was no way Travis could drive in this dust storm faster than I could run. My eyes gritted up and my lungs hurt almost immediately. It was impossible to see more than two steps ahead. I wrenched my T-shirt up over my mouth and nose – hoping it would filter out some of the crap and took off after Travis.

22

Travis's van had left tyre marks in the sand which I could see if I leaned down towards the ground. As the tracks headed up the hill, I followed, breaking into a jog. The roar of the wind made it impossible to hear anything else – it was eerie. There was no way Travis could drive any faster than I was moving without the risk of colliding with something or running off the track. The smart part of my brain was telling me to quit and wait for Ravic – the angry part wasn't listening. I wanted some kind of karma to kick in – or was it the ugly cousin to karma – revenge? I kept seeing the bloodied stump of Carol's finger – and Beautiful struggling desperately to stay afloat in the well – and it made my jaw hurt from clenching my teeth. It suddenly occurred to me that as I'd left the cottage, Travis's gun wasn't on the floor – he must have picked it up as the dust and sand blew in when he opened the door. Good. There was no way I could shoot him unarmed.

The wheel tracks headed downhill and then travelled off the track which I was grateful for as the dust storm grew thicker and louder. It meant Travis was having trouble seeing where he was going. Good. I was growing more tired by the minute and I knew I wouldn't last much longer but the thought of Travis getting away drove me on. I picked up my pace and thought of Phillipa – how betrayed she would feel. I wondered whether people like Travis ever considered how much they hurt others.

Ahead, the tiniest flash of white through the dust stopped me in my tracks. The rear of Travis's van. Not moving. I dropped to my hands and knees, grabbed the Smith & Wesson and began crawling alongside the van. For the first time I was grateful for the cover of the dust storm. Near the driver's side door, I halted. If I moved closer, and he was in the van he would see me. I flattened out on my stomach, the gun held out in front of me, and wriggled forward slowly focusing on the driver's window. I thought about firing a few shots through the door where I guessed he might be. I still couldn't do it – shoot in cold blood. I wriggled closer. On the sand in front of me there were unmistakable footprints. They led away from the van. I took a deep breath and leapt upwards alongside the car window, pointing the gun inside. Empty. And then I noticed why the van had stopped. The front was crumpled into the driver's side of Worland's Lexus which in turn had hit a massive hardwood post-and rail fence. A fence which I recognized. It was part of the yard to Edgar's camel compound.

I checked out the Lexus – it was empty. There was a splash of blood across the steering wheel and dashboard. It had to be Girard's. Great. It looked more like an accident than an intentional crash – Travis's van running into the side of the Lexus and pushing it into the fence. Both cars write-offs.

Where were they? I spun around with the Smith & Wesson pointed into the swirling dust and sand. What was Girard doing here? He'd given me more time than this to voluntarily transfer the money. Was he connected to Travis? But Travis seemed to be telling the truth about not knowing that Worland and Girard were after the money? Could Girard just have been following me to protect their investment – and got lost in the dust storm? Jesus. What a mess.

Travis's legs were unlikely to be strong enough to walk far – especially in this wind. I checked out the footprints in the sand and they didn't meet up. Good. Unlikely they're working together. Girard's prints disappeared as the ground became firmer and there were spots of blood at every step. Travis's tracks headed towards the compound's barn. Not so good. The camel barn was massive. I forced myself to focus on remembering what the inside of the barn looked like. It had several nursery pens separated by solid brick walls, and individual stalls to keep the males apart. There were concrete feeding and watering troughs built in around the stone floor, and higher up, there was a loft-like gallery for storing feed which had stairs and an elevator system to lower and lift heavy deliveries. There were plenty of places to hide – plenty of places to be ambushed. Would he have expected me to come after him? Probably. I calculated that even if Ravic had picked up my voice message soon after I'd hung up, and even if he'd left immediately, it would take him three to four hours or longer to get here through the storm.

I followed Travis's footprints to the large bi-fold doors to the barn, and paused. This was a dumb place to enter. It was where he would be waiting. I steadied my breathing, checked the police gun had one in the chamber and edged my way around the side of the building, running my hands along the brick wall to guide me. The opening to the loading bay was somewhere high up along the side wall but it was impossible to see in the dust. I continued feeling my way along the wall until I reached where the loading bay might have been. I could see old wheel ruts for delivery vehicles etched into the ground. The gantry arm might be above me but there was no way I could see it, let alone reach it. Okay, that meant back to the front doors. Perhaps I could push through the doors quickly and get lucky. Yeah right.

I leaned back against the wall and wiped at the grit in

the corners of my eyes. Close up to the brick I noticed a small chiselled out section the size of a teacup. I felt the wall higher up. Another one. And another one higher again. They felt like deliberate cuts – could they be toe holds? Had someone carved them to climb up to the gantry? I felt it again. It made sense – maybe they needed to reach the gantry arm when the thing jammed or a pulley rope got stuck.

I tucked the gun back into my belt and jammed my foot into the first hole, my fingers into the third one, and lifted. It felt precarious – my sneaker just getting enough purchase – but it could possibly work, the opening wasn't that high. I inched my way up the wall and lost sight of the ground. Between gusts, I looked upward and there above my head was the loading bay. I felt around for something to grip and found the base of the gantry. It was solid. As quietly as I could, I lifted myself upwards onto the timber platform of the opening. I had an immediate flush of pleasure – I was inside – how clever was I?

I wriggled forward on my stomach across the platform and peered down into the building. It was hard to see anything, the only light available coming through old cracked and stained fiberglass panels in the roof. Travis could be anywhere. I could sit in place until help came. It made sense to wait. Unfortunately, I didn't make sense all that often. I tried to see where the steps from the loading bay down to the barn might be. My eyes were growing accustomed to the dark a little and a few shapes were becoming visible. I could see what looked like a handrail and I headed for it, wriggling on my stomach until I reached the top of a set of stairs. Looking down the twenty or so steps I knew I had a problem – old timber stairs were notoriously squeaky. May as well stick a candle on my head and whistle. The idea of whistling suddenly reminded me of my phone and I scrambled to switch it off. Christ. Focus. I was now seriously sweating – the barn was hot, humid and stunk of mould and camel crap.

I decided to test the stairs by leaning my weight very slowly onto the second top step. I tensed, waiting for the creak. Nothing. The step felt solid as stone. Woo hoo. I looked closer and saw that they were very thick timber planks set into a solid steel frame. They weren't going to move if an elephant bounced on them. Below, there was nothing I could hear moving apart from the obvious camel noises, and it was too dark to see. Good. This meant I couldn't be seen unless I was less than a sneeze away. I sat on the top step and moved slowly down on my butt, step by step – the gun out in front of me. Nothing squeaked or moved and I felt clever again and thanked the gods.

At ground level, I flattened again to my stomach and wiggled forward. I tried to think like Travis might: wait out the dust storm – then get a vehicle – maybe the publican's – and get the hell away as fast as possible – meanwhile be prepared for the idiot, junior detective, Frankie Bennetti to come through the door and get a bullet to the head. Okay. That sounds like a plan. If I was Travis, I would want a clear view of the front doors – which would mean he would be somewhere in the front half of the building – hopefully looking for those big front doors to open.

On my hands and knees, I headed in the opposite direction, away from the front. I skirted a feed trough and an empty enclosed stall. The concrete floor was rough and hurt my knees. I crawled up to the pen where Carol had excitedly shown me the baby camel named after her. She was sitting with her legs folded under her, staring at me. "Hello, Carol," I whispered as I passed.

The anger washed back as I was reminded of Carol and Beautiful but I couldn't afford to indulge that now, and immediately cleared my mind. Towards the end of the barn I heard movement, possibly a camel. I slowed my pace and moved as soundlessly as possible towards it, Karl's gun held out in front of me. An odd sucking, breathing sound came and went directly in front of me. I stopped and considered. Should I take no chances and fire three or four shots directly at the sound? And what if it was a camel? And what if it was Travis? I strained to see in the dark, my finger moist on the trigger. Slowly a shape formed as I inched forward. It was Girard with his back against the wall, his feet out in front of him. I pointed the gun at his head and he gave me an odd smile.

"Frankie," he whispered. "You never cease to surprise me..."

I moved closer and saw blood on his shirt but no gun pointing at me.

I whispered back. "The other guy, where is he?"

"No idea.. Too dark."

"What's wrong with you?"

"Van came out of nowhere...crumpled the door into my chest..."

I could tell he was in pain and his voice and breathing sounded odd. "Where are you hurt?"

"Ribs...might have done something...not good to my lungs..."

"Okay, help is on its way."

"Not in this dust storm."

"Sshh." I held my finger to my lips and listened to hear if there was any movement in the barn. Nothing. "Listen, the guy that ran into you... I think he's in here... he'll kill us if he finds us."

"You're really pretty..."

"Whaa? Jesus, Girard. Have you got your gun?"

"I would have fallen for you, Frankie...when I was younger..."

"Jesus, we get out of here alive, I'll lick butter off your entire body."

"Hah ha ha...oww.."

"Now have you got your gun?"

"No use."

"What do you mean?"

He held up his gun by the barrel. "Magazine and trigger got crushed in the accident against the steering wheel."

"Great."

"But I found this..." He held up a rusty but very sharp looking sickle.

"Okay, great – if we find a hammer we can join the Communist Party..."

"Hah ha ha...oww... Don't make me laugh...it hurts. So, who is it that's going to kill us?"

"You remember the guy in the wheelchair – used to visit Phillipa Ericsson in jail?"

"Hah, really. I told Worland not to trust him...something wrong about him."

"You were right. And by the way, he can walk, he cheated about that too."

We sat silently for several minutes, listening intently for any movement. Nothing. An occasional camel noise, and the wind creaking the old building and rattling the roofing. My heart rate steadied. Maybe Travis didn't come into the barn – maybe he came and went.

"So, Girard," I whispered, a few inches from his ear. "The money in that account – where did it come from?"

"Hardly think it matters now."

"Maybe not to you..."

"Good point."

I tried provoking. "You don't know, do you?"

Girard shook his head. "Frankie, you are the most persistent human being I have ever come across."

"So?"

"The short answer – some very big shots in the military overseas – maybe Brits or Americans or Australians, figured a way, using some clever software, to pay local suppliers of food, vehicles, labour etc. that didn't exist. Their only problem was they needed the auditing company to be on side so that it would all be passed okay. Enter Heyden Ericsson and his company." Girard grimaced and held his breath for what looked like a wave of pain.

"You okay?"

"No."

"So what went wrong?"

"Old Heyden skimmed off a little too much into his own account – probably for a couple of years before they figured it out."

"Do you know who they are – these military guys?"

"No. Even Worland didn't know – we operated through a middleman and got paid obscene amounts to do what they wanted."

"Sshh!" I whispered. "I thought I heard something..."

Out of the darkness, a thin white light flashed across the wall behind Girard and stopped on my chest. With surprising speed Girard's arm shot out and knocked me sideways. Three quick gunshots exploded in succession – pieces of brick exploded off the wall where a half second before sat Girard. We both crawled behind a stack of feed bags. I fired two shots in the direction of the flashlight and felt Girard's hand pulling down on my arm.

"Don't waste shots on luck," he whispered.

My heart was hammering in my ears. "Thanks... for the.. you know, for the quick thinking."

"We should split up," he said.

"We've only got one gun between us..."

"I've got my little friend here." He held up the rusty sickle.

"Does it stop bullets?"

He smiled.

"The bastard has a torch," I said.

"He's not going to use it until he's close because he makes himself a target," Girard said softly, speaking with difficulty. "You should move away to the side and when he comes at me – you should shoot him – body shot, once – head's too small a target – then move three quick steps sideways and body shot again... How good are you with that gun?"

"Never fired it till today. Some bald-headed maniac took my baby Glock..."

"Hah ha ha... Give it to me, and you take this." He

handed the sickle to me and as he reached for the gun, a bright light flashed blindingly in my eyes. Girard whacked me with his arm and my head smacked against the feed bags as gunshots rang out. I fired the Smith and Wesson in the direction of the light until I heard the click click of an empty magazine. Girard grimaced and shook his head at me. Not good. I tried to see into the darkness.

"Listen to me," Girard whispered. "He'll come for us now. When I move towards him, he'll focus on me – that's the only chance you'll get."

Slowly, Travis's shape began to emerge, his gun appearing first, moving back and forth from me to Girard as he came closer.

"Frankie, sounded like you might be out of ammunition.. and luck. You don't know when to quit, do you? And this must be your dangerous friend I bumped into outside?"

I held out my car keys. "Here, you can have my car, it's parked near the hotel."

"Why didn't you just let me go, Frankie?"

I let my breathing steady. "Good question, Travis." I glanced at Girard. "Someone once said to me – 'We are who we are - the cat will torture the mouse and the dog will bite the cat'." Girard laughed and then groaned. Travis raised a puzzled eyebrow.

"You look a bit broken up, fella..."

Girard ignored him and turned his head to me. "You remember what I told you?" he whispered to me. I nodded.

"Frankie tells me, I should be afraid of you..." Travis said to Girard. "If what she told me is true, and you blew Worland's brains out... I have to thank you."

"Maybe you shouldn't thank me just yet. And maybe you should be afraid of me."

"Ah, but I have the gun," Travis said, enjoying himself.

"You know what Thoreau said about guns?" I said. Both Travis and Girard stared at me as if my nerves had cracked and I was losing it. "'A gun gives you the body, not the bird'." It took a few seconds for it to sink in.

"Guess I'll take the body, then," Travis said.

"Then you'd be a fool..." Girard said, as he smiled at me, pursed his lips and blew me a kiss. I knew what it meant.

With lightning speed, Girard leapt at Travis who overreacted, stumbling backwards and firing repeatedly into Girard's body. I was on my feet, reaching for Travis – as in slow motion, Girard fell through the air to the ground and Travis turned the gun on me and fired and pain shot through my chest and I swung with hate and fury – the sickle making a perfect, swooping arc through the air. And I saw the gun floating and floating and falling towards the ground – and Travis screaming and running, leaving a bloody trail across the floor from where his hand lay, fingers still twitching as they gripped the gun. And then nothing. Everything fell away to nothing.

23

There is something about hospital air that is unmistakably, hospital – antiseptic and cleaning fluids and death. And the feel of stiff, cotton bed sheets. I wanted to stay submerged, asleep, unconscious to the real world of violence, and loss and the pain of how people hurt and disappoint. And in my dark dream I was being gently kissed along my neck by a stranger I couldn't quite see or resist but who I knew was gentle and kind and gorgeous – who moved along my face and stopped at my lips – whose breath smelt of steam and... and... dog food?? I opened my eyes to Beautiful being held by Carol and licking my face.

"Frankie!" Carol squealed. "You're awake!"

Beautiful leapt out of Carol's hold and onto the bed and went nuts with excitement.

"Tell me he's going to turn into a prince," I said.

Carol laughed. "I'm not supposed to let him near you. How are you feeling?"

"Like someone drove a stake through my chest."

"You're in the prison hospital... you've been in an induced coma for days. They took a bullet out of you...you almost died."

"Hello Beautiful," I said, which sent him into raptures of leaping and kissing again. "Sit!" I said. Beautiful obediently sat on my stomach and stared lovingly at me. He weighed a ton – but I loved him.

"They found you in the baby camel pen at Wondabeyer..." Carol said.

That brought reality back with a rush. "What else did they tell you?"

"They didn't tell me anything – I overheard Officer Ravic talking to mum. They've dropped the charges against her and she's home now."

"Ah Carol, eavesdropping... you've already passed half the investigators training course."

Carol laughed. "There was a man there, Frankie...he was dead..."

Oh God, Karl, I thought...he didn't make it. "Did they described him?"

"They said he was from the city and had a bald head."

Okay, this made me want to cry. Why would I cry for someone who tried to kill me? Maybe because he was also the person who kept me alive. I figured I was just emotionally unstable at the moment.

"They found another guy – a detective who was shot, and he's in intensive care in the city... and there's something else...something kinda gruesome... I probably should let Officer Ravic tell you..."

"Don't make me get out of bed and shoot you, Carol," I said.

Carol stifled a laugh. "It was a hand...holding a gun...it was like cut off. It wasn't the bald-headed guy's or the detective's..."

"So, do they know who's hand it was?"

Carol's face darkened as she sat on the bed and reached for my hand. "They didn't say... but I think I know whose it was."

I squeezed her hand in support. Her eyes moistened with tears. "You don't have to talk about this, Carol," I said gently.

"I think it was Travis's." She looked squarely at me. "It was Travis who cut my finger off, wasn't it?"

I thought as rapidly as my thick brain would allow – should I try and protect her – evade an answer – let her mother tell her? Then I remembered how much I hated being left out of important information when I was a kid.

"Yes, it was," I said.

She burst into tears. "It's like a part of me knew it, Frankie...even at the time... I just couldn't..." She slumped her head on the pillow beside me and cried for several minutes.

"Did they find the rest of him?" I finally asked.

This struck Carol as particularly weird and funny – she almost choked, coughing and laughing and crying at the same time. "No," she said.

I was surprised. How far could you run with blood pumping out of your severed wrist?

Phillipa and a nursing sister appeared in the doorway. "Oh, you're awake," the sister said with a scary smile that said: 'why didn't you tell me – you idiot patient'. "Please take that dog off the bed."

"Get down, Beautiful," I told him and he jumped off the bed.

Phillipa rushed over to me. "Thank God you're all right, Frankie," she said. She hugged me and Carol together as best she could. "Carol and I want you to stay with us as long as you need."

There was a high-pitched squeal at the door and Roxy flew into the room. "Oh my god, Frankie... you're okay. I almost died when they brought you in..."

"You almost died? Stop hogging my sympathy..."

"Jesus, you look like shit. You want me to get you some make up?"

"Thanks, Rox...but that's pretty low on my list at the moment."

Edgar appeared at the door. "Hey Frankie," he said.

"What did you do to my camels? They're a bit shaken up – they got that military thing – whaddyacallit... post-dramatic stress disorder..."

For a few seconds I thought he was serious, I had this picture of depressed camels and it made me laugh which hurt my chest – which also made me laugh.

#

It took two weeks lying beside the pool and walking Beautiful and watching movies in Phillipa's home cinema before I began to feel something like normal. The hospital was delighted to offer me a free wheelchair – Travis's, which I protested about at first until I decided to accept it as part of the irony of life.

Apparently, no one came to collect Girard's body and he was buried in the little cemetery on the edge of town. I took some flowers and sat with him for a while, staring at the sad little white marker with his name stencilled on it. "Well, Girard, thanks to you I'm above ground," I said to him. "And you were wrong – sometimes the dog chooses not to bite the cat. Anyway, the good news is, you finally made it into the promised land." I fancied he found it funny.

Karl came out of intensive care and wanted to see me to explain why he thought it was okay to steal from thieves. I assured him I wouldn't tell the cops – it wasn't a serious enough crime for a basically good cop to lose everything. But I didn't feel the same about him. It wasn't so much the moral/ethical thing – God knows I'd danced around that line myself a few times. But that he hadn't told me what he was doing – that he hadn't trusted me, and now I couldn't trust him. It didn't matter that he insisted he was protecting me. My idea of him had changed and it wasn't coming back any time soon. But hey, I'm a repeat offender in the forgiving stakes – and I know he's really a good guy. And to be honest with you, I think about that steamy, sexy shower moment at Wondabeyer, all the time – a girl has her needs.

Travis's body couldn't be found. It was assumed he ran off into the desert and maybe the sand storm covered up his body. They even tried tracker dogs but to no avail. Phillipa had several nights of crying – I could hear from my room. Once, in the middle of the night I found her just sitting and staring into the dark and she said to me, "Frankie, what do most people think money will do for them?"

"Ah Phillipa, you're asking the wrong person, I've never had enough to find out."

"Seriously," she said.

"From what I've seen, most of us act like it's the magic elixir – the missing part that'll make us happy, and powerful and we can buy lots of stuff, and everyone will envy us and we'll never die."

"Do you know what I've seen, Frankie? Money just amplifies who you already are – the good, bad, kind and mean that's already there."

#

The following morning, I went with Carol to the bank. She begged me not to reveal to her mother or the police or anyone else how much was in the security account so that her father would never be implicated. I tossed and turned the night before, considering the pros and cons of telling the police and decided that whoever had done this in the military, were obviously smart enough and powerful enough to cover their tracks. On a more selfish level, I knew that the police would put me through the endless torture of questioning, form filling and suspicion – and would probably pull my license. The deciding factor: I hatched a plan for a little revenge of my own.

245

After a dozen forms were filled out, Carol was able to operate the account. I had a list that Roxy compiled for me of seventeen charities that listed electronic deposit details. It took an hour to deposit $174,624,210 in various amounts to the different charities. When it was done, I saved one dollar and forwarded it to the account Girard had instructed me to, along with copies of the amounts sent to the charities. I included a message for the bastards at the top of the food chain: 'get stuffed'. Okay, I know – not classy, not smart, and maybe not a good way to stop them coming after me – but oh, so satisfying. My reasoning was that once the money was gone, there was nothing to gain by hurting any of us. They would realize I hadn't gone to the police so the smartest move for them would be to move on.

It felt good walking away from the bank – the three of us Carol, Beautiful and me – all wounded, but significantly, still walking.

#

Now I needed cheering up. How I'd done that in the past was to take on something ridiculous, something risky, something that was exciting – an adventure – something that could kill me. I bought a motorbike. A fast one. A Ducati with lots of numbers in its name. Rodney, the now dating-a-sexy-prisoner, previously agoraphobic, very grateful mechanic, got it for me. I rode around in sensible circles, and up and down back roads for a week until one day, on the sealed highway – the part of me that wanted to always go as far as possible – needed to go fast. I opened up the throttle and slammed rapidly through the gears – the highway was as straight as a laser beam. The engine whined, the wind screamed past my helmet. The roadside and reality melted into a blur – just what I needed. I was alive. And every part of me could feel it. I had much to pull me forward into the future – Roxy was about to come work for me, full time. Carol was coming next month for a week of her holidays. And Beautiful was welded to me. I had the idea of having a special harness and seat made to be fixed behind me on the motorbike – both Beautiful and me wearing black leather jackets with printing on them: 'mongrel' and 'bitch' – not sure who should get which. I laughed into the wind as the world raced by.

24

Roxy's date and dance night went brilliantly. Hundreds of people showed up from farms and small towns and mining communities. Two busloads of female prisoners evened up the gender imbalance. Edith, with her bird calls had her moment of glory, Rodney sang, 'Everybody Loves Somebody Sometime', and Hugo Ravic kept dancing way too close with the slightly tipsy warden.

Towards the end of the night, I sat outside under the stars with Beautiful leaning up against me, watching through the open doorway as people danced together, holding onto each other, nervous, thrilled, hopeful. I remembered reading: 'all happiness or unhappiness depends upon the quality of the objects to which we are attached by love' – maybe it was Spinoza. It struck me as the best way to approach life – hold onto someone or something that means something to you, even if you're frightened and doubtful….and keep hoping.

"Hey, I'm coming back – *and*
I'm joining a motorcycle gang..."

Frankie: Book 2

Join Frankie Online:

hello@frankiefoxybabe.com
Twitter: @robbycart, @frankiefoxybabe
Facebook.com/frankiefoxybabe
www.frankiefoxybabe.com

dw
publishing